HIGH PRAISE FOR
ROBERT J. RANDISI
AND *BLOOD OF ANGELS*!

"[Randisi] doesn't waste a phrase or a plot turn…. His prose is supple and never flashy."
—*Publishers Weekly*

"A fine crime novel." —*Booklist*

"Robert Randisi is a master of the genre. He's one of the best."
—Michael Connelly, author of *Chasing the Dime*

"A riveting, increasingly suspenseful plot. Recommended!"
—*Library Journal*

"A skilled, uncompromising writer, Randisi knows which buttons to press—and how to press them."
—John Lutz, author of *Single White Female*

"Randisi knows his stuff and brings it to life."
—*Preview Magazine*

"Randisi has a definite ability to construct a believable plot around his characters."
—*Booklist*

THE NEXT VICTIM

The Observer watched from the street with the other onlookers as the body was finally pulled from the water. He'd just been asked by a uniformed if he'd seen or heard anything and he said no. The man moved on, questioning everyone who was craning their necks in the hopes of seeing blood.

Once they loaded the body into a van he turned and made his way through the crowd. His work was done, time to move onto the next one.

The Ice Man was waiting.

COLD BLOODED

ROBERT J. RANDISI

LEISURE BOOKS NEW YORK CITY

For Marthayn,
who keeps my blood anything but cold.

A LEISURE BOOK®

November 2005

Published by

Dorchester Publishing Co., Inc.
200 Madison Avenue
New York, NY 10016

ISBN 0-8439-5574-0

The name "Leisure Books" and the stylized "L" with design are
trademarks of Dorchester Publishing Co., Inc.

Printed in the United States of America.

Visit us on the web at www.dorchesterpub.com.

COLD
BLOODED

PROLOGUE

The average age of the members of the Coney Island Polar Bear Club was sixty-two, and that was because the youngest member, Bobby Kelly, was only fifty-eight years old.

As the nine men spread out on the beach and discarded their clothing, Kelly looked over at eighty-four-year-old Walter Dunham, who was wearing the skimpiest bathing suit of all of them. There was entirely too much of his pale, slack skin in sight.

"What the hell is that?" Bobby asked.

Dennis Hasselbeck turned and looked over in Walter's direction.

"Those are his French-cut trunks," he said. "His wife got them for him."

"His wife?" Bobby asked. "Ain't she even older than him?"

"Yeah," Walter said. "Louise is eighty-six. She calls Walter her boy toy."

"Yuck," Bobby said. He was hopping around on one foot, trying to get his other pant leg off, and almost toppled over before recovering his balance.

"Whatsmatta?" Walter asked. "He's skinny enough to wear 'em." The man touched his bulging belly. "Wish I was."

"How old are you, Walter?"

"Sixty."

"Be happy you ain't so old and senile enough to wear somethin' like that."

The rest of the Polar Bears got their pants off and began hopping from foot to foot, rubbing their arms to ward off the twenty-five degree cold. Bobby shook his head. If these old geezers couldn't take this, what were they gonna do when it got down to zero? Of course, they weren't as young as he was, but it was kind of pathetic for a guy to come out here alone and swim in the cold water off Coney Island, and they were the only group of its kind on this beach. He could have joined a couple of clubs on Jones beach, but he hated Jones Beach. It reminded him too much of when he was a kid, having his parents drag him there in the summer when it was wall-to-wall people. This was the way to swim on the beach, when you had it all to yourself.

"Okay, Polar Bears," Sammy Saperstein shouted. "Into the water!"

Saperstein was the president of the club, and he always called for them to get in the water like he was Napolean at Waterloo ordering his troops to battle.

Bobby looked up and down the beach. As usual there was seaweed and driftwood in either direction, not to mention garbage. There was even an old mattress that had drifted in from somewhere. He remembered the days when this beach was spotless. Even when he hated being on Jones Beach at least it had been clean. These days if you wanted a clean beach you had to go to Jamaica, or Hawaii or someplace like that, and Bobby Kelly was not about to spend that kind of money.

Bobby headed for the water with the rest of the men. Experienced Polar Bears, they did not hesitate or stop when they stepped into the icy water. They kept on going until they were waist-high, then chest-high, and finally swimming in the Atlantic.

Bobby enjoyed the shock to his system as the cold made its way to his bones. What people didn't realize was that once you were in the water it felt colder when getting out. The true bone-chill occurred when you made your way back to the beach, where the wind met the wet on your body.

Bobby looked over at Walter, wondering how many more years the older man could last before the cold gave him a heart attack. He also had to wonder if he'd still be doing this—or even be around—when he was the age of some of these other duffers, let alone Walter Dunham.

Bobby felt something swirling around his feet as he swam. He didn't know if it was seaweed or fish or garbage, but it made him head back to shore before the others. He did not, however, exit the water at the same point where he had entered it. The waves had carried him farther down the beach, and as a result he came out near the water-soaked, garbage-covered, discarded old mattress.

Only there wasn't just a mattress there. As he came out of the water he spotted something else lying on the beach. He squinted, wiped salt water away from his eyes and slowly approached the debris. He thought he knew what he was looking at, but he was hoping he was wrong.

"Hey, Kelly," Sammy Saperstein shouted. "What are ya doin'?"

Bobby waved Saperstein away impatiently and continued to approach the mattress.

"Hey Bobby," Dennis Hasselbeck called. "You lookin' for a place ta lie down?"

Kelly ignored the others as they all joined in to toss catcalls at the youngest of their number for leaving the water first, but he didn't hear them. As he got closer he realized that he was, indeed, seeing what he thought he was seeing, and the chill that he felt no longer came from the cold water or the icy wind.

When he reached his goal, he stopped and stared at the arm that was draped over the mattress. He was surprised that it looked so gray. In fact, he couldn't tell if it was a man or a woman, black, white or Mexican, but it was definitely a person.

"Bobby, whataya got?" Hasselbeck asked, coming up behind him. He came up next to Bobby and stopped short. "Jesus! Who is it?"

"I dunno," Bobby said.

They stared at it for a few moments, long enough for Saperstein and some of the others to join them. Before long they had formed a circle around the body.

"Somebody's gotta take a look at it," Hasselbeck said. "What if they ain't dead?"

"Of course they're dead," Tony DeMarco said. "Lookit the color of the skin. Ain't you ever seen a dead body before?"

"We gotta check, anyway," Saperstein said. "Bobby, you found it. You check it."

Bobby didn't mind. Suddenly, he was the center of attention.

"Okay," he agreed, "but you guys gotta move the mattress so I can take a look."

They all looked at each other, and then Saperstein said, "Well, come on, grab the edges and let's move it."

"Wait, wait," DeMarco said, "don't touch nothin'.

4

We should just call the police. They're gonna be pissed if we move somethin'."

"Tony," Hasselbeck said, "this person could still be alive."

"I'm tellin' ya, they're dead—" DeMarco replied.

"Move the damn mattress so I can take a look!" Bobby yelled.

Four of the men—Saperstein, Hasselbeck, Eddie Delaney and old Walter Dunham—each grabbed a corner of the mattress and lifted. But it was so water-logged it was too heavy and sagged in the middle. Two more Polar Bears stepped forward and grabbed hold and the six of them finally shifted the thing and uncovered the body.

"What is it?" somebody asked as Bobby leaned over it. "Man or woman?"

"Jesus," Bobby said.

"What?" Saperstein asked.

"What is it, Bobby?" Hasselbeck asked.

"Can we put the mattress down?" Walter asked.

"It's a man," Bobby finally said, "a kid, from the looks of him."

"How long you think he's been in the water?" De-Marco asked.

"Not long," Bobby said. "Except for the color of his skin he looks like he could be . . . sleeping. Except for one thing."

"What?" Saperstein asked. "What thing?"

"Lookit him," Bobby said, pointing. "He's got ice on him. He's frozen stiff."

The Observer watched from the boardwalk as the members of the Coney Island Polar Bear Club gathered around the body on the beach. This was his fourth morning in a row watching and waiting for the body to wash ashore, and for someone to find it.

His research of the tides here had told him the body would wash up somewhere along this stretch of beach.

"What's going?" a young man asked, coming up next to him.

"Dunno." He pulled the woolen cap farther down on his head. "Looks like they found somethin'."

"Yeah? Like what?"

Before he could answer, a young woman came up next to the second man and asked, "What's goin' on?" She'd been running along the boardwalk, wearing a sweatshirt and shorts to show off her runner's legs. She was also wearing headphones, which were hanging from her neck now. The Observer ignored her, because she disgusted him.

"We don't know," the second man said. "Looks like the old farts found somethin'."

"I wonder what it is?"

The Observer remained silent, but not so his two companions, and before long he was standing in the center of a line of people who were watching and waiting . . . and were still doing it when the first police car arrived.

PART ONE

1

Detective Sergeant Dennis McQueen stopped his car behind an EMS van on the Coney Island boardwalk. In addition to that vehicle he saw the medical examiner's van, a Crime Scene Unit vehicle, an unmarked Precinct Detective Unit car and a 60 Precinct radio car, obviously the first car on the scene, since it was penned in by all the others.

He was driving his own car, a three-year-old Toyota, rather than an unmarked department car because there had been a shortage of cars recently—cars that would run, that is. Although he was a boss and entitled to first pick over other detectives, he preferred to use his own car and leave the department autos available to his men.

He got out of the car as his partner, Ramon Velez, exited the passenger side.

"Goddamn," Velez said. He didn't say another word but McQueen knew he was complaining about the cold. Winter was his partner's least favorite season, and they were right in the middle of it. This was

9

the coldest New York January in recent history. They were lucky there had been no rain or snow to go with it, but that didn't cut much slack with Velez. He never really complained when it was wet, just when it was cold.

"Yeah," McQueen replied. He pulled his cheap Burberry knockoff close around him and headed for the beach.

McQueen thought that the sand of Coney Island's beach felt like concrete beneath his feet the closer they got to the water. That's what below-freezing temperatures did, turned even the softest of things hard.

His partner was cursing about what the sand was doing to his expensive new shoes. McQueen didn't care what happened to his shoes, because he had an identical pair at home. He'd bought them both when they were on sale at Pay Less Shoes. Ray Velez would never have been caught dead buying shoes on sale. That wasn't the only difference between the two men, but they worked together remarkably well. That had been why McQueen had managed to take Velez with him when he was transferred from a precinct-level detective unit to the Brooklyn South Homicide Squad. At least that way, starting a new assignment didn't mean breaking in a new partner.

McQueen stepped around a frozen puddle as he made his way toward the water's edge, where the tide coming in and out had kept ice from forming. Here and there, however, there were patches of ice where the water had been trapped in a sandy depression.

"Well, step back, boys," a man in a back trench coat announced. The coat was belted, but the wind had it flapping around his legs. "The Homicide Squad has arrived. This mess is all yours, Dennis."

"Parker," McQueen said, greeting the 60 Precinct detective. "Where's your partner?" Parker usually worked with a man named Franks. Both of them had better than twelve years in.

"I think he went to see if he could find somebody to fire up the Nathan's grills early. Nothing like some hot dogs and fries for breakfast. Whataya say, Ray?"

"I say you don't need any more hot dogs, Parker," Velez replied. "That belt is about to pop."

"Fuck you," the other man responded good-naturedly. "We ain't all got your Latin metabolism."

"You got that right," Velez said.

Parker looked at McQueen.

"You catch this?"

"It's mine."

"Then I'm handin' it off to you," Parker said, with a bow. He had caught the case originally on a precinct level, and it was he who had put out the call for Homicide.

"Don't forget to copy me on your reports."

"I'll get to them as soon as I get back to the house."

"What made you call us, Parker?" McQueen asked.

"Hell, Dennis," the other detective said, "this boy's dead, and he was murdered."

"How do you know?"

"Instinct."

If it had come from anyone else McQueen would have labeled the call for Homicide to the scene as premature, but Dan Parker was one of a handful of detectives in the department whose instincts he truly respected.

"Duty Captain get here?"

"Not yet."

"Who is it?"

"Don't know."

"Okay," McQueen said. "I've got it, Dan. You better go and find your partner before all the hot dogs are gone."

"No chance of that," Parker said. "Don't worry. We'll leave some for you boys."

He moved past McQueen, touching him lightly on the arm, then waved to Velez and started across the beach to the boardwalk.

2

When McQueen and Velez reached the body the M.E. was already crouched over it. The Crime Scene techs were standing around, waiting their turn impatiently. As far as McQueen was concerned, the advent of all the *C.S.I.* TV series had given them an exaggerated idea of their own importance. It made them arrogant, and more difficult to deal with. He didn't watch TV cops shows himself, but colleagues who did preferred the *Law & Order* series to the *CSIs*. McQueen thought they were all crap, and that went for *NYPD Blue*, as well. When he watched TV he preferred sitcoms. He worked with cops all day, he certainly didn't want to watch TV shows about them at night. Besides, he still felt that the best and most accurate cop show on TV had been *Barney Miller*. He'd seen nothing since that one went off the air to change his mind.

He looked back up at the boardwalk, which was not only clogged with vehicles but with rubbernecking observers, as well. The boardwalk was lined with them, but since they weren't in the way he disregarded them. The killer—if there was one—could have been standing among them, but he left that sort of psychological mumbo jumbo to others.

Dr. Ethan Bannerjee looked up at McQueen and said, "Detective."

"Doc."

"Got a cold one here," Bannerjee said, "real cold."

"What can you tell me?"

"Not much until I kept him someplace warm," the medical examiner said. He stood up to his full height, well over six feet. McQueen liked the man in spite of the fact that his thin physique always made the larger detective feel clumsy and even bigger than he was when in the medical man's presence. In his late forties, the doctor was only four or five years younger than McQueen, but somehow the years had not managed to etch a single line onto the man's face.

"The body is a young male in his twenties, naked and dead."

"Wow," McQueen said.

"I earn the big money," Bannerjee said.

"You can't tell me what killed him?"

"Like I said, not until I thaw him out. Can't even guess at a time of death, not with this cold. Let the fancy boys here have a look and then we'll move him."

By "fancy boys" he meant the Crime Scene techs. There was no love lost between Crime Scene and medical examiner personnel, for obvious reasons. Still, McQueen remembered how arrogant a lot of the members of the M.E.'s department had gotten during the run of Quincy. The techs were just having their turn.

McQueen looked at the uniformed officer who was standing nearby.

"First on the scene?" he asked.

14

"Yes, sir," the man said. "Me and my partner. I'm Smith, he's–"

"Jones?" Velez asked.

Smith frowned and said, "Uh, no, he's Acosta. Why would you think—"

"Forget it," McQueen said, as Velez shook his head sadly. "Who found him?"

"Polar Bears."

"Come again?" Velez asked.

"The members of the Coney Island Polar Bear Club," Smith said, pointing. Both detectives turned and looked down the beach where a group of men stood huddled with blankets around them and Officer Acosta standing nearby.

"All of them?" McQueen asked.

"Well, one man spotted the body, and then the others gathered around."

"They move anything?"

"The mattress," Smith said. "They wanted to see if the vic was still alive."

McQueen knew a lot of the younger officers, like Smith, were using words like "perp" and "vic," which they'd picked up from movies and television. McQueen didn't think he'd ever said "vic" in his life.

"Ray," McQueen said.

"I'll go and talk to them."

McQueen nodded and Velez walked off down the beach. McQueen turned and saw that the techs were at work. He hunkered down by the body, across from one of the techs, who gave him a dirty look.

"Who're you?"

"McQueen, Detective Sergeant," he replied. "It's my call."

The man looked annoyed that he wasn't going to be able to tell McQueen to go away.

"I'm Cahill. Bad scene, here," he said, instead. "Contaminated. Water coming in and out, it's bound to have carried something away."

McQueen looked down at the body's legs, genitals, torso. There weren't any clothes around anywhere, but as the tech had suggested, they could have been carried out by the tide.

"Think he was carried down here?" McQueen asked. "Or did he wash up onto shore?"

"Hard to tell. The sand is cold and hard, and where it did pick up tracks, those old geezers trampled it."

McQueen watched as the tech took a small chunk of ice from the body and dropped it into a jar. He was glad to see that the man seemed to know his job.

"Can you get me a report on that ASAP?" he asked.

"Fast as I can," the man said. "This is my third scene today."

"I'd appreciate it."

"You Homicide?"

"That's right."

The man nodded, packed up his kit.

"Soon as I can," he said. He turned to the M.E.'s boys, who were waiting impatiently. "All yours."

"Are you gonna take the mattress in?" McQueen asked the tech.

"Yup. Soon as these boys have removed the body, we'll take the mattress. We know our job."

"I'm sure you do," McQueen said.

As the tech walked away McQueen said to the M.E.'s guys, "Okay, stop."

"What?" one of them said.

"The duty captain hasn't been here," he told them. "You'll have to wait."

"Ah, shit."

"Yeah."

"When's he gonna be here?"

"I don't know," McQueen said. "I don't know who's got the duty, so I can't predict it. We'll all just have to wait."

"Can we still have the mattress?" one of the CSU techs asked.

"Sure, you can take it," McQueen said.

The techs smirked at the M.E. workers. Where it had taken six Polar Bears it took only two of the techs to lift the mattress and remove it without dragging it on the beach. The M.E.'s boys gazed after them enviously.

"Cold as shit out here," one of them said.

"Imagine how they feel," McQueen said, jerking his head down the beach at the shivering Polar Bears.

"Yeah," the man said, "but they came out here willingly."

"Not to stay this long in their bathing suits," McQueen said.

McQueen took out his cell phone, a new model Nokia with a digital camera, and started snapping shots of the body.

"Whataya doin'?" the other man asked. "Crime Scene took photos."

"Might as well take advantage of the technology available to us," McQueen said. "I like to get my own."

He'd only started doing this recently. He hated cell phones, but when they started combining them with cameras he changed his mind about them. He could have also accessed the Internet if he wanted to, but he hadn't carried his dependence on technology that far, yet.

He noticed some movement up by the boardwalk. Another car had joined the others on the boardwalk. "You might be in luck," McQueen said. "Looks like the duty captain's arrived."

They watched as the driver got out, put on his hat, then went around to the other side to open the passenger door.

"Oh, no," McQueen said.

"What?" the other man asked.

"Hartwell's got the duty."

"How do you know that? He didn't even get out of the car yet."

"Captain Hartwell is the only one who requires his driver to open the door for him."

"You're kidding."

"I'm not."

The man turned to watch.

Captain Eugene Hartwell got out of the car and looked around. He paused long enough for someone—anyone—to see that his driver had opened his door for him. It was a status thing for him, and wasn't any good unless somebody saw it.

Satisfied that he'd been noticed, the man put his hat on carefully and instructed two other arriving officers to disperse the crowd. He then followed his driver off the boardwalk and onto the beach. The officers made no move toward the collection of onlookers that had built up two or three deep on the boardwalk. It was an impressive turnout for that time of morning. Why deprive them of the entertainment? Besides which, they knew they'd be the ones stuck with canvassing the area later for information. They'd have a better chance of finding something out if they didn't piss everyone off by making them move, right now.

3

"We'll get you out of here as soon as we can," McQueen promised the M.E.'s man as the captain approached.

"Sergeant," Hartwell said, when he reached the water's edge.

"Sir."

They'd been to enough crime scenes together that they knew each other on sight, and although they had spent very little time together in other venues, there was an innate dislike between the two men. For one thing, McQueen hated pretentious people, and Hartwell stood tall at the top of that list. Hartwell also did not appreciate the fact that McQueen was not awed by him.

"I saw the Crime Scene boys lugging a mattress to their van," the captain said. "What's that about?"

Briefly, McQueen explained what they had, giving his superior all the details he thought salient.

"You shouldn't have allowed them to remove the mattress until I'd arrived, Sergeant," Hartwell said, when McQueen was finished. "You know better than that."

"Yes, sir." McQueen could have offered several arguments for not needing the captain's approval to remove the mattress, but decided to simply back off and let the man have his way. They'd all get off the cold beach quicker that way.

"The M.E. has examined the body?"

"Yes, sir."

"Any conclusions?"

"The state of the body and the cold weather precluded that, sir," McQueen said. "He won't be able to get us any more until he takes the body back to the morgue."

"Statements?"

"My partner is taking them now, sir," McQueen said, pointing down the beach.

"That's the Polar Bear club?"

"Yes, sir."

"Foolish old farts," Hartwell said, shaking his head. "They're all just begging for a heart attack."

"Yes, sir."

Hartwell took off his hat just long enough to run his hand lightly over his expensively cut gray hair, thereby bringing it to everyone's attention. Satisfied that his haircut had been properly shown off, he put his hat back on.

"Stupid old men," he continued, even though at his age he would have fit right in with them—or, perhaps, because of it.

"Sir, the M.E.'s office would like to get the body someplace warmer as soon as they can."

"Of course, of course," Hartwell said. He looked down at the body, walked around it a bit, made a show of leaning over and examining it. "All right, you have my okay to move the body."

McQueen looked at the impatient men from the M.E.'s office and said, "Go."

"Who's your superior, Sergeant?" Hartwell asked as the men moved forward and began to bag the body.

"Lieutenant Jessup runs my squad, sir."

"All right," the captain said, "carry on."

Hartwell looked at his driver and nodded, and the man led his boss back up the beach to the boardwalk. The driver opened the car door for Captain Hartwell, then trotted around, got inside and backed out.

"Asshole," one of the M.E.'s men said.

"No comment," McQueen said.

As they hauled the body up to their van, McQueen walked down the beach to where his partner was talking to the shivering members of the Polar Bear club.

"I'm about done, Dennis," Velez said. "Can we let them go get dressed and go home?"

"I want to talk to the one who actually saw the body first," McQueen said.

"That would be me," Bobby Kelly said.

"Okay," McQueen said to Velez. "Let the rest go and find their clothes and go home, as long as you have their addresses."

"And phone numbers," Velez said. "I learned that in detective school."

"Sorry, Ray."

"You were talkin' to Captain Hartwell, weren't you?"

"Yep."

"Then I forgive you."

"Mr. Kelly," McQueen said, "take a walk with me."

"Sure."

Kelly fell in next to McQueen, holding a towel tightly around him.

"You seem somewhat younger than the rest," McQueen said.

"I am," Kelly said, "but they were the nearest group."

"What's the kick?" McQueen asked. "I don't understand the appeal of freezing."

"Don't think I could explain it to you," Kelly said. "It's just . . . invigorating."

"Tell me about finding the body."

"What's to tell?" Kelly asked. "I came out of the water and there it was."

"What do you do for a living, Mr. Kelly?"

"I'm a stockbroker."

"And the others?"

"All different professions," Kelly said. "Your partner took all that information."

"No one noticed the mattress before you all went in the water?" the detective asked.

"I did," the man said. "I mean, I saw something, but you always see things on the beach these days. Garbage just . . . washes up. Besides, it was farther down the beach from where we were going in. I just happened to come out . . . well, in the right place, I guess you'd say."

"Or the wrong place," McQueen said. "All right, sir. We'll be in touch. You can go."

As McQueen started to walk away Kelly said, "You didn't ask me if I knew the dead guy."

"I assumed if you did, you would have told me."

Kelly stared at him for a moment, then turned and started off toward his fellow club members, who were donning their clothing with quick, jerky movements.

McQueen found Ramon Velez sitting on the steps to the boardwalk, slapping his shoes together in an attempt to get all the sand out of them.

"Goddammit, I hate the beach."

"Don't you take your kids in the summer?"

"Only when Cookie makes me."

He slammed the shoes down on the step, slapped them together again, then ran his hands over his socks before putting the shoes back on. Finally, he stood up.

"Ready to go?" McQueen asked.

"What about canvassing?"

"Let the uniforms do it," McQueen said. "I'm hungry. Figured while we're here we might as well hit Nathan's."

"I'm with you on that," Velez said. "Let's go."

They climbed back up onto the boardwalk and back to McQueen's car, which was blocking in the M.E.'s van. He waved his apology to the driver, backed his car out and drove around the corner to the original Nathan's Famous.

When the two detectives got into their car and pulled away from the boardwalk, the Observer decided his job was done. Even before the rest of the crowd dispersed, he made his way through them, head low, hat pulled down, and left the area.

This assignment was finished. On to the next one . . .

When they were standing at the Nathan's counter, each armed with a couple of hot dogs and an order of fries, the detectives discussed their new case.

"What'd Dr. G say?" Velez asked.

"Not much," McQueen said. He explained that the body had to be warmed—almost thawed—before the M.E. would be able to find anything.

"No obvious wounds?"

"None," McQueen said.

"I hate tough cases."

"We got no case at all, Ray, unless the M.E. tells us so," McQueen said. "We've got no other cases, right?"

"Not right now," Velez said. "We closed out that one last week, and this is the first one we've caught since."

"Then all we've got to do right now is eat hot dogs and wait for the M.E.'s report."

Velez ate the last bite of his second dog and said, "Then we need two more?"

"Absolutely."

4

"Dennis," Lieutenant Alan Jessup said. "My office."

McQueen finished out the day filing and answering phones at the Homicide office on Snyder Avenue, on the second floor of the 67 Precinct building. They shared the floor with the regular precinct squad, which was not a situation either squad enjoyed.

McQueen's shift finished at six P.M., but at five forty-five Lieutenant Alan Jessup walked in and uttered those words.

Velez looked across the desk at McQueen and asked, "Want me to come in?"

"What for?" McQueen asked.

"Moral support."

"Relax, Ray," McQueen said. "Finish what you're doing and go home."

"Did we get anything from the M.E.'s office, or the lab?" Velez asked.

"Not yet," McQueen said, standing up. "Maybe in the morning. Go home to Cookie and I'll see you then."

"Right."

Velez stood up and grabbed his jacket from the back of his chair while McQueen went into the lieutenant's office.

"What's up, boss?" he asked.

"Shut the door and have a seat."

McQueen did so, taking a chair across from the lieutenant. Jessup was ten years younger than McQueen, and on the fast track to making captain. It didn't bother him to take orders from the man, though. He'd never wanted to be a boss, and only backed into becoming a sergeant when he was put in command of a task force several years before. He'd had plenty of chances to push for a promotion to lieutenant since then, but McQueen was happy with his present rank. In fact, he'd only accepted the move to the Homicide Squad on the condition he could still catch cases, and not just supervise.

"I had a call from Captain Hartwell today."

"What'd he want?"

"Seems he doesn't feel he got the proper respect from you at the Coney Island crime scene this morning."

"I 'yes, sirred' him up the ass, boss."

"Well, apparently he thought it was less than heartfelt," Jessup said. "Thought you were being sarcastic."

"I'll try and watch it next time," McQueen said, sarcastically.

"And there was somethin' about a mattress?"

McQueen closed his eyes.

"The lab was waiting to take the mattress that had been covering the body," McQueen said. "It's all in my report, Loo."

"I read the report," Jessup said. "Look, we have to deal with him, Dennis, so just deal with him, okay? In the future just wait for him to get to a scene before you let anybody or anything go."

"Jesus Christ," McQueen said. "Is he going to haul me up on charges?"

"No," Jessup said, "he's leaving it to my discretion."

"That's white of him."

"Just watch your p's and q's when he's around, okay?"

"Okay, sure," McQueen said, "I got it, boss. Is that it?" He started to get up.

"No," Jessup said. "Sit back down."

McQueen dropped back into the chair. Jessup picked up a personnel folder and dropped it on his sergeant's side of the table. He then pushed his chair back from his desk and slumped comfortably in his chair.

"We're getting a replacement for Jackson tomorrow."

"What are they doing with him?"

"Dropping him back in the bag."

The "bag" was uniform.

"Good," McQueen said, "he never should have been made a gold shield, anyway."

"I agree," Jessup said, "but it took a while to get others to see it, too."

"Who are we getting?"

"There's the file," Jessup said.

McQueen picked it up and opened it.

"When is he getting here?"

"Tomorrow morning."

"Detective Bailey Summers," McQueen said, reading the file. "Ten years in, gold shield two years ago, worked in the sixth for a while, then Sex Crimes. Thirty-two. Five-six, kinda short, but that's okay. At least he's got some experience on him. Should be an improvement over Jackson."

"You missed something."

"What?"

"Keep reading," Jessup said. "You're a detective— detect."

McQueen shrugged and went back to the folder. He scanned the pages again, and then saw it, the "F" under sex.

"A woman," he said.

"Yes," Jessup said. "She'll be the first woman ever in this squad. Will you have a problem with that?"

McQueen closed the folder and kept it on his lap.

"It's the twenty-first century, Loo," McQueen said.

"Does that mean yes or no?"

McQueen had twenty-five years on the job, which meant he'd worked with guys who had come into the department during the late 1950s and early 1960s, when the department was totally different. But women had been in the department a long time, and the first woman had made it into a homicide squad over twenty years ago. Still, there were men in the department who hung onto the belief that this was a man's job, and women still had to put up with some crap.

"I won't give any problems, boss."

"But you think somebody will?"

"We've got good detectives in this squad, Loo," McQueen said, "but a couple of them can be assholes. They'll put her to the test."

"Well," Jessup said, "maybe she'll win them over."

"Any idea what she looks like?"

"You think that matters?"

McQueen looked at the personnel file again. Five-six, red hair, a hundred and thirty pounds.

"In a perfect world it wouldn't matter, Loo," he said, "but if this girl is hot it could add to the problem."

"Well, right now there's no problem to add to, Dennis," Jessup said. "We're gettin' a new detective in the squad, and that's that. Let's just wait and see if a problem materializes, and not go lookin' for one."

"I agree."

"Okay, then there's one more thing."

"What's that?"

"I want you to work with her."

"Right away?"

"Yep, put her on this case with you."

"The Coney Island thing?"

"Yeah."

"But she wasn't there, Loo."

"You were, and you're the primary," Jessup answered. "Just let her assist you."

"What about Ray?"

"Put Velez with Cataldo," Jessup said. "He needs a partner now that Jackson's gone."

"Loo—"

"After she works this case with you, and gets some experience, you can put her with Frankie and take Velez back."

"I'll let her work with me," McQueen said, "but I'm not sure Frank Cataldo is the right partner for her."

"Frankie's a good man."

"He's a good detective, that's for sure," McQueen said, "but—"

"Then it's settled." Jessup pulled his chair forward and sat up straight. His body language was unmistakably dismissive.

"Okay, then," McQueen said. He stood up and maintained his hold on Detective Bailey Sommers's personnel file. "I'll just take this with me."

"Fine. I'll see you tomorrow, Dennis."

"Yeah, boss. Good night."

McQueen went right to his desk and dropped the folder on it so he could address it first thing in the morning. While his partner would arrive for his ten-to-six tour, McQueen, as a sergeant and second in command in the squad, would arrive earlier than that without seeking any overtime pay. It was one of the benefits, or alternate benefits, of being a "boss"— even a second-in-command one.

He wasn't looking forward to the arrival of Detective Bailey Sommers, and it had nothing to do with the fact that she was a woman. He just never looked forward to breaking new people in, especially when he was starting work on a new case. He would have preferred to assign her to one of the other detectives in the squad and let them break her in. Now he was going to have to do both at the same time.

Seated at a corner desk were Detectives Diver and Dolan, the Double D boys of the squad. They had been working together for three years, and told anyone who would listen that this was the best partnership either had ever had in their years in the department—and both had been on the job for more than fifteen years. McQueen felt the same way about his partnership with Velez, but that was going to have to be put aside, at least for a short while.

He waved good night to the Double Ds, and left the building.

5

Detective Second Grade Bailey Sommers exited the subway on the corner of Church Avenue and Rogers Avenue in front of a Carvel Ice Cream store. She paused and looked around, spotted a donut shop, a newspaper stand, a restaurant, a luncheonette and an OTB parlor, among other things. A Manhattanite all her life, Brooklyn was a new experience for her. She'd had a couple cases that had taken her there before, but not for any extended period of time. Working in Brooklyn was definitely going to be something new, but it was the only place there had been an opening in a homicide squad.

Her directions told her the precinct was two blocks away, on Snyder Avenue. She passed a Chinese take-out along the way—a particular favorite of hers—but would soon hear the story about the half a mouse that had been found in a can of soda there.

When she turned into Snyder Avenue she saw the precinct building, a three-story thirty-year-old structure which, at that time of the morning, was taking in and belching out blue-and-white cars and cops in uniform and plain clothes. She was doing a nine-to-five tour of duty that day rather than a ten-to-six, because she was doing to undergo orientation. More than punctual throughout her life, though, she was arriving before eight A.M., which was why she was encountering some traffic.

She entered the precinct lobby with a garment bag slung over her shoulder. It was the way most cops arrived at a new command. She had her uniform in there, and another change of clothes. When she presented herself at the front desk, the sergeant there looked at her expectantly.

"Yeah?"

"Detective Sommers reporting."

"You new in the unit?" he assumed she was newly assigned to the Precinct Detective Unit.

"Uh . . . the homicide unit."

He waved her off.

"Then you don't need to report to me. You're not assigned to this command. Homicide is separate."

"Well . . . where are they?" she asked.

"Second floor," he replied, and promptly ignored her.

She was about to ask how to get there but remembered passing the elevator on the way in.

"Thanks, Sarge," she said, and the man grunted.

She passed a couple of uniforms on the way, who stopped and looked at her.

"Maybe we're gettin' a looker in the PDU," one of them said.

"Be better than lookin' at all them guys," the other said.

"Hatcher's a chick."

"Coulda fooled me," the other said.

Sommers ignored them and headed for the elevator.

* * *

McQueen had stopped for dinner at the Italian restaurant he lived above the night before. It had taken him a couple years after his divorce to actually stop living in basement apartments and find something decent but now, almost half a dozen years since the divorce, he was satisfied with where he was living. Maybe not completely satisfied with his life, yet, but after four years he was settled in his small apartment. And it was only one precinct over from where he worked, an easy drive.

His transfer to the Brooklyn South Homicide Squad had been almost a lateral movement. His previous assignment had been with the 67 Squad, so he was still working in the same building. The only difference was that he didn't have to report to the C.O. of the precinct. His immediate boss was his lieutenant, who in turn reported to the chief of detectives.

Returning home the previous night after dinner he'd given the new case of the frozen body on Coney Island Beach a few moments of thought, but went to bed after deciding to put off any thought until after he got the M.E. and crime scene reports. No point in treating it as homicide until he had to.

The next morning he woke thinking about the new detective who had been assigned to the squad. He hoped that her hundred and thirty pounds was distributed in a lumpy fashion over her five-foot-six frame. The last thing they needed in the squad was a distraction.

He got to work early so he could clear up some paperwork and see if the reports were in on the frozen guy. He also wanted to be there when Detective Sommers arrived. As it turned out he got there just about ten minutes before she walked in.

He was relieved to see that she was wearing a

parka, and her hair was pinned atop her head. Her face looked plain and she could have been lumpy beneath the parka. The night watch guys, Vadala and Silver, looked up as she entered.

"Sergeant McQueen?" she asked, looking at the three men in turn.

"That's me," he said.

She turned her attention to him.

"I was told to report directly to you," she said. "Detective Bailey Sommers."

"We've been expecting you, Sommers," McQueen said. "That's Pat Vadala over there, and Billy Silver."

Both detectives waved, then collected their jackets from the backs of their chairs.

"We were just going off," Silver said. "Good luck on your first day."

"Thanks," she said.

Both men walked past her, and didn't look back as they went out the door.

"Come on over here," McQueen said. "You got your ten card?"

"Sure thing."

She approached his desk, put down her garment bag and dug her ten card out of her pocket. On the card was listed each of the firearms she owned, along with their serial numbers. It would be kept on file and she would not be allowed to carry any other weapons.

As she came closer to hand him the card, McQueen saw that she was prettier up close. It was the lack of makeup that made her look plain. He turned his gaze from her to the card. Her service revolver and a 9mm Glock were the only guns on the card. His first instinct was to ask her if these were the only two guns she owned, but he decided not to. Most cops had another gun stashed somewhere.

"The lieutenant will be in later," McQueen said, putting the ten card down. "I'll introduce you then."

"Okay."

"You'll be partnered with me."

"With a sergeant?"

"I catch cases around here," McQueen said.

"What about the partner you have now?"

"He'll be reassigned temporarily. We lost a man recently—he was reassigned, like you."

"Fine with me," she said, with a shrug. "Is there someplace I can stow my gear and get changed? Fix my face? Will I have a locker?"

"I'll show you where the lockers are," he said. "For now it'll be with the others, but we'll have it moved so you have some privacy."

"Maybe the guys'll want privacy."

"Everybody shows up already dressed, Detective," McQueen said. "The lockers are really just for uniforms, coats in the winter—like now. We don't have any showers up here. You want a shower you'll have to take it at home, or go down to the precinct and use theirs. You have a problem with any of that?"

"No, sir."

"If you're gonna be changing your clothes today do it now. Day shift won't be here for a few minutes."

"Yes, sir."

"I'll show you where."

He took her out of the squad room and walked her down a hall to a makeshift locker room. Since they weren't assigned to the precinct, the homicide detectives were not given lockers in the basement with the rest of the precinct personnel. McQueen had often thought that basing the squad here was something that had not been given very much thought.

"There's a bathroom down the hall," he told her. "When you're ready just come back into the squad room. I just caught a new case yesterday, and I'll brief you on it."

"Yes, sir."

"And cut that out," he said. "We're gonna be working as partners for a while, so you don't have to call me sir."

"Yes, Sarge."

"Just call me Dennis, Detective," he said, and left her to get herself ready for work.

When he returned to the squad room he saw that the door to the lieutenant's office was open. Since it was usually closed when the man wasn't there, he wasn't surprised to find his boss inside.

" 'Mornin', boss," he said, sticking his head in.

"Dennis," Jessup said. "The new detective in yet?"

"Nice and early."

"Good. Can I meet her?"

"She's getting settled," McQueen said. "I'll bring her in as soon as she's ready."

"Fine. What's happening with the frozen guy case?"

"No reports on my desk," McQueen said. "I'll probably have to go down to the morgue, and to the crime lab, and get the results myself. Big surprise."

"Well, make sure you take Detective Sommers with you."

"She'll be with me every step of the way."

"Have you told Velez about the change in assignment yet?" Jessup asked.

"I'll let him know when he comes in."

"You didn't call him at home last night?"

"This is business, Loo," McQueen said. "Why ruin his night?"

"Okay," Jessup said. "Your call. Uh, what's Sommers look like, by the way?"

"Couldn't really tell," McQueen said. "She was wearing a parka, and no makeup. I'll let you decide for yourself when I bring her in."

"Fine," Jessup said. "Just bring her on in when she's ready."

"Yes, sir."

McQueen left the lieutenant's office and went back to his desk. Detective Cataldo had arrived and was seated at his desk, and at that moment Ray Velez walked in.

"Ray, Frankie," he called out. "Can I talk to you guys for a minute?"

Bailey Sommers checked herself in the mirror and thought she had done a decent job making herself presentable, under the circumstances. She was wearing a cream-colored sweater and black pants, had her holster clipped to her belt and had dabbed on a little makeup. The only thing she wasn't happy with was her hair, but she didn't have the time to try to do more with it, so she put it in a ponytail that didn't quite hang to her shoulder blades.

She squared her shoulders, checked herself in the mirror one last time and, satisfied that she looked businesslike, headed back to the squad room.

"Do either of you have trouble with the new assignments?" McQueen asked.

Cataldo shrugged and said, "I don't much care who I partner with."

"No," Velez said. "No problem."

"Good," McQueen said. "Then let's get to work."

Cataldo turned immediately and headed for his desk. Velez didn't budge, leaned over and dropped his voice.

"I have a problem."

"I thought you said you didn't."

"I lied," Velez said. "Come on, Dennis, I couldn't say anything in front of him but . . . come on. Me and Frankie?"

"I know he's not the perfect partner, Ray," Mc-Queen said, "but it's not for very long. Just work with me."

"Why don't you work with Cataldo and give me the new guy?" Velez asked.

"The lieutenant asked me to partner with Detective Sommers," McQueen said. "In fact, it was an order."

"Fine."

And one other thing," McQueen said, as Bailey Sommers entered the squad room again, "she's not a guy."

6

When Detective Bailey Sommers reentered the squad room, McQueen sat back in his chair and closed his eyes. Whatever she'd done to herself had changed her appearance drastically. She'd gone from plain and kind of stocky to the kind of woman who turned men's heads. In her sweater and pants she looked shapely rather than stocky. The parka had done a lot to hide that. And with the addition of makeup her cheekbones suddenly became very noticeable, as did her full-lipped, sexy mouth and blue eyes. This was the kind of woman who'd had to endure all kinds of verbal abuse in the police department over the years, through no fault of her own. The job had changed, bringing more women into prominent jobs, and nobody was to blame, least of all them.

He was going to have to keep a close eye on the squad for the next few weeks, to see if her addition was going to lead to any trouble—for her, or anyone else.

"Sergeant—I mean, Dennis," she said, approaching his desk. "I'm ready to go to work."

"The lieutenant would like to meet you, but first . . . Frank!"

"Yeah, boss?" Cataldo looked up from his desk.

"This is Detective Sommers," McQueen said. "She's just been assigned to the squad."

"Is that a fact?" Cataldo asked, looking her up and down. "Welcome."

"Nice to meet you," she said, neutrally.

"And this is Ray Velez," McQueen said. "Usually my partner, he's gonna work with Frank for a bit, while you work with me."

Sommers looked at Velez and said, "I hope that won't cause any problems?"

"Why should it cause any problems?" Velez asked. He put his hand out. "Welcome to the squad."

She shook his hand and said, "Thank you."

Velez looked at McQueen.

"What about the Coney Island frozen guy?"

"I caught that, so Bailey and I will follow that up."

"Bailey," Velez said. He looked at Sommers again. "Odd name for a woman."

"It was my mother's maiden name," she said, with a shrug.

"Yeah, well," Velez said, "parents do some odd things to their kids with their names."

"Yes, they do," she agreed.

"Some day I'll tell you my whole name," Velez said, and walked over to Cataldo's desk.

Sommers looked at McQueen, who said, "It's long . . . real long. Come on, I'll introduce you to the boss."

"What's this about a frozen guy on Coney Island?"

"I'll fill you in, after you meet the boss."

He led her across the room to the open door of the lieutenant's office. He entered without knocking.

"Boss, here's Detective Sommers."

Jessup looked up from his desk, then stood up. He stared at Sommers for a moment, and McQueen knew the man was replaying in his mind the physical description he'd been given of the new detective in his squad.

"Detective Sommers," he said, finally.

"Sir," she said. "I'm very happy to be here."

"And we're happy to have you," Jessup said. "Getting settled in all right?"

"Yes, sir."

"Has Sergeant McQueen told you that you'll be partnered with him for the time being?"

"Yes, sir," she said. "I'm looking forward to working with him."

"Are you familiar with the sergeant, Detective Sommers?" Jessup asked.

"Yes, sir."

McQueen looked surprised, exchanged a glance with his boss.

"And how is that?" the lieutenant asked.

"When I found out I was being transferred here, I did some research," she explained.

McQueen and Jessup both waited, and when nothing else was forthcoming the lieutenant asked, "And?"

"I read about the serial case a few years back," she said, "where the killer was working from his dead wife's diary. Killing people as a result of some of her fantasies?"

It was the case that had gotten McQueen promoted to sergeant so he could be second whip on a task force. McQueen had tracked the killings and decided they were being done by the same man, a distraught husband named Turner.

"It was primarily Sergeant McQueen's work that led to the killer's capture and conviction," she said.

41

She tossed a brief look McQueen's way. "I was impressed by what I read, sir. Originally I was just happy to be transferred to any homicide squad. The fact that this was the only one with an opening didn't matter to me, but after I did my research . . . well, I'm anxious to work with Sergeant McQueen, as I said before."

"Well . . . good, then," Jessup said, after a moment, "good. Why don't the two of you get to work, then?"

"Yes, sir," she said.

"Come on, Sommers," McQueen said. "I'll fill you in on the body we got yesterday."

"If you have any problems, Sommers," Jessup said. seating himself again, "just let me know."

"Yes, sir, I will," Sommers said. "Thank you."

She turned and followed McQueen out.

7

"What was that about?" McQueen asked.

"What was what about?"

McQueen waited until they were at his desk to speak again.

"All that stuff about wanting to work with me?"

"It's true, Dennis," she said. "I did the research. You did a hell of a job in that case. It couldn't have been a fluke, could it?"

"It sure could have," he said.

"But it wasn't, was it? You're good at this, aren't you?"

"Yeah, I am."

"Then I want to learn," she said, "and I might as well learn from someone who, if he's not the best, at least is good."

McQueen looked across the room at Velez and Cataldo, to see if they were hearing any of this. They seemed oblivious.

"Okay," he said, "have a seat."

McQueen seated himself behind his desk and

43

Sommers took a seat across from him. He took out the report he had typed the night before, about the body on Coney Island beach, and tossed it across the desk.

"What we have is in there, but I'll give it to you briefly," he said, and outlined everything that had happened the day before, what they knew, and what they didn't know.

"So we don't know yet if it's a murder or not," she said.

"Right."

"When will we know?"

"Normally when we get a report," he said, "but since you're new I think I'll take you down there so we can find out firsthand."

"To the lab?"

"And the morgue."

She was quiet.

"You have been to a morgue before, haven't you?" he asked. "Seen dead bodies?"

"Yes."

"What was your last assignment?"

"Sex Crimes."

He got up, grabbed his jacket from the back of his chair.

"What you'll see at the morgue can't be any worse than some of the stuff you saw there."

"Probably not," she said.

"Well then, go get your parka and we'll get going."

"Right."

She ran down the hall and came back ready to go.

"Where first?" she asked, in the elevator.

"Morgue," McQueen said. "We're gonna find out if we have a murder on our hands."

* * *

44

They found Bannerjee in his office in the morgue in Kings County Hospital, on Clarkson Avenue in the confines of the 71 Precinct.

"I was going to call you," the doctor said, looking up at his visitors.

"I'll bet," McQueen said. "Dr. Bannerjee, this is Detective Sommers. New to the Brooklyn South Homicide Squad. Detective, Dr. Bannerjee."

"My pleasure," the handsome doctor said.

"Nice to meet you," Sommers said. The doctor's good looks had not escaped her notice.

"What have we got, Doc?" McQueen asked.

"I have a dead body," Bannerjee said. "You have a murder, I think."

"You think?"

"Perhaps we should look at the body."

"Lead the way."

The doctor stood up, excused himself politely as he slipped past Sommers to go out the door. They followed him out, down the hall and through dual swinging doors. There was a gowned doctor at the other end of the room working on a body.

"Do we need gowns?" Sommers asked. "Masks?"

"I've already autopsied our body," Bannerjee said.

He walked to a table, grabbed the edge of the sheet that was covering the body, then paused and looked at Sommers.

"Are you ready?"

She swallowed and said, "I'm ready."

"Me, too," McQueen said, unnecessarily.

Bannerjee pulled the sheet down to the waist, leaving the bottom half of the body covered, from the genitals down. McQueen figured if he'd been there alone, or with Velez, the sheet would have come completely off. Ever the gentleman, the good doctor. As it was,

Sommers had a good look at the Y incision in the torso.

"The body was pretty cold when we got it," Bannerjee said, "In fact, frozen in some areas. We had to thaw it out."

"He froze to death?" Sommers asked.

"Ah," Bannerjee said, "there's the odd part. I found something very interesting when I removed the lungs and examined them."

"You put them back, right?" McQueen asked. He didn't think they needed to see the actual lungs.

"Yeah, but I kept enough tissue samples."

"And what did you find, Doctor," McQueen asked, "when you examined the lungs?"

"There were two very interesting things."

"So how was he killed?" McQueen asked impatiently.

"Well, from the condition of the lungs I'd say he died in a fire," Bannerjee answered.

"He was burned to death?" Sommers asked.

"Not quite," the doctor said. "As you can see, there are no burns on the body."

"So he didn't freeze to death, or burn to death," McQueen said. "Should we just keep guessing? Do this by process of elimination? Hit by a car? Fell out of a tree?"

"He's very impatient," Bannerjee said to Sommers. "You'll learn that about him the longer he's your partner."

"He's not really my partner," she said. "It's just . . . like . . . orientation."

"Good for you," Bannerjee said.

"Doc?" McQueen said, feeling and exhibiting the impatience he'd been accused of.

"Oh, right," Bannerjee said. "Well, he died of smoke inhalation. I found evidence of not only smoke but other—"

"So he was in a fire," McQueen said, cutting him off.

"Apparently."

"So somebody dropped a dead body off at the beach?"

"Yes, but—"

"That still doesn't make it murder."

"Ah, to that." Bannerjee reached behind the head of the corpse. "If you look at the back of the skull—"

"Doc," McQueen said.

"Okay, okay," Bannerjee said, "I'll tell, not show."

"Thank you."

"He was hit on the back of the head. Blunt force trauma."

"Hard enough to kill him if he hadn't died of smoke inhalation?" McQueen asked.

"Yes."

"Could the injury have been caused by a fall?" Sommers asked.

"Possibly," Bannerjee said, "but there are other bruises on the body, on the torso, and around the kidneys. I think he was beaten, or in a fight, and then somebody hit him on the back of the head with . . . something. They then apparently left the body somewhere—in a building—in a car—something that they either set on fire, or was on fire—"

"Hit him with something like what?" This time it was Sommers who cut him off. "A hammer?" She asked.

"No, something blunt," he said. "A club of some kind."

"A baseball bat?" she asked.

"Possibly."

"A shillelagh?" McQueen asked, half serious, or less. Bannerjee frowned.

"I suppose so . . . although I'm not really sure about the shape of one of those."

"Don't worry about it," McQueen said. "The important thing is that you're calling this a murder."

"Yes, I am," Bannerjee said. "You'll have my report on your desk by later today. It will have all the details that you, uh, have not allowed me to elucidate for you now."

"Having it in a report will be fine, Doc," McQueen said. "This is all we need to get started."

"Well, there is that other interesting thing I mentioned," Bannerjee said, as McQueen turned to leave.

"And what's that, Doc?" He was half in, half out the door.

"Something else about his lungs," Bannerjee said. "They were frozen."

"From being in the water?" Sommers asked.

"Definitely not."

"Why definitely?" McQueen asked.

"The lungs were frozen solid," Bannerjee said, "and covered with ice crystals. I examined the crystals and guess what I found?"

"Doc—" McQueen said, but Sommers was more willing to play the game.

"Freshwater?" she asked.

"Give the lady a prize," the M.E. said.

"So . . . he was frozen first, and then dropped in the water?" McQueen stepped back into the room.

"I believe so," Bannerjee said. "I see evidence that he was in the water, not just dropped on the beach. Also . . . well, have a look."

They walked back to the body with the doctor, who turned the man over onto his side.

"See that?" he asked, pointing.

McQueen bent to have a look.

"A scratch?"

"Exactly."

It was down around the small of the back, horizontal, about four inches long. It seemed deeper at the top than at the bottom.

"From something in the water?"

"No," Bannerjee said, letting the body down on its back again. "There is blood in the scratch, but not his. He was dead when he went into the water, so he was not scratched then. In fact, whenever the scratch was inflicted, he was dead, and so did not bleed."

"So when? And with what?"

"Still working on that," the doctor said.

"About the lungs, Doc," McQueen asked. "Why would they still be frozen?"

"Have you ever taken a turkey out of the freezer and thawed it for Thanksgiving, Sergeant?" Bannerjee asked.

"What's that got to do—"

"I have," Sommers said, catching on. "The outside can be thawed, but when you slide your hand inside it's still frozen solid and covered with crystals of ice."

"Exactly!" Bannerjee said, happily. He looked at McQueen. "She's sharp, this one."

"So the body was in a freezer?"

"That's what I think," Bannerjee said. "That's why I can't figure out the time of death. After he was killed he was stored in a freezer, and then disposed of, days . . . perhaps even weeks later."

"Well, that's just great," McQueen said. "Doc, when you get something more from that scratch, let me know, huh?"

"You'll be the first."

"We gotta go," McQueen said.

"Detective Sommers," Bannerjee said, executing a small bow, "it's been a pleasure."

"Thank you, Doctor," she said, with a smile.

"Sommers!" McQueen called from the hall.

* * *

"Where to now?" she asked from the passenger seat.

"One Main Street," McQueen said.

"What's there?"

"Crime Lab," he said. "We're chasing down their results, too."

"What about fingerprints?" she asked. "To ID the body so we can have a name and address on the victim?" She made points with him by not saying "vic."

"That's one of the things we're after."

"And what else?"

"Whatever they got from the body, or the mattress," he explained. "How are you doing?"

"I'm fine," she said. "Why?"

"Well, unless you've been in a homicide squad a detective wouldn't have a lot of experience with the morgue," he said. "Ever sit on a ripe one while on patrol?"

"I saw one, once," she said. "I never . . . sat on it."

"The morgue is a lot different from seeing D.O.A. on patrol."

"I saw that," she said, "and I'm fine."

"Good."

They rode in silence for a while and then Sommers said, "Can I ask a question?"

"Sure, why not?"

"Why wouldn't you let the doctor finish what he was saying?"

McQueen hesitated a moment, then said, "This is not a TV show, it's real life. There's no reason for the doctor to go into great detail about what he found. All I need is the results. They can save all the computer-generated guts for the TV audiences."

"I take it you don't watch much TV?"

"Not cop shows."

"I'll keep that in mind for future conversations," she said. "What do you like to talk about?"

"I'm not famous for my conversational skills, Bailey," he said. "Sorry."

"That's okay," she said. "I'm here to learn the job. Can I ask questions about that?"

"All the questions you can think of," he said, glad she hadn't decided to try to engage him in something more personal.

8

Upon arrival at the crime lab, McQueen presented himself and Sommers to the clerk at the desk and asked for the tech he'd spoken to at the scene, Cahill.

"Marty Cahill?" she said. "Sure, he's here. Hold on."

She picked up her phone, spoke to Cahill and then hung up.

"He'll be right out."

While they were waiting Sommers asked McQueen, "What do you expect to find from the mattress?"

"I don't know," he said. "I just want to know if they did find something. It's possible the mattress floated in and covered the body by accident and has nothing to do with the case. I'm hoping this guy will tell us."

A man McQueen recognized from Coney Island Beach appeared in the hall, approaching him and Sommers.

"Sergeant McQueen?" He extended his hand.

"Cahill," McQueen said. "This is my partner, Detective Sommers."

Cahill gave Sommers a frank appraisal and obviously liked what he saw.

"My pleasure, Detective." He did not offer to shake hands with either of them. He said to McQueen, "I thought you had a different partner yesterday."

"That was my regular partner," McQueen said. "This is a temporary situation, but Detective Sommers will be my partner for the duration of this case."

"Excellent." Cahill was tall, slender, in his thirties, a good-looking young man who had been with the Crime Scene Unit for about five years. He had an easygoing manner that McQueen thought would probably take him far. It probably helped him with women, too, if the look on Sommers's face was any indication.

"We're here about your findings," McQueen said.

"I figured," Cahill said. "Come on back. I'll show you what I've got."

As they walked down the hall with him, McQueen said, "I thought I'd get a written report."

"And you will," Cahill said. "As soon as I can get the time to sit down and write reports. I'm working six different cases from all over Brooklyn, and that's just my case load. In here."

He took them into a small room with two desks. Apparently one belonged to him and one to another tech.

"Sorry there's not much room to sit," he said. "Sergeant, you can sit behind that desk, Detective, you can have my chair. I'll just perch right here." He sat on the edge of his own desk.

"Did you get anything off that mattress?" McQueen asked.

Cahill picked up a folder and opened it.

"The mattress was soaked," he said. "Any trace evidence that might have been on it had been destroyed by the seawater."

"That figures."

"But it also looked like the mattress had nothing to do with the body, anyway," Cahill went on.

"It washed in?"

"Looks like it."

"And landed on the body?"

"Maybe."

"What do you mean maybe?"

"They may have drifted in together."

"But not connected to each other?"

"No."

Fine, McQueen thought. The man *was* confirming his thoughts.

"So the body wasn't dumped on the beach?"

"No," Cahill said. "And another thing. I took a piece of ice from the body's, uh, genitals. It was stuck to his pubic hair."

"Freshwater?" Sommers asked.

He looked at her and asked, "How did you know?"

"The M.E. found freshwater ice in his lungs," McQueen said.

"Well," Cahill said, "I'll tell you what I think it means. I think the body was encased in a block of ice and dropped into the sea."

"Doctor G says he thinks the man died in a fire," McQueen said.

"Then somebody must have frozen the body after it was dead."

"Tell me something, Cahill."

"My name's Marty."

"Okay, Marty," McQueen said. "Answer me this. A block of ice like that would float, right?"

"Right."

"So if somebody, say, dumped it off a boat and watched, they'd see that it was floating."

"You'd think so."

"Wait a minute," Sommers said. "Then whoever put it in the water knew it would float."

"Right," Cahill said.

"And knew it would eventually wash ashore."

"Maybe not," Cahill said. "Maybe whoever did it figured the ice would melt and then the body would sink."

"Then why freeze it in the first place?" she asked. "Why not just dump it in the water, weigh it down, make sure it'd sink?"

Cahill closed the folder.

"That's your job to find out," he said.

"He wanted us to find it," McQueen said.

"What?" Sommers asked.

"He wanted the body found," McQueen said.

"Why?"

"It's the only thing that makes sense," he said. "Like you said, Bailey, if he didn't he would have weighed it down."

"Scott Peterson weighed Laci down and she still washed ashore," Cahill pointed out. "Most bodies do. They deteriorate, pieces fall off, and they bob to the surface. Or bottom feeders get to them and nibble at them until they come to the surface."

"So why don't we just have a dumb killer," she asked, "who doesn't know any of this?"

"The body died in a fire, then was frozen and finally dropped in the ocean," McQueen said. "There's too much going on here for us to be dealing with a stupid killer. No, somebody wanted this body found. They're proud of what they did." He looked at Cahill. "What about prints?"

"Apparently, this young fella was never arrested," he said. "We're running the prints through AFIS now. We'll let you know if and when we come up with a hit."

"What about putting his picture in the papers?" Sommers asked. "Asking people to ID him?"

"We don't want his family finding out that way if we can help it," McQueen said. "We'll hold off that way for a while. Meanwhile, we'll call Missing Persons and give them the description. Maybe they can match it up."

"Sorry we couldn't give you more to go on," Cahill said.

"You did your job," McQueen said, standing up. "That's all I could ask."

Sommers stood up and came around Cahill's desk. The tech got up at the same time and McQueen couldn't tell if it was by accident or the man's design that Sommers had to brush up against him to get out.

"It was nice meeting you," Cahill said when he and Sommers were chest to chest.

"Yeah, me too," she said.

Outside McQueen said, "You drive."

"Me?"

"You can drive, can't you?"

"Of course."

"Then do it."

In the car she asked, "Back to the house?"

"Yeah," McQueen said. "When we get there you can call the kid's description in to Missing Persons."

She sat behind the wheel for a few minutes.

"It helps if you turn the key," he said.

"I'm just getting the route right in my head."

"Want me to give you directions?"

"No," she said. "I paid attention while you were driving."

He decided to go ahead and give her the chance to find her way back.

After a few minutes she said, "Sergeant?"

"Yeah?"

"You buy what Cahill said? I mean, about the body being encased in a block of ice?"

"Far-fetched," McQueen said. "I'll go with the M.E.'s findings. The body was frozen, but not encased in a block of ice. The logistics of that—of transporting something like that—makes it too unlikely."

"Sounded far-fetched to me, too."

"And yet, lots of murders are far-fetched," McQueen said.

"I'd sure like to catch this guy and find out the whole story."

"We'll catch him," McQueen said, "but I wouldn't count on getting the whole story."

"Why not?"

"Doesn't always happen that way," McQueen said. "Even when we have the killer, we don't always get all the answers."

"Must be frustrating."

"Stay in homicide long enough," he said, "and you'll find out."

9

Back at the office McQueen put Sommers to work calling Missing Persons and having them check the description of the dead man against some of their reports. Both Velez and Cataldo were out, presumably after catching a case. Homicide was called in on any case involving a death, and given the sheer volume of callouts, the number of cases that actually turned out to be homicides was small. In fact, the number of actual homicides that needed to be investigated had dropped in Brooklyn from about 247 in 1993 to just under 100. New York City itself—once considered crime-riddled—was now ranked 211 out of 230 cities nationwide. McQueen almost expected the department to disband the unit at any time and give homicides back to the precinct squads.

For the time being, though, it was still his job to investigate murders in the Brooklyn South, and according to the M.E., he now had one.

Lt. Jessup was in his office, so McQueen stuck his head in.

"Back, boss."

"Close the door," Jessup said.

McQueen obeyed, stood in front of the man's desk. "How'd she do?"

"She was fine at the morgue," McQueen said. "Came up with some good questions at the lab."

"Good, good," Jessup said. "What about the Coney Island thing?"

"Murder, according to the M.E."

"All right, then it's yours and your new partner's," Jessup said. "Frankie and Ray went out on a call, but it sounds like a suicide."

"We're checking with Missing Persons now, to see if they have any reports on someone matching our dead guy's description."

"Nothing on his prints?"

"No."

"We do have prints?"

"Yeah," McQueen said. "Apparently he wasn't in the water long enough for them to be ruined."

"How long was he in the water?"

"That'll be in the written report," McQueen said. "I should have it before I go home."

"Okay," Jessup said. "Copy me, as usual."

"Yes, sir."

"That's all. You can close the door on your way out."

"Close it?"

"Yeah, Dennis," Jessup said, "close it."

McQueen almost asked him if everything was all right, but they didn't have that kind of relationship. He didn't think he had that kind of relationship—or friendship—with anyone but Ray Velez.

"Yes, sir," he said, and closed the door behind him.

"Sarge?" Sommers said, approaching him as he exited the office.

"Sommers," he said, "just call me Dennis."

"Yes, sir," she said. "Dennis . . . Missing Persons is going through their reports. They'll get back to us if and when they find anything."

McQueen felt foolish, as he had felt when the lieutenant had asked how long the body had been in the water. That was something he should have gotten from Dr. Bannerjee. Instead, he'd have to wait for the written report.

"All right," he said. "When the doctor's report comes in you can call them back and tell them how long the man's been dead. Might give them a ball-park figure of how far back to look."

"Yes, si—Dennis. I, uh, also put in a call to the Arson Squad to see what fires they've had in the past week."

"That was good thinking, Bailey," he said, wishing he'd thought of it. The body had obviously died in a fire, although there were no burns on the body. Checking with the Arson Squad was a smart thing to do.

"Meanwhile," he said, "all we have are the names and addresses of the men who found the body. We can go out and question some of them again, now that they're home, and warm. Maybe one of them will remember something he saw."

"All right."

"We've only got half a day left, so we might be able to get half of them done."

It would give McQueen a chance to see how she interacted with the people she was interviewing. At some later date he'd find out how good she was at actual interrogation.

"Get your coat," McQueen said. "We might as well start now."

Getting out of the office would also accomplish leaving the lieutenant alone, to deal with whatever he was dealing with. He rarely, if ever, closed the door while he was in the office.

By the time they returned to the office again, a half hour before their tour was to be up, McQueen was impressed with the way Sommers had handled the interviews. Of course, they had talked to four men and no women, and all of the men—even the eighty-four-year-old Mr. Dunham—had been smitten with her. They hadn't found Bobby Kelly home, so she hadn't had a chance to speak with the man who actually found the body.

"Should I do my D.D. Five before I leave, Dennis?" she asked. This was the detective's follow-up report.

"How good a typist are you?"

"Good, and fast," she said.

"All right, then. Get to it."

She turned to go to one of the desks, then stopped, as she hadn't really been assigned one yet. She'd made the phone call to Missing Persons from a handy phone, earlier, as no one else had been present, but now Cataldo and Velez were back at their desks.

"Use that one," McQueen said, pointing to the desk that had been used by Jackson. "And here." He plucked a yellow sheet of paper from his in-box. "Here's the original report from the 60th Precinct. You'll have to reference the 61 number." The report was referred to by its form number, UF 61. Each report, as it came in, was given a number on the precinct level. Copies were then sent out to the borough office, the squad involved, and to police headquarters.

"Thanks," she said, taking it from him. "Um, did you ask me if I could type so I could do your report, also?"

McQueen bristled.

"I do my own reports, Detective."

"I—I'm sorry," she said hurriedly. "I didn't mean to offend you. It's just that, in the last squad I worked, they usually had me do the typ—"

"You're a detective, not a secretary," he said, cutting her off. "Just take care of your own reports."

"Yes, sir."

As she walked away he said, "Bailey?"

"Sir?" she turned.

"I'm not offended."

"Yes, sir."

She went to her new desk and started going through the drawers to familiarize herself with it.

"Dennis?"

McQueen turned to face Velez.

"What've you got, Ray?"

"That's up to the M.E. but it looks like a suicide to me," Velez said. "Old fella with cancer swallowed a shotgun. Wife said he'd been talkin' about it ever since he got home from the hospital."

"Not much of the head left, then," McQueen said, wincing. "You'll have to spend a few days on it, talk to his friends and relatives. The M.E.'s not gonna be able to tell much."

"Yeah, okay," Velez said, "we'll put in some hours. What about the Coney Island thing?"

"Dr. G says it's murder," McQueen said, and quickly outlined the doctor's findings. "In fact, his report is supposed to be here . . ." He scanned his desk and found an intra-office envelope from the M.E.'s office. "Here it is. He messengered it over. I'll have to give it a read before I leave, and do my report."

"Well, have fun," Velez said. "I'm headin' out."

"How are you getting along with Frank?"

"If we don't talk," Velez said, "we get along just fine."

"Okay," McQueen said, "it won't be for long, Ray. I promise."

"I'm gonna hold you to that, Dennis. Good night."

"Good night."

Velez headed for the door, but stopped short, turned his head and said, to Sommers, " 'Night, Detective."

She looked up, smiled at him and said, "Good night."

As Velez left he had to slide by to let Diver and Dolan enter. McQueen stood up to introduce Sommers to the Double D boys before one of them said something stupid.

10

After Sommers finished her report she gave it to McQueen, who told her to go on home. While he was finishing up his own report the lieutenant came out and said to good night to them all. That left McQueen in the squad room with Diver and Dolan, until they were called out. Alone, he read through Sommers's report and his own before he tore the copies apart and sent the yellows and whites on their way. He was about to leave when the phone on his desk rang. It was the direct line to the squad, and not the line from the switchboard downstairs.

"McQueen, Homicide," he answered it.

"This is Detective Jack Orson from the Arson Task Force," a voice said. "I'm returning a call we got from a . . . Detective Sommers?"

"Yeah, she's assigned here," McQueen said. "I'm her sergeant. What have you got, Detective?"

"Hey, Sarge, how ya doin'? We got a call askin' about a body . . ." he went on to give McQueen the description that Sommers had sent out to Missing Persons and the Arson Squad.

"Are you lookin' for somebody like that?" McQueen asked.

"Well, we had a fire in Red Hook a couple of weeks ago," the detective said, "and after it was put out a body came up missing. A fella named . . . Wingate, Thomas Wingate."

"Tell me about the fire, and the man."

"I can do better than that," Orson said. "I can fax you the report, complete with a photo."

"Photo?"

"Yeah, we got it from Wingate's mother."

"His mother? How old was he?"

"We got him as twenty-two, still living at home," Orson said. "You got a fax number?"

McQueen gave him the number of the precinct downstairs. He'd pick it up on his way out and take it home with him.

"After you read it, gimme a call back if you think it's him," Orson said. "I'm goin' off duty now, but I'll be back tomorrow at noon."

"Noon?"

"Yeah, I'm doin' noon by eights this week," Orson said.

"I'm doin' a ten by tomorrow," McQueen said. "I'll get back to you then."

"Okay," Orson said. "We been workin' this case a week, one more night ain't gonna hurt."

"Thanks, Detective. I appreciate the call."

"Hey, if this is the same guy I'll thank you. It'll be your case, or Brooklyn North Homicide's, however you guys wanna work it. 'Night, Sarge."

" 'Night."

McQueen hung up, couldn't help but feel some admiration for Detective Bailey Sommers. She had not only taken it upon herself to call the Arson/Explosion Squad, but the Arson Task Force, as well. The task force worked commercial arsons that were committed for profit. It was good thinking on her part.

Detective Orson was right. If it turned out to be the same guy Brooklyn North Homicide probably would claim it. At the moment, he wasn't sure how he'd feel about that. Might as well wait and see.

He went downstairs to pick up the fax.

McQueen drove to his apartment on the corner of Nostrand Avenue and Avenue S, and stopped into the Italian restaurant for an order of baked ziti. He took it upstairs, got situated in the kitchen with a beer and started reading the faxed file. When he'd finished eating, he made some coffee and carried a cup and the file to the desk in the front room.

The apartment was only three rooms, the eat-in kitchen, the bedroom and a front room he used as a combination living room and office.

According to the faxed photo the dead body did seem to be Thomas Wingate. The only way to make sure, though, was to have the mother identify the body. That was not something he looked forward to, but it was going to have to be done.

The thing that puzzled him was the fact that the body was supposed to be two weeks old. He'd checked with the M.E., but it was likely that freezing the body had preserved it. The question was, why? Why preserve it, and why dump it in or near the ocean two weeks later, knowing it would be found?

He turned his attention to the property that had burned. It was a commercial building, and the fire was deemed suspicious by the fire marshal. It was then assigned to the Arson Task Force, since it investigated

fires that appeared to have been set for profit. Even if
the murder went to the Brooklyn North Homicide
Squad, or stayed with McQueen, the Arson investigators would continue to run a parallel investigation.

McQueen left the file on the desk and went back to
the kitchen for more coffee. Under normal circumstances he might have called Ray Velez to talk some
of this out, but for the time being Velez wasn't his
partner. And he couldn't call Bailey Sommers because
he didn't have her phone number with him. He was
going to have to make a point of copying it down
when he got back to the office in the morning.

Armed with a second cup he went back to the living room but didn't make it to the desk. He plopped
down on the sofa and turned on the TV. There was no
point in thinking about the case anymore tonight.
There would be time enough to work on it in the
morning. Besides, there was the possibility that it
would be taken away from them.

Normally, he only watched the news or sports, but
last year he'd become involved in a show he never
would have thought he'd watch. It was a guilty pleasure for him, in the true sense of the definition of the
phrase—something he'd never want anyone else to
know.

He found the right channel, then set the remote
down and settled in for a new season of *America Idol*.

11

The Observer knew that the Ice Man was anxious for another victim. But the Ice Man wasn't out here looking for them. This was his job. It was only after the intended victim was turned into an actual victim that the Ice Man got the body.

So the Ice Man would just have to wait until the Observer found the perfect victim. In order to do this he had to be out there, out in the streets where the people were. He had to watch them, and wait for the likely ones to point themselves out by their actions. This wasn't just a simple matter of trolling for victims. This was a very careful selection process.

He was sitting in the window of a new coffee shop in the Sheepshead Bay section of Brooklyn, watching the people go by. Inside, they were enjoying their lattes and other fancy, foamy coffee drinks. Outside, they were bundled up against the cold, but they didn't know what true cold was. To the Ice Man the cold was a tool, and he wielded it very well. The Ob-

server sometimes envied the others. They got to act, and all he ever did was watch,
    observe,
    choose.
The one he most envied was the Killer.

12

By the time Bailey Sommers walked from the train station to the precinct her nose was bright red. If this assignment was going to last she was going to have to think about moving to Brooklyn, just to be closer. Maybe get a car, too. She'd recently taken the sergeant's exam. If she passed, the extra income would allow for the car, but she didn't have time to wait to decide about the move. She'd have to find a place to live, once she was sure she'd be staying in Homicide.

Women had come a long way in this department, but there were still no squads with a woman in command. In fact, there were no women above the rank of captain, and there was only one of those. However, all she wanted at the moment was an assignment she'd find interesting, and become good at.

When she got to the squad room McQueen was already there. The door to the lieutenant's office was closed, and she'd already learned that meant he wasn't in.

"Sarge," she greeted McQueen. He gave her a look. "I mean, Dennis."

" 'Morning, Sommers," he said.

"What's on for today?"

"We might have an ID on our victim from Coney Island," he told her. "That call you put in to the Arson Task Force panned out. That was good work."

"Thank you."

He told her about the call from the task force detective, and the case file fax.

"I put it on your desk, but you won't have time to look it over," he added. "We have to go and talk to the mother. She'll have to make an ID on the body."

"Shit," she said, then, "sorry."

"That's how I feel, too," he said. "I'm gonna call the morgue and alert Dr. G that we'll be bringing someone down to view the body. Then we'll get going."

"Yes, sir."

"Might as well peruse the file while I do that," McQueen said.

"Mind if I take it in the car?" she asked.

"You can," he said, picking up the phone, "but you're gonna be driving."

He dialed the morgue and when the phone was answered asked for Dr. Bannerjee.

Evelyn Wingate lived in a house in Marine Park, a large, two-story home on a large corner lot. It was over thirty years old, which is why so much land went with it. Most people in the area were living in tiny houses on small twenty-two by a hundred lots, the homes built claustrophobically close together. Some of them were even semi-attached, so they were sharing the lot. However, just a few blocks away the dynamic changed. The streets were wider, the homes larger and fewer, and none of them were attached. There was also a decent amount of space between them.

The Wingate house was in the section that nestled between the two dynamics. It was larger than any of the neighboring homes.

Sommers parked McQueen's car in front of the house and put on the emergency break, even though the car was not on an incline. It told him something about her.

During the ride she'd asked him for some advice about finding a new place.

"I'm the wrong guy to ask," he'd said. "I've got a small apartment in the Six-One precinct and it took me a long time to find it. Plus, you're younger than I am, you'd be looking for something different."

"Maybe not," she'd said. "I just want someplace quiet."

"Ask some of the other women working in the precinct," he'd said. "They can help you better than I can."

Now they got out of the car and walked up the path to the front door. McQueen rang the doorbell, then turned to look around.

"Quiet neighborhood," Sommers said.

"Changes every few blocks," he said. "Old homes, newly renovated homes, people who have lived here forty years, others who have just moved here. Some clubs over on one of the streets, older ships the other way."

"What's the ethnic mix?" she asked.

"Lots of Russians of late, some Hassidics . . . sort of a microcosm of the whole borough."

"Have you lived in Brooklyn long?" she asked.

"All my life," he said. "I don't live all that far from here, right now. I used to live—"

He stopped when the door behind them opened,

and they turned to face the woman in the doorway. She appeared to be in her sixties, but well-preserved, well-dressed, makeup expertly applied to fend off the years. Her hair was brown, streaked with gray.

"Yes? Can I help you?" she asked, without opening the storm door.

"Ma'am, we're with the police," McQueen said. "I'm Sergeant McQueen, this is Detective Sommers." He held out his ID and badge for her to see.

She opened the door and asked, "Is this about Thomas? About my son?"

"Yes, ma'am."

She took one step outside.

"Did you find him?" she asked. "Is he all right?"

The worry on her face was giving the makeup a run for its money, and she suddenly looked her age.

"Please . . ." she said.

She reached a hand out. McQueen backed away from reflex, but Sommers reached out to the woman and grabbed her hand.

"Mrs. Wingate," she said, gently, "we need you to come with us."

The woman stared at Sommers's face, then said, "Yes, yes . . . of course. I—I just need to get my coat and my purse."

Sommers said, "I'll come inside with you."

The two women went into the house and McQueen waited on the doorstep.

McQueen drove them to the morgue. Sommers sat in the back with Mrs. Wingate, holding tightly to her hands. When they came out Sommers had whispered to McQueen that there was no Mr. Wingate. The woman lived alone. She had a daughter, and she allowed Sommers to call her and ask her to meet them at the morgue.

By the time they arrived the daughter had not yet shown up.

"Do you want to wait for her?" Sommers asked.

"No," the woman said, "but . . . would you come in with me?"

"We'll both come in with you, ma'am," McQueen said. He felt bad for backing away from the woman when she reached out.

"Thank you," she said.

The three of them went in to view the body. The woman collapsed when she saw her dead son, and this time McQueen reacted and caught her before she hit the floor.

"Miss Wingate?" McQueen asked.

There was a strong resemblance between mother and daughter. Same height, same jaw line. It was entirely possible the mother had been as beautiful as this woman thirty years ago.

"I'm Mrs. Dean," she said. "Mrs. Wingate is my mother. Where is she?"

"She's all right, Mrs. Dean," McQueen said. "She's lying down. My colleague is with her."

The daughter had the same expertise with makeup, only it wasn't hiding anything, it was enhancing what she had.

"My name is McQueen," he said, "Sergeant McQueen."

"Sergeant," she asked, "do you have my brother here?"

"I'm afraid we do, Mrs. Dean."

"Then he's dead."

"He is."

She was wearing a long fur coat, beneath it an expensive-looking suit. She had her purse clasped in both hands, and now she held it even tighter.

"Did he die in the fire?" she asked. "Where's he been?"

"He did apparently die in the fire, Mrs. Dean," McQueen said. "Smoke inhalation, according to the medical examiner. As to where he's been, that's one of the things we're going to try to find out, along with who killed him."

"Oh, I know who killed him." When she said it she looked as if she was in a trance.

"What?"

She stared straight ahead, then suddenly seemed to come to. She looked directly at him.

"I'd like to see my mother now."

"Of course," McQueen said. "We can talk later."

He took her into the room where the doctor had allowed the woman to lie down. Sommers watched as the woman entered and went to her mother's bedside. She stood up so the woman could sit down next to her mother, and even handed her mother's hand to her.

"Thank you."

McQueen crooked a finger at Sommers, who followed him into the hall.

13

McQueen pulled Sommers aside and told her what Mrs. Dean had said.

"Did you find out who she means?" Sommers asked.

"No," McQueen said, "but I don't want to let her leave here without calling her on it."

"How do you want to play it?"

"I want you to take the mother, talk to her," McQueen said. "I'll do the same with the daughter."

"Okay," she said. "Where will you be doing this?"

"The hospital has a cafeteria for the employees," McQueen said. "I thought I'd take her there."

"Is there a place I can take the mother? She can probably use a cup of tea."

"There's also a trendy sort of snack bar or coffee shop at the front of the hospital," McQueen said. "Take her there. When you're done, meet me back here."

"Okay."

When the two women were ready they led them away from the body of their son and brother, and the two detectives separated them.

"I need to stay with my mother," Mrs. Dean said.

"Detective Sommers is very sensitive, Mrs. Dean," he said. "She'll stay with your mother while we talk."

"Talk? About what?"

"Ma'am," he said, "just a few minutes ago you told me you knew who killed your brother?"

"Did I?"

"Yes."

The woman pressed two fingertips to the center of her forehead. McQueen had a feeling this was a practiced gesture on her part.

"I didn't mean—"

"Ma'am, I'm sure you want to do all you can to help us find whoever killed your brother."

"Of course, but—"

"I suggest we have a talk now, while we have the chance," McQueen said. "Come on, I'll buy you a cup of tea."

"I'd prefer coffee," she said.

"Fine," he said. "Let's go to the cafeteria."

"My mother—"

"Like I said, Detective Sommers is very compassionate. She'll look after your mother. This way . . ."

McQueen led the way to the cafeteria. He'd been there many times before alone and with Dr. Bannerjee on occasion. It was a good place to eat because everything was free for employees—and if you were eating in there, they assumed you were an employee, especially when your face was familiar.

"How you doin'?" one of the cafeteria women asked him as he went to get coffee for himself and Mrs. Dean. He thought he probably should have taken her to the trendy new place in the front of the hospital and let Sommers take the mother here.

"There you go," he said, setting the coffee in front of her.

"Thank you." She had removed her coat and set it on one of the other chairs. McQueen figured her for a very well-preserved thirty-five or so, maybe more, but she had a well-toned tennis body—or maybe Pilates.

"Mrs. Dean," he said, "do you have any other siblings?"

"No," she said. "For a lot of years I was an only child, but then . . . Thomas came along late in life. I was almost nineteen when he was born."

"And how old was Thomas?"

"He is . . . was twenty-two."

McQueen did the math. She was older than he'd originally thought, but still very attractive.

"You're doing the math," she said.

"What?" Caught, he felt his face flush.

"Don't be embarrassed," she said. "I'm not. I'm forty-one."

"You look very . . . I mean, you don't—"

"Are you trying to tell me I'm well-preserved, Detective?"

"I didn't mean—"

"You know, women my age are not considered old anymore," she interrupted him. "Fifty is the new forty now, so I'm considered to be the new thirty."

"Ma'am, who am I to say anything," he replied. "I'm older than you are, and I look my age."

"Do you mind if I smoke?" She reached into a small clutch purse for a pack of cigarettes and a gold lighter. On the front of the purse was a stylized silver "L."

"I believe this is a nonsmoking cafeteria," he told her.

She didn't say anything, but her mannerisms betrayed her annoyance. She set the cigarette pack and lighter down with a thump.

"Detective," she said, "I'm sure my mother needs me."

"I'll make this quick then, ma'am," he said. "Earlier you said you knew who killed your brother. What did you mean by that?"

She fidgeted uneasily, picked up the cigarettes as if to take one out, then remembered she couldn't and put them down again.

"Well, I didn't mean that I literally knew who killed him," she said, finally.

"What did you mean, then?"

She took a deep breath and let it out slowly before replying.

"I think—I believe—that my husband was responsible for the fire that killed my brother."

"In what way? Did he actually set the fire?"

"No," she said. "He owned the building. It was our business."

"What kind of business?"

"Clothing."

"Selling, or manufacturing?"

"Both," she said. "I'm a designer. My husband did the manufacturing, and controlled the sales force. We've had some . . . setbacks recently." She touched her forehead again in that way that she had.

"You believe your husband had the building torched for the insurance?"

She hesitated, then said, "Yes."

"Then I guess I'd better speak with your husband, Mrs. Dean," he said. "Where can I find him?"

"You can't," she said. "When he heard that the fire department found the fire to be deliberate, he disappeared." She looked McQueen right in the eye then, for the first time, which caused him to believe her last statement more than any other.

"I have no idea where he is."

14

When McQueen and Mrs. Dean returned to the morgue area, Sommers was already there with the victim's mother. As soon as they approached her the woman reached out and grabbed hold of McQueen's forearm. Her hand felt like a claw and the touch creeped him out in that moment. He wanted to pull away, but resisted the impulse.

"You'll find who killed my son?" she asked. "Please? Promise me?"

"We'll find the killer, Mrs. Wingate," he said. "I promise."

"Come along, Mother," Mrs. Dean said, and she pried her mother's hand off of McQueen's arm. Before leaving though, she fixed him with a hard stare and said, "We'll hold you to that promise," and then led her mother away.

"What did you get?" McQueen asked Sommers when they got in the car.

She started the engine, pulled away from the curb

and said, "Mother and daughter definitely have problems. The son, Thomas, was the baby, and the favorite."

"She told you that?"

"Not in so many words," she said. "I mean, a mother never admits to favoring one child over another, but I was able to read between the lines. How about you?"

He told her what Mrs. Dean had said about her husband paying to have the building professionally torched, and disappearing when the word got out.

"What was the boy doing in the building?"

"Mrs. Dean says her husband gave him a job," McQueen said. "Apparently, he has a habit of getting fired from jobs."

"Well," she said, "if that's true, and he did have someone start the fire, who took the body out of the building, kept it stored somewhere on ice for two weeks, and then discarded it two weeks after the fire?"

"That's a very good question, isn't it?"

"I guess now that we've found the body and identified it," Sommers said, "and it originated from the crime scene in Brooklyn North we'll have to hand the case over, right? So somebody else will be getting those answers."

"Technically speaking, I suppose that's true."

She stole a look at him—something he'd noticed she rarely did while she was driving—"Technically speaking?"

"I find this case interesting," he said. "When there's this many squads involved—Arson, ours, Brooklyn North, and the fire department—it gets to be a real mess if one person doesn't keep control."

"And you want that to be you? How are you going to manage that?" she asked.

"I don't know," he said. "I'll have to talk to the lieutenant when we get back."

"By the way," Sommers said, "it's Lydia."

"What?"

"Mrs. Dean's first name," she said. "I get the feeling you didn't ask her. It's Lydia."

"We'll have to check out Lydia Dean and her husband," he said. "You can started on that when we get back to the office, while I'm talking to Jessup."

"Okay."

McQueen figured he didn't need to tell her how to do that. She must have run background checks before, when she was in Vice.

Back at the office Sommers went right to her desk while McQueen went into the lieutenant's office to give him a verbal report on what they had so far.

"Write it up, Dennis," Jessup said, "and ship it over to Brooklyn North. It's theirs."

McQueen made a face, but said nothing.

"Okay," Jessup said, sitting back in his chair, "I can see it all over your face. Make your pitch."

"We have a fire that happened two weeks ago," McQueen said, "and Thomas Wingate showing up on the beach in Coney Island two weeks later. We don't know where he died."

"He died of smoke inhalation, right?"

"Yeah, but that could've happened anywhere."

"Was he reported missing after the fire?"

"Mrs. Dean said she was advised to do that," McQueen said. "We checked with Missing Persons but they haven't gotten back to us yet."

"So, it could be their case. It's not even definitely murder, is it, Dennis? I mean, he could've died in the fire accidentally, right?"

"Somebody moved the body, though," McQueen said. "Most likely to hide it."

"So why does it show up two weeks later?"

"They might have tried dumping it in the ocean, and it washed up on the beach."

"Your initial report said the body could have been dumped there."

"Could've been, right. Loo, I'm just not comfortable giving this case up, yet."

"Dennis . . ." Jessup said, shaking his head. "How's your case load?"

"This is the only case I have, right now."

"Okay," Jessup said, "talk to everyone else involved, see how they feel. Try and work it out and get back to me. But if anyone balks, we'll have to hand the case over."

"What about a task force?"

Jessup shook his head and said, "Not to solve one murder of a kid. I'd never get the okay for that."

"Okay," McQueen said, "then I'll be satisfied with that. I'll talk to Arson and Brooklyn North. I can tell those commanders that I have your okay?"

"In principle," Jessup said, "yes."

McQueen stood up.

"Thanks, Loo."

"Dennis," Jessup said, "you know that the Arson Task Force will send a D.D. 5 to Brooklyn North."

"Yes, sir," McQueen said. "I thought of that. I could keep the case by simply not filing a report until I'm sure where the victim was killed, but once Arson sends a five to Brooklyn North they'd be looking for it."

"So why not do that? Buy yourself some extra time?"

McQueen shrugged.

"I thought I'd play it straight, for once."

"Well," Jessup said, "I hope it works out for you."

McQueen stood up and walked out of the office.

As he did Sommers hung up her phone and waved him over.

"What've you got?"

"Missing Persons confirmed that Lydia Dean reported her brother missing after the fire," she said. "I talked with Detective Brennan from Missing Persons. He's satisfied to let us and Arson fight over the case. Says he's swamped."

"That's fine," McQueen said.

"What'd the lieutenant say?"

"If I can get everybody to agree, we can keep the case."

"Good," she said.

"Why?" he asked.

"I figure my first homicide case might as well be an interesting one," she said.

"You get anything on Lydia Dean and her husband?"

"Victor," she said. "I'm still running checks. I've got to go down to the precinct to use their computer."

"You want me to arrange that?"

"Already did," she said. "I called down. That's where I'll be for a while, okay?"

"Get going," McQueen said. "I've got my own phone calls to make."

"Talk to you later, boss."

"Don't call me boss," he called after her as she went out the door.

15

McQueen spent the next two hours on the phone, trying to talk to the appropriate people in Brooklyn North Homicide and the Arson Task Force. He got Detective Jack Orson on the phone at Arson again, but Orson said McQueen would have to talk with his lieutenant. Then when he finally got somebody on the phone at Brooklyn North it was a police aide who said everybody was out. McQueen left a message for someone—preferably somebody in authority—to call him back. When he hung up he wondered why they didn't have a clerical aide to help them with phone calls and filing and stuff like that?

It was getting on toward the next tour and both Frank Cataldo and Ray Velez were at their desks typing up reports, getting ready to head home. Sommers was still out of the office, presumably still working on the precinct's computer.

When somebody from Brooklyn North finally called him, it was somebody he knew, Detective Don Santo.

ROBERT J. RANDISI

"Hey, Donnie," McQueen said, "I'm glad it's you."

"Well, don't be," Santo said. "My lieutenant wants to know what the hell is going on, Dennis? You got a case for us or not?"

"Let me go over this with you, Donnie," McQueen said. "I'm pretty sure I can make this clear."

"Well, make it clear to him, then," Santo said. "I'm about to hang up and go home. He says for you to come by early in the morning and talk to him."

"What's his name?"

"Lieutenant Howard Campanella."

"I don't know him," McQueen said. "What's he like?"

There was hesitation at the other end and McQueen could envision Donnie Santo looking around before he answered.

"Dennis, he's a lightweight who thinks he's a hard ass," Santo finally said.

"What about your sergeant?"

"Ain't got one, right now," Santo said. "We been waiting a month since Bassett returned."

"George retired?"

"You're behind the times, Dennis," Santo said. "Put his papers in last month, and they rushed it through for him. He's got cancer."

"Jesus," McQueen said. "Okay, Donnie, I'll come by in the morning and see if I can plead my case."

"He'll try to push you, Dennis," Santa said. "If you push back hard enough he'll fold like a cheap suit. You didn't hear that from me."

"Gotcha. Thanks, Donnie."

As he hung up the phone Sommers walked in with some print-out sheets in her hands. Velez and Cataldo had already left for the day, and Jessup was still in his office. The Double Ds had not yet arrived or, if they had, were downstairs, shooting the breeze with some of the precinct cops.

"Tell me," he said, leaning back in his chair.

"The clothing line is called Lydia Studios," she said, "and they are in so deep it's no wonder the husband torched the place."

"What about their personal assets?"

"Seems like the husband poured it all into the business," she replied. "They don't have much left besides the house, a couple of cars and some other possessions."

"And they won't get any insurance money, either."

"Right," Sommers said. "They're done."

"Did you check out the old lady?"

"Yeah, she's got money. Lots of it. Her husband died a few years back. The insurance on that just gave her more money."

"Why hasn't she given some to her daughter?"

She sat down opposite him and placed the printout sheets on his desk between them.

"That's not in her, but like I said, I was reading between the lines earlier. She's got no use for her son-in-law, blames him for the rift between her and her daughter."

"Seems to me there's more to it than that," McQueen said, "especially if the son was the favorite."

"I'm an only child," Sommers said. "I wouldn't understand that kind of thing."

"No children?" he asked.

"No," she said, "never been married, never been pregnant."

"I have a daughter," he said. "She's an adult now, and we don't talk much. Started drifting apart after the divorce."

"That's a shame."

"Yeah," he said, "it is."

"How'd your phone calls go?"

He told her he was going to have to go and talk to the C.O. of the Brooklyn North Homicide Squad in the morning.

"I'll have to make my case, and make it well," he said. "There's money in this case, so it's liable to become high profile once the press catches on. Brooklyn North may not want to give it up."

"There may have been money here," Sommers said, "but they weren't high society. They pretty much kept to themselves, stayed in Brooklyn."

McQueen knew that the paparazzi prowled Manhattan for their high-society stories and photos. If these people stayed in Brooklyn—and stayed away from the new "trendy" Brooklyn, where some shutterbugs had taken up residence—then maybe it wouldn't be as high profile as it could have been.

Sommers had spent a good portion of the day either on the phone or the computer. She rubbed her eyes, then her entire face.

"Go home, Bailey," he said. "Get some rest. Tomorrow morning we'll head over to Brooklyn North."

"I'm going with you?"

"You're my partner, aren't you?"

"Yes, sir."

"Get out of here, then," he repeated. "I'll see you in the morning. Don't be late."

"I won't." She stood up. "You want me to write something up before I go?"

"No," he said, "let's put it off for now."

"I've got no problem with that," she said. She went to her desk, grabbed her purse, then waved and went down the hall to her locker for her coat.

He decided he should have told her she'd done good work. She'd been good with the old lady, better

than he could ever have been. He'd been better with
the daughter, who hadn't needed much in the way of
sympathy—at least, not over her brother.

He'd make a point of telling her in the morning.

16

Lieutenant Howard Campanella had been a pencil-pushing, clipboard-carrying, stat-keeping desk jockey for so long he was determined to make the most of his assignment as C.O. of the Brooklyn North Homicide Squad. His appointment was one of those decisions made higher up the ladder that no one could understand. He'd made lieutenant at forty and now, at fifty, was stuck in the same rank. Circumstances beyond anyone's control had left the Brooklyn North Squad without an experience sergeant, or lieutenant. Campanella knew he'd been out here as a stopgap measure, but a big case would go a long way toward keeping him here.

That's why he was royally pissed when Detective Santo told him that Sergeant Dennis McQueen of the Brooklyn South Homicide Squad was coming in to see him about a case.

"What about it?" he asked. "Is it our case?"

"Well," Santo said, not wanting to screw Dennis

McQueen too badly, "apparently it's supposed to be, but—"

"But nothing," Campanella said, cutting Santo off. "If it's our case it's our case. What is it?"

"I don't know, Loo," Santo said. "I knew you'd want him to talk to you about it."

"Damn right!" Campanella said. If it was a good case, he was thinking, there was no way he was going to give it up.

No way.

When they arrived at Brooklyn North on Wilson Avenue, McQueen introduced Bailey Sommers to Donnie Santo.

"Nice to meet you," Santo said. "The lieutenant is waiting for you, Dennis."

"What did you tell him?" McQueen had the existing file in his left hand, shook hands with Santo with his right.

"Everything I know," Santo said, "which ain't a lot. Come on."

Santo showed them to the lieutenant's office, at the back of the squad room.

"Donnie," he said, "why don't you get Detective Sommers a cup of coffee?"

"My pleasure," Santo said. "Come on, Detective. Do you want real milk, or that powdered crud . . ."

McQueen knocked on the closed door.

"Come!"

He opened the door and entered. The man behind the desk stood and glared at him with all the malevolence his five foot six could muster.

"Detective McQueen?"

"Sergeant McQueen."

"Yes," the man said, "sorry. My name is Lieutenant Harold Campanella."

"Lieutenant."

"Have a seat, Sergeant," Campanella said. "I understand you have a case that belongs to me. Is that the file?"

"It's what we have so far," McQueen said, putting the file on the desk between them.

Campanella ignored it.

"Why don't you summarize it for me, Sergeant?"

McQueen did so, starting with the fire two weeks before, on through the body washing up on the beach in Coney Island and ending with his talk with the mother and sister of the victim at the morgue.

"Well then," Campanella said, placing his hand on the file, "I assume there's a D.D. 5 in here transferring the case here, where it belongs."

"Not exactly."

"And why not?"

"I'm not sure that would be in the best interest of the case."

"Perhaps not, Sergeant," Campanella said, "but it would be proper procedure, wouldn't it?"

McQueen had already decided to try honey before vinegar.

"Sir," he said, "maybe I can make a case for letting me keep this, uh, case."

"Perhaps I should read the file before you do that, Sergeant."

McQueen figured if Campanella read the file and found out that there was money in the family he'd never want to give the case up.

"The Arson Task Force will continue to work on the fire," he explained. "They found no bodies in the rubble, but did determine that the fire was suspicious. I've found out from another source that it's very

likely the owner of the building—and the business—
hired a professional to set it."

"For the insurance money."

"Yes, sir."

"Well, now he won't get it."

"He obviously knows that," McQueen said, "and
he's disappeared."

"So he's Arson's problem."

"Yes."

"But the murder is my problem," Campanella said,
"or it belongs to whomever I assign to it."

"Sir, I'm not all that certain that the victim was
killed in the fire," McQueen said.

"How was he killed?"

"Well," McQueen said, "he died in a fire, that's
true—or, at least, from smoke inhalation, but he was
moved."

"What are you trying to tell me, Sergeant?"

"Sir, I just think I have a handle on this already
and, for the sake of continuity, the case should stay
with me." He was aware that in his attempts to
spread honey he was repeating himself.

Campanella pulled the file over to his side of the
desk and opened it.

"Sergeant, why do I get the feeling this has all the
earmarks of a high-profile case?"

"I don't think it does, sir."

"Then why do you want to keep it?"

"As I said, sir," McQueen answered, "continuity."

Campanella studied McQueen for a few moments,
then snapped, "Bullshit!"

"Wait a min—"

"I don't know a man on my squad who wouldn't
give up a case if they could," Campanella said. "For
you to want to keep this one means there's something
in it for you."

"Can't it just mean I want to solve it for the sake of solving it?" McQueen asked. "Finish what I started?"

"That would make you different from most men I know."

"And?"

"Not likely."

McQueen moved quickly, leaping to his feet and snatching the file from the desk.

"Hey."

"It's my file."

"That's my case—"

"No, it's not," McQueen said, "not until I send it over to you."

"Sergeant," Campanella said, "I'll have your badge for this."

"I'll write out my reports and refer the case to you when the time comes, Lieutenant," McQueen said. "Consider this a courtesy call."

"Arson will send the case to me before you do," Campanella said. "Then I'll take it from you."

"Until then," McQueen said, "it's still mine."

"Do yourself a favor, Sergeant," Campanella said, getting to his feet. "Put that file back on my desk and walk out."

"Not a chance," McQueen said, "sir."

"By the time you get back to your squad I'll have talked to your C.O.," Campanella said.

"That'd be Lieutenant Jessup," McQueen said. "Give him my regards."

McQueen walked out, ran into both Donnie Santo and Sommers in the hall.

"What happened?" Santo asked.

"Don't go in there for a while," McQueen said. "He's a little more hard-nosed than you thought."

17

McQueen held his anger until they were in the car, and then he pounded his fist on the dashboard.

"That was a bad idea!" he said.

"What happened?"

"I'm getting too old and soft," McQueen said. "I should have just kept my mouth shut and worked the case as long as we could. Now this dickhead lieutenant is gonna be trying to take it away."

"What did you tell him?"

"That it was our case," McQueen said, "and when the time came that I thought it was his I'd send it over."

"You can do that, right?" Sommers asked. "I mean, you can make that decision, right? As long as you're the lead detective on the case?"

"I don't honestly know," he said. "I never tried to do this before."

"Well, then," she said, starting the engine, "I guess we're going to find out, right?"

He hesitated a moment, then said, "Right. Let's get back to the house."

By the time they walked into the squad room, the word had already gotten around. In fact, McQueen had the feeling that it had spread to the precinct level, and that they were being watched as they walked in the front door to the elevator.

"The lieutenant wants to see you, Dennis," Velez said.

"I figured." He looked at Sommers. "Wait here."

He stuck his head into the lieutenant's office.

"You want to see me, Loo?"

"Come in," Jessup said. "Shut the door."

McQueen did both, fidgeted uncomfortably. He really didn't want to get into it with his own lieutenant, not after he'd managed to hold it together with Campanella.

"I got a call from Lieutenant Campanella from Brooklyn North," Jessup said. "He wants me to take your badge and shield."

"You want 'em?" McQueen asked.

"Don't be such a fucking smart-ass with me, Dennis," Jessup said. "You should have used that on him."

"Yes, sir. What did you tell him?"

"I told him I had complete confidence in my men to know when they should refer a case," the lieutenant said.

"Did he buy that?"

"Did he buy it?" the man asked. "Shit, I don't even buy it. But I do have confidence in you, Dennis."

"Thanks, Lo—"

"Confidence not to fuck me while you're trying to fuck him," Jessup added.

"I'm not tryin' to fuck anybody, Loo," McQueen said. "I'm trying to solve a case."

"Yeah," Jessup said, "he told me you said that to him, too. Luckily, I believe you."

"So where does that leave us?"

"Work your case as long as you can," he said.

"And how long will that be?"

"As long as nobody above my head comes down on my head, Dennis," his boss said. "I'll cover for you, but I won't give up my career for you. Not over this."

"Don't worry," McQueen said. "I'm not gonna give up my job over this, either."

"Good," Jessup said. "As long as we both keep things in their proper perspective."

"Yes, sir."

"Then you better get moving."

"Yes, sir."

"What's goin' on with this case?" Velez asked Sommers.

"I'm not really sure," she said, but told him everything she knew. Then she asked, "Why's he doing this? I mean, why's he fighting for this case?"

"I don't know why Dennis does anything," Velez said. "I guess we'll all have to just wait and see."

They both turned toward the door of the lieutenant's office as McQueen came out.

McQueen saw the two detectives waiting for him.

"So?" Sommers asked.

"You still got your badge and gun?"

"Both," McQueen said. "Campanella's just another fuckin' lieutenant."

"What happens when somebody higher up takes a hand?" Velez asked.

"Then what?"

"Then I'll hand the case over," McQueen said. "I'm not crazy enough to lose my job over one case."

Sommers didn't know McQueen well enough to know if that was true.

Ray Velez knew him only too well.

18

While Sommers was at her desk, Ray Velez walked over to McQueen's and perched his hip on the edge.

"Don't get stubborn about this, Dennis."

"Stubborn?"

"Don't tell me you never get stubborn," Velez said. "I know you too well."

"That's got nothing to do with it, Ray."

"What, then?" Velez asked. "Why do you want to hang onto this case?"

McQueen shrugged and said, "It's interesting." He didn't bother to tell Velez that he'd promised the victim's mother that he'd catch the killer, and that the victim's daughter—his very attractive sister—told him they were going to hold him to that promise. That was the kind of statement that had made Ray Velez shake his head more than once over the past few years.

"Interesting."

"Yeah," McQueen said.

"Okay," Velez said. "Okay."

"How are you and Frankie gettin' along?" McQueen asked.

"We're not talkin' much," Velez said.

"What cases are you workin'?"

"We had that suicide," Velez said. "We put the report on your desk."

"Nothin' else?"

"Not right now."

"I may have you do some interviews for me, then."

"Sure, why not?" his once-and-future partner asked. "Just don't have us do them together."

"Don't worry," McQueen said, "I'll give you separate assignments."

Briefly, McQueen told Velez what he wanted him to do. Canvas the area of the fire, find out who saw what. Also, find out who saw the victim last.

"What are you gonna have Frankie do?"

"Sommers and I didn't finish reinterviewing the Polar Bears," McQueen said. "I'll give him that."

"Well," Velez said, "you give him the news, and I'll go out and get started." He started away, then turned back. "What do I say if I get called for being off my patch?"

"Refer 'em to me," McQueen said. "I'll take care of it."

Velez gave McQueen a small salute and headed out.

McQueen walked over to Cataldo's desk and gave him his assignment.

"I'm on my own?" the man asked.

"That's right."

He thought about that, shrugged, then smiled and asked, "Why don't you send the broad with me?"

"I would," McQueen said, "but if you called her a broad she'd probably smack your face. Here are the addresses. Get goin'."

"Sure, Sarge."

Cataldo grabbed his jacket from the back of his chair, and went down the hall to get his coat from his locker.

McQueen walked over to Sommers's desk as she was hanging up the phone.

"What've you been doin'?"

"I made some calls, checking to see if there were any other bodies found in the city that might've matched ours."

"And?"

"There was one in Central Park that was found frozen to death," she said, "but he was a homeless guy. They figure he just . . . froze in his sleep."

"Any others?"

"No," she said. "I'm waiting for some callbacks, though. I called some precincts with ponds and beaches and ocean access—even Rockaway."

"That was good thinking," he said.

"Where'd everybody else go?"

"They had no cases of their own, so I've got them canvassing and doing follow-ups."

"And what are we going to do?"

"I think I'd like to take a look at where the victim lived, check his room," McQueen said. "Also, have a look at where the brother-in-law lived, check his home office, if he has one. Might find something that'll lead us to the torch."

"Wanna split up?" she asked.

"Since we're short on time," he replied, "that'd make sense."

"So I guess I'll go talk to the mother," she said, "get her to show me her son's room."

"Okay," McQueen said. "I'll go and have another talk with Mrs. Dean."

"Don't forget."

"Forget what?"

"Lydia," Sommers said. "Her name's Lydia."

"I'll try to remember."

She turned to grab her jacket from the back of her chair, then looked at him and said, "I meant to ask earlier."

"Ask what?"

"Do you think it was a good idea to promise the mother you'd find her son's killer?"

"Making a promise like that is never a good idea."

"Then why'd you do it?"

He shrugged.

"I just wanted to get her hand off my arm."

He shivered again at the thought of the woman's hand clutching him like a claw.

19

McQueen had gotten Lydia Dean's address from her when they were in the hospital cafeteria. He'd told her he might need to come to her house for further information. What he didn't tell her was that it would be so soon.

Lydia and Victor Dean lived in an expensive condo in Brooklyn Heights. When she answered her door and saw McQueen standing on her doorstep, her surprise was obvious.

"Detective," she said.

"Sergeant, actually." It was the first time he'd corrected her.

"McQueen, isn't it?"

"That's right."

"Well . . . you did say you'd be stopping by, but I had no idea it would be so soon."

"Actually, neither did I," he said, "but it turns out to be the next logical step. I'd like to look at your husband's things, if it's not inconvenient."

"Well . . . all right," she said. She stepped back to

ROBERT J. RANDISI

allow him to enter, then closed the door. They were in a hardwood floor foyer. There were doorways on either side, and a stairway leading up.

He turned to face her. She was as expertly made up as she had been at the hospital. Her lipstick was dark red, her eye makeup did not make her eyes look brittle, as it did with most women her age that he met. She seemed to know how to use cosmetics to play up the benefits of her features—high cheekbones, a prominent nose, full lower lip, but thin upper. He liked that she didn't use lipstick to widen that upper. He always thought that looked silly.

She was wearing an expensive-looking purple sweater and black pants. Her feet were bare, which he found odd. The floor they were standing on was some kind of tile, and must have been freezing.

"Cold feet," he said.

"What?"

He pointed.

"You must have cold feet."

She looked down and wriggled her toes. He found it a playful thing to do, and so an odd thing.

"The rest of the house has rugs," she said. "I like to keep my feet bare."

"Well," he said, "we should move into another room so they can warm up."

"That's very considerate," she said. "Please . . . come this way."

She led him to a warm living room, furnished with overstuffed sofa and chairs. The heat wrapped itself around him and he opened his coat.

"I keep it hot in here, I know," she said. "Can I take your coat?"

"Thanks." He took it off and handed it to her.

"I have some coffee made," she said. "Can I offer you a cup?"

"That'd be great," he said. "Thanks."

"I'll be right back."

He was surprised that she was being so hospitable. It was not what he would have expected after talking with her at the hospital.

When she returned it was with a mug of coffee in each hand. He'd expected her to come back with a tray and china. He was liking her better than when they first met. He wondered what she thought of him, and suddenly he felt . . . big and clunky, and clumsy.

"Thank you," he said.

"I didn't know what you took in it," she said. "I could get some sugar or milk—"

"Black is fine," he told her truthfully. "It's how I usually take it."

"Please, sit down."

They each sat in an armchair, the sofa an empty line of demarcation between them.

"I came to ask you some more questions about your husband," he said, "and to ask if I can have a look around."

"For what?"

He shrugged.

"Something that might tell me where he went. That is, unless you know, and want to tell me."

"Detec—Sergeant," she replied, "if I knew where he was I would tell you."

"You'd turn your husband in?"

"Yes."

"Why?"

"It's because of him our business went bust," she said. "Because of him the building was burned down, and because of him my brother is dead."

"Were you close with your brother?"

"No," she said. "He came late in life to my parents. There were too many years between us. But that doesn't mean I don't—didn't love him. I'm sorry he's dead."

He studied her face, but there were no tears forming in her eyes.

"You're looking for tears," she said, surprising him. "You won't find them."

He didn't comment.

"It's not because I don't want to cry," she said. "It's the . . . anger. The . . . the absolute rage I feel for my husband. It's keeping the tears at bay."

He hesitated, took a moment to taste the coffee. Again, surprised that it was good.

"I don't know if that's good, or bad," he said.

"I don't either," she said.

They drank their coffee in silence for a few moments, then she said, "I suppose you'll want to start with his office."

"Yes," McQueen said. "Does he have a lot of business records there?"

"Some," she said, "but most of them were lost in the fire."

"That's . . . too bad."

"Well," she said, placing her coffee mug on an end table. He looked for a coaster, didn't find one, and followed her example. "This way."

20

Victor Dean's home office was on the second floor. McQueen followed Lydia up the stairs. Her butt swayed so much as she ascended that he thought she must have been doing it deliberately. No woman could have that much motion naturally, could she? He also found himself wondering if she was wearing clothing she had designed herself.

"This is Victor's office," she said. "It's small, but he spent a lot of time in here."

"Did he close the door when he was in here?"

"Yes."

"Lock it?"

She hesitated, then said, "Sometimes."

So there were times when he was doing something in the office he didn't want his wife to see. That could have been something illegal, or if could have just been Internet porn.

McQueen entered, looked around. The walls were lined with bookshelves, but only half were filled with books. On the small oak desk was a Gateway computer.

"Do you know how to use that?" he asked.

A small smile came to her lips. "I can turn it on and play solitaire, but that's it."

He turned to face her.

"Did you do that while he was out of the house?"

"Yes," she confessed.

The desk top was remarkably clean, as if it had been recently dusted. Even the screen of the computer.

"Do you have a cleaning woman?"

She nodded and said, "She comes in three times a week. My husband hates dust."

McQueen frowned. If there was anything incriminating in the room Dean wouldn't want anyone messing around there, not even to clean. In fact, a cleaning woman would probably be even more thorough than somebody searching the place.

"I'm going to do downstairs and take the mugs into the kitchen," Lydia said. "Can I bring you another cup of coffee?"

"No, I'm fine," McQueen said.

"I'll leave you to it, then." She turned to leave, then stopped and turned back. "I don't suppose I should have asked for a warrant?"

"Only if you have something to hide," he told her. "I can get one."

"No," she said, "I have nothing to hide. Go ahead."

After she left, he went through the desk, found remarkably little in the drawers other than some office supplies. In one of the bottom drawers he found a few copies of *Playboy*, *Penthouse* and *Maxim*.

The books on the bookshelves were mostly nonfiction reference books, some computer books and some novels he'd never heard of. The room did not look like one that anyone ever did work in. There were no ashtrays, no glass rings, no paper clips lying about, or Post-it notes. He was starting to think that all Victor Dean might have done in here when the door was locked was read men's magazines.

He pulled out the ergonomically correct chair, sat down in front of the computer, found the ON button and pressed it. The machine whined into life and, slowly, the monitor glowed. He waited until Windows launched and a bunch of icons appeared, but he didn't know what to do with them. Then he remembered that one of the books on the shelves was a yellow one called *Windows for Dumbbells*, or something like that. He stood up, took the book down from the shelf and in a few minutes was able to negotiate the icons. He stayed away from the ones that were for the Internet—apparently, Victor Dean had accounts with more than one provider—and found the ones that the man would have used for business. By the time Lydia Dean reappeared, McQueen had gone through some of her husband's accounts. He didn't really understand them, but by using the book he was able to transfer them to a disk, which he put in his pocket. Lucky for him Dean had a box of blank formatted disks on the desk.

He was standing, had turned the computer off and returned the book to the shelves by the time Lydia returned.

"Is everything all right?" she asked.

"Fine." He didn't mention the disk he had in his pocket, because he actually would have needed a warrant to remove it from the house. "I'm done in here."

"Did you find anything helpful?"

"I'll tell you what I didn't find," he said, as he followed her out into the hall.

"What's that?"

"A phone book," he said, "or address book of your husband's. Did he have one?"

"He had a filo-fax in the office at work," she said. "And I'm sure he has an address book somewhere. It might have gotten burned up in the fire."

Walking down the stairs behind her he noticed the scent of her perfume. He either hadn't noticed it before, or she'd put some on after she left him in the office.

When they reached the entry foyer they stopped. He noticed she had put some purple socks on to protect her feet from the cold tiles.

"Is there anything else I can do for you, Sergeant?" she asked. There was nothing overtly sexual, or flirtatious, in her words or manner, so maybe he imagined that she was coming on to him. She was standing a bit hip shot, though, as if showing off her body to him. He remembered her swaying butt as he'd followed her up the stairs, earlier.

He took a business card from his pocket and said, "If you think of something helpful, or hear from your husband, I'd like you to give me a call."

"All right," she said, accepting the card. She didn't do anything sexy with it, like tap her teeth with it or slip it into her shirt, so it had to be him. He was just getting a vibe from her, as the kids said. "I don't expect to hear from him, though."

"Why not?"

"We'd had a big argument and I kicked him out of the house," she said.

"You didn't tell me that before."

She studied him for a moment, then said, "I wasn't comfortable with you before."

"And you are now?"

"Oh, yes."

110

Okay, he thought, now that's obvious.

"Mrs. Dean," he asked, "when did you have the fight and kick him out?"

"I guess this is important," she said, with a shrug. "It was the same day of the fire."

21

Bailey Sommers was having a dissimilar experience at the mother's house. Mrs. Wingate let her in and agreed to let her look at her son's room. She offered tea, but Sommers refused, so they went right up to the room together.

Unlike Victor Dean's office, Thomas Wingate's room was a mess. There were clothes strewn about everywhere, empty microwave soup and noodle containers everywhere, as well as empty Snapple bottles.

"Mrs. Wingate, how old was your son?"

"Twenty-two."

Sommers nodded and continued to look around without moving from the spot she was standing in. Posters on the wall ran the gamut from Britney Spears to monster trucks and Formula One. It had all the appearances of a teenager's room.

"He still lived at home?" she asked.

"Yes."

"Didn't move out, and then come back, maybe?"

112

"No," Mrs. Wingate said, "no, he still lived here. He never moved out."

"Why was that, ma'am?"

The woman looked confused.

"This was his home."

"But he was twenty-two, ma'am," Sommers said. "Young men don't usually live at home until that age."

"I—I don't—didn't see anything wrong with it," she said. "Besides, I liked the company. Ever since my husband died . . . if Thomas had moved out, I would have been . . . lonely."

"Did he have a job?"

Mrs. Wingate hesitated, then said, "He had lots of jobs."

"Your daughter said he was in the building when the fire started," the detective asked. "Did he work for your daughter and son-in-law?"

"I—I don't know," she said, "He didn't tell me what job he had. I just knew he had . . . different ones."

Sommers looked around the room again. She didn't think she was going to be able to find anything helpful in there. It looked like a cyclone had hit it, and she wouldn't have wanted to touch anything without gloves, anyway.

"What are you looking for?" Mrs. Wingate asked.

"Just something . . . helpful."

"I'm afraid he's not a very neat boy," she said.

He wasn't a boy, Sommers thought, he was a man—or he was supposed to be.

She wasn't going to find anything in the room, but maybe she could still find something out from the mother.

"Maybe I'll have that cup of tea now, Mrs. Wingate."

* * *

Before leaving the Dean residence McQueen asked Lydia, "Did your brother work for you and your husband?"

"He was working for us at the time of the fire."

"Doing what?"

She shrugged.

"Nothing, as far as I know," she said. "Thomas wasn't very good at anything. He certainly wasn't good at keeping jobs. So we put him on the payroll."

"Doing what?"

"Like I said, I'm not sure."

"Then why would he have been there?"

She sighed.

"Victor said that if he was going to pay Thomas then he had to be around—you know, for errands."

"So he was an errand boy."

"I guess you could say that."

"And your husband," he asked, "he didn't have time to find another place to live, did he?"

"I think he did," she said, "but he would have only been there a couple of days when he heard that the fire had been deemed suspicious. After that I never heard from him again."

"Does he still have clothes here?"

"Yes, he does," she said. "He only packed a single bag to take with him that morning."

"And would he have any friends he might have stayed with?" McQueen asked.

"I'm afraid my husband didn't have those kind of friends," she replied. "He was not a very friendly man."

"Okay then, Mrs. Dean," McQueen said, "we'll be talking again."

"I'm sure we will, Sergeant," she said, "but in the future, why don't you just call me Lydia?"

"All right, Lydia," he said. "My name is Dennis."

"Nice to meet you, Dennis," she said, shaking his hand. "I'm afraid I wasn't at my best when we first met. I think I was rude."

"That's all right," he said. "It was a shock, I know."

"And thank you for the compassion you and your partner showed to my mother."

"Don't mention it," he said. "I've got to get going now, but like I said, we'll talk."

"Yes."

She showed him to the door, and closed it behind him before he reached the bottom of the porch steps.

22

McQueen got in his car and fished out his cell phone. Doing so reminded him that he'd never had the photos he took of the scene in Coney Island "developed." Didn't much matter now, though.

Before leaving the office he had arranged two things—an unmarked car for Sommers to drive, and an exchange of cell phone numbers so they could stay in touch. He took his out now and made one call before calling her, to the Arson Task Force.

"Orson."

"This is Sergeant McQueen, from Brooklyn South Homicide?"

"Hey, what can I do you for, Sarge?"

"I'd like to get a look at the scene of that fire we talked about," McQueen said. "What are the chances of you meeting me there?"

"When?"

"Within the hour."

"No chance," Orson said. "I'm outta here in fifteen to do some interviews."

"On this case?"

"No, another one," Orson said. "But if you're interested in info about the fire why not have the fire marshal meet you there? I don't know squat about the fire. I'm lookin' into the fraud end of it, you know? Lookin' for the owner, gonna lock his ass up for having the fire set."

McQueen had a feeling the guy just didn't want to meet him, but he actually liked the idea of speaking with a fire marshal.

"You got his number?"

"Hold on," Orson said. McQueen heard some pages being turned. "Here ya go." Orson read off the number and McQueen jotted it down. Then Orson gave him a name: Willis.

"Okay, got it. Thanks."

"So you got Brooklyn North to let you keep the case?"

"In a way, yeah."

"Hey, keep in touch, okay?"

"You do the same," McQueen said.

He hung up, dialed the number for the fire marshal's office. When the phone was answered by a man he asked for Fire Marshal Willis.

"Why do you want Willis?"

McQueen explained who he was and what he wanted.

"Within the hour?"

"If possible."

"Sure," the man said. "Willis will be there."

"Okay," McQueen said, surprised. "What's your nam—"

The man hung up and McQueen stared at the phone in surprise, then dialed Sommers's number.

* * *

Bailey Sommers left the Wingate house after having a long conversation with Thomas's mother in her kitchen. The woman was obviously in denial about her son who, by all appearances, was something of a bum, not to mention a slob and a mooch. He lived with his mother and worked for his sister. Not exactly the catch of the day for any woman. But to his mother he was a sensitive boy who was misunderstood by everyone he worked for, including his sister and brother-in-law. Mrs. Wingate's disgust for her son-in-law, Victor, was obvious, and also obvious was the fact that she didn't get along with her daughter. Sommers thought she'd be interested to hear the daughter's side when she got back and talked to McQueen.

She left the house and walked to the unmarked unit McQueen had managed to get for her. It was cold out, and the engine didn't turn over right away but she finally got it running. It would be a while, though, before the heater started pumping out hot air.

She touched her cell phone in her coat pocket and, as if by magic, it rang.

"Sommers," McQueen said, when she answered. "Where are you?"

"In my car, in front of the Wingate house. I finished talking with the mother."

"I'm done here, also," he said. "Meet me at the scene of the fire."

She got the address from him and then asked, "What are we going to do there?"

"We're gonna talk to the fire marshal who called it suspicious," he said, "and, hopefully, get some answers."

McQueen pulled his car to a halt in front of the burnt-out building that was walking distance from Gold Street, where Brooklyn Central Booking was located.

He got out of his car and approached the front. The outside of the brick building was intact, but the inside had been gutted by the fire, and by the fire department's attempts to control it. Sometimes he thought the fire department did more damage than they had to do, but that feeling might have just been a result of the natural rivalry between the departments.

He turned at the sound of a another car, saw that it was Sommers's unmarked unit. She parked and got out, approached him.

"Fire marshal not here yet?" she asked.

"I guess not."

"I'm here," a voice said from behind him.

He turned and saw a woman come out of the building. Had she been the one who spoke? There was still some police tape here and there, blowing in the wind in some places like yellow streamers. When he saw the short, stocky woman approaching him with her hands in her coat pockets he thought she was going to ask direction. She surprised him.

"Sergeant McQueen?"

"That's right."

She extended her hand and said, "Fire Marshal Willis."

23

"They didn't tell you I was a woman," Willis said.

"No."

"They think that's funny," she explained.

McQueen hurriedly offered his hand, to make up for his surprise.

"Glad to meet you."

"Yeah, me too," she said.

"This is my partner, Detective Sommers."

The two women simply nodded to each other.

"You wanna go inside?" Willis asked.

"Absolutely," McQueen said.

They went into the building, ducking under some crime scene tape. McQueen and Sommers followed Willis in.

"What was the make up of the building?" McQueen asked.

"Three stories, offices on the top floor, manufacturing on the second floor, first floor and basement used for warehousing."

"Where'd the fire originate?"

"Basement," she said. "I'll take you down."

They picked their way through the debris and followed her down some stairs to the basement. It was one, long continuous room down there, used as a warehouse. McQueen could see among building debris lots of cloth materials, and packing crates.

Deeper into the basement they found the room where the fire had started. The floor, walls and ceiling were badly scorched, but intact. There was more debris around from the company's product, here and there some overturned metal clothing racks.

"The fire originated here and spread throughout the building. That's why they had to fight most of the night to keep it contained. We're still trying to find out why it was so hot."

"And?"

"This fire was started by someone who almost knew what they were doing. Just the right amount of accelerant, the alligatoring—"

"The what?" Sommers asked.

"Come here."

They followed her to a wall and looked where she was pointing.

"See the charring of the wood? That's alligatoring. These markings indicate an intense fire. And there was obviously some flashover."

"Which means what?" Sommers said.

"Flashover," she said, "is when the heat in the room becomes so intense that the flame can travel on it, spreading over the entire area."

"So this fire was not set by a pro?" Sommers asked.

"A talented amateur is more like it."

"Why do you say that?" McQueen asked.

"There's too much fingering." When she saw their blank looks she added, "I'll explain. The fingering is the splash effect of the accelerant. There's too much

121

of it here for a real pro to have been involved. Also, it got out of hand."

"So the guy was good, but too sloppy?" Sommers asked.

"Exactly," she said. "He overdid it."

"Why were there not any bodies?" Sommers asked. McQueen answered before Willis could.

"It was Saturday morning," he said. "They were closed."

"But the Wingate boy . . ."

"Was apparently working overtime," Willis said.

Sommers looked at McQueen. This didn't jibe with the picture she had formed of the victim.

"About the accelerant," she said. "It wasn't gasoline?"

"No," she said, "or kerosene, or anything else we could readily identify by the smell, like naphthalene."

"Like what?" McQueen asked.

"It comes from mothballs."

"You can smell that?"

"If you're experienced."

"Is that what you smell here?" McQueen asked.

"No," she said, "this wasn't quite that homemade."

"So how do you ID it?" McQueen asked.

"Our lab will work on it," she said. "Part of the problem is that extra smell."

"The . . . what? Packing material?"

"Or whatever it is," she said, wrinkling her nose. "I can usually ID an accelerant from the smell, but that other odor is interfering."

"What all was in here?" Sommers asked, looking around.

"Well, as you can see it was mostly empty," she said. "There were some crates and racks of clothes against that wall, but the fire started right here, dead center."

McQueen and Sommers looked around, then at each other. They weren't learning much, here.

"I understand you found a body you think came from here?" Willis asked.

"We found the younger brother of the woman who owned this place with her husband." He told her where, and under what circumstances the victim had been found.

"Burns?"

"None," McQueen said, "but smoke in his lungs."

"He might have died on one of the upper floors," she said. "Smoke would have killed him before the flames got to him . . . but how did the body get out before it was burned?"

"That's what we'd like to find out," McQueen said. "Mind if we have a look at the upper floors?"

"I wouldn't wander around the building without me," she said. "If you want to have a look, I'll take you there."

"I thought you said the flames didn't get up there?" Sommers commented.

"I said the smoke would have killed your victim before the flames got there," she said. "Obviously, somebody got him out first, but the flames did get there. The entire interior of this structure could go at any moment."

McQueen and Sommers both looked up at the ceiling.

"If you want to look at the upper floors, you better hurry."

"No," McQueen said, "that's all right. Why don't you walk us out of here . . . safely?"

McQueen and Sommers were still standing in front of the building after Fire Marshal Willis had left.

"She had a lot of personality," Sommers said.

"She's probably had a hard time getting to where she is," McQueen said. "I'd think if anyone would understand that it would be you."

"You don't have to become a machine," Sommers said. "You can still maintain your personality."

"Have you maintained yours?" he asked.

"I have," she said. "You just haven't known me long enough to notice."

McQueen looked up at the burnt-out brick structure.

"Who was here?" he wondered aloud. "Who was here with the kid to pull him out? And if he was dead, why pull him out?"

"I've got another question," she said.

"What's that?"

"What was he doing here?"

"Like Willis said, maybe working overtime."

"No," she said, "that doesn't fit. Just talking to the mother I can see that he was a total waste."

"She said that?"

"Hell, no," Sommers answered. "She had nothing but good things to say about him, but she's in total denial. He was still living at home, sponging off Mom, and couldn't hold a job. A bum. What did his sister have to say about him?"

"They weren't close," he said. "Her husband gave him a job, but the mother hated the husband, and she and the mother didn't get along all that well, either."

"So why bother giving him a job?" Sommers asked. "It was a joke."

"Sounds like the whole family was a joke," McQueen said. "But maybe . . ."

"Maybe what?"

"Maybe the sister gave him a job just to stay in the will," McQueen said.

Sommers nodded and said, "That would fit. She's

got a pretty good bank account. The sister seem like that type?"

"I was getting mixed signals."

"Like what?"

"Like suddenly it seemed like she was . . . hitting on me."

"That surprised you?"

"Well . . . yeah. You saw her."

"So?"

"So why would a woman like that hit on me?"

"You don't think it could be because you're a man?"

"More likely it's because I'm a cop," he said. "The cop in charge of finding out who killed her brother."

"She blames her husband, right?"

"That's right."

"Convenient, since he's in the wind. You think she was in on it? Setting the fire to defraud the insurance company?"

"I'm not sure, right now. I can't get a read on her."

"Maybe I should talk to her," Sommers said.

"Maybe," McQueen said. "We'll see. We better get back to the office."

As they started walking to their cars, she asked, "You think maybe she did the husband?"

"The husband and the brother?" McQueen asked. "She'd have to be one cold bitch."

24

When they got back to the office they found Velez and Cataldo back from their assignments. When they asked McQueen if he wanted to hear what their interviews had turned up, he said, "Write it all up, leave it on my desk before you leave."

Cataldo said, "But Sarge, I can tell you—"

"Write it up, will you, Frankie? Thanks."

"Fine," Cataldo said, "no skin off my nose. I didn't get nothin', anyway."

As Cataldo went back to his desk McQueen said to Velez, "What did you get?"

"You don't want me to write it up? But Frank—"

"I gave Frankie busy work, Ray," McQueen said. "None of those Polar Bears knows anything. What did you find for me?"

"Not much," Velez said. "It was Saturday, so a lot of the other buildings were empty. Did you know the place was a few blocks from Central Booking?"

He did, but he said, "No."

"Well, it is," Velez said. "Also not that far from Junior's. I stopped and had a piece of cheesecake. Still the best in the country."

McQueen had lived in Brooklyn all his life but had never been to Junior's. But he wasn't a big cheesecake fan, anyway.

"Ray—"

"Huh? Oh, yeah, well . . ." He opened his notebook. "I did manage to find one person who saw somebody go into the building that morning."

"Who?"

"A lady who lives about a block away," Velez said. "She walks her dog every morning at the same time. She said she saw a young man go into the building about nine A.M."

"That's it? He just went in? Was he carrying anything?"

"She didn't think so," Velez said.

"Did they speak?"

"No."

"What else did she see?"

"That's it," Velez said. "He went inside."

"How did he get in?" Sommers asked.

Velez looked at her.

"Front door."

"Did he have a key, or was it open?"

"I asked her that," Velez said. "She said it looked like he opened it with a key."

"Did she see the fire? Or smoke?"

"Not until later, when she heard the fire engines," Velez said. "She said she came out to see what was going on, and the building was ablaze."

"What about smoke?" McQueen asked.

"She said there was lots of it coming from all the windows."

"Okay," McQueen said. "Type it up and leave it on my desk. Thanks, Ray."

"Hey, Dennis," Velez said, "I didn't spend that much time having cheesecake, you know? I was all over those streets, but she was the only one I found."

"I know it, Ray," McQueen said. "Don't worry about it. Just write it up."

"Okay."

Velez turned and walked to his own desk.

"That didn't help us much," she said.

"Well, we know that the kid let himself into the building with a key, and that he was alone when he went in."

"So?"

"So that means nobody took him there against his will, or at gunpoint."

"Do you think he set the fire and got caught in it?"

"Could be, I guess," McQueen said, "but did you find out anything about him that might indicate he could do it?"

"I don't think he could light a cigarette without burning his nose," she said.

"Right. So he's still just a victim, and our best suspects are still the missing brother-in-law."

"And the sister, right?"

McQueen hesitated, then said, "Right, and the sister."

McQueen was still in the office with the Double Ds when Lieutenant Jessup came back in.

"Dennis, my office," he said, without breaking stride.

McQueen got up and followed the man into his office.

"What's up, boss?"

Jessup stood behind his desk, facing McQueen.

"I've got to take this case away from you."

"Why?"

"Orders."

"From who?"

"Lieutenant Campanella went to the C-of-D with this," Jessup said. "The chief called me in. He says it's a Brooklyn North case."

"Loo—"

"I argued for you, Dennis," Jessup said, "but I told you I wouldn't put my career on the line for you. Not for this."

"I understand, Loo," McQueen said. "I wouldn't put my own badge on the line for it, either. It's just one case. I just wanted to finish what I started."

"Write it up, get all the reports together, and ship it over to Brooklyn North."

"Yes, sir."

He turned to leave and Jessup said, "Dennis."

"Sir?"

"Campanella just wins this time. That's all."

"Yes, sir," McQueen said. "I'll take care of it first thing in the morning."

"Good enough."

As McQueen went out, Jessup sat back in his chair and shook his head. He didn't like letting any of his men down, but this just wasn't important enough to go up against the chief of detectives.

McQueen went back to his desk and sat down. In addition to sending the case files over to Brooklyn North, he'd have to notify Sommers that they were off the case, as well as Detective Orson in the Arson Task Force and Willis at the fire marshal's office. Those calls could also be made in the morning, but he felt it necessary to call Mrs. Wingate tonight—now—and let her know that finding her son's killer was going to be someone else's responsibility.

PART TWO

25

Two weeks later . . .

Two weeks into February and it was colder than ever.
McQueen stopped his car behind one of the blue-
and-whites and set the emergency brake. He wasn't
on an incline, it was just force of habit.

He was riding alone, responding to the scene in a
supervisory capacity. He and the lieutenant had decided to shake the squad up a bit after they shipped
the Coney Island case out to Brooklyn North. Actually, Jessup told McQueen he wanted him to start taking on some more responsibility as a supervisor, so
they hooked Ray Velez up with Bailey Sommers as
partners. McQueen thought he might have been being punished for getting the boss in dutch with his
boss, the chief of detectives, but he didn't bitch about
it. In fact, he'd started thinking recently that it might
be time to put in his papers and retire. He just had to
figure out what he'd do with his life after that.

He was responding to a call from Sheepshead Bay

of a floater, but in fact this was Velez and Sommers's catch. The word had gone out for Homicide to respond, and then he got a call from Velez, who said, "Dennis, I think you better come out here."

McQueen hadn't been on the streets at all during those two weeks, and was starting to feel rooted to his desk. Even retirement was preferable to permanent desk duty. He thought that might end up being a strong factor in his decision.

In any case, he was happy to be out from behind the desk. He got out of his car, which he left in front of Randazzo's—where he'd had seafood more than once—and walked across the street to the docks. Fishing boats left from there each day—not so much now as in the spring and summer—as well as excursion boats. He saw Velez and Sommers at the end of one long concrete pier and, hands thrust deeply into his pockets and the collar of his coat turned up, he walked out to them.

Sommers and Velez were red-faced from the cold, and both were glassy-eyed, as well. In addition, Velez's nose seemed to be running badly, and he sniffed after every few words.

As Velez started to tell him what they had, McQueen held up his hand to stop him.

"I can't understand, with all the sniffling," he said. "Sommers?"

"It's my case, anyway, but I can show you better than I can tell you," she said. "Come with me."

He followed her to the end of the pier, where she pointed into the water. McQueen looked down and saw the body of a man floating there. Someone had used rope to lash it to the pier so it wouldn't drift away.

He turned his head to look over his shoulder. The pier was crowded with official personnel from the

M.E., the Crime Scene Unit, blue uniforms, boat captains and crew and—farther down, toward the street—civilian onlookers. There was also a police boat tied to the pier, with men in uniform wearing baseball-type blue caps with police insignia on them standing by.

"No duty captain?" he asked Sommers.

"Not yet."

Somebody from both the M.E.'s office and the Crime Scene Unit came up to him. "Can we get the body out of the water, yet?" the M.E.'s man asked.

"Yes," McQueen said. "Get it up here on the pier—" He stopped talking, because beyond them he saw that the M.E., Dr. Bannerjee, had arrived. He waved at the doctor to come over to him, then repeated what he'd started to say to the other men before continuing "and make the rest of your examination as quickly as possible. The duty captain should be here soon and he'll release the body."

"No danger of it thawing in this cold," Bannerjee commented, "even when we get it out of the water. Is this connected to that one in Coney Island last month?"

"That's what I want to find out," McQueen said.

The M.E. leaned over to look at the body in the water.

"Looks like his face is unmarked," the doctor said. "Young man, too, like that other one."

"I see that."

"Okay," Bannerjee said, "let's get it out of the water . . ."

By the time they'd pulled the body from the water and the M.E. had made his cursory examination, the duty captain had arrived. McQueen was pleased to see that it wasn't Captain Hartwell, but the much more congenial Captain Bill McAffey.

Before the captain reached him, and as the M.E.'s guys were carting the body away, McQueen pulled Bannerjee to the side.

"Is there a scratch on his back?"

"Yes, there is."

"Did you ever find out about the blood on the other one?"

Bannerjee looked embarrassed.

"We became extremely busy, and once the case was shipped to Brooklyn North—"

"Okay, never mind," McQueen said. "Not your fault. Just let me know if the scratches are identical, and try to find out about the blood. Also look for any other . . . similarities, all right?"

"I'll let you know ASAP," Bannerjee promised, and followed his men.

"Who's catchin'?" McAffey asked.

McQueen had already determined that Sommers had been up when the call came in.

"Detective Sommers, Cap," McQueen said.

McAffey looked at him. In his forties, his blonde hair had begun to turn gray, but his eyebrows were, as yet, untouched by gray. His eyes were blue, and they bored into McQueen's.

"I know you," he said. "McQueen, right? Brooklyn South Homicide?"

"That's right, Cap."

"Which one's Sommers?" McAffey asked, looking past McQueen at the two detectives standing at the end of the pier.

"The lady."

"New?"

"Fairly new to the squad, sir."

"Okay," McAffey said. "I'll talk to her."

COLD BLOODED

"Yes, sir."

"Why are you here?" the superior office asked. "Why'd they need a boss?"

"This case might be connected to one I caught last month, sir."

"That right? You still workin' it?"

"No, sir."

"Why not?"

"I had to turn it over to Brooklyn North."

McAffey opened his mouth to ask another question, then said, "Fuck it. I don't want to get involved, do I?"

"No, sir, you don't."

"I'll talk to your lady detective."

"Yes, sir."

As the captain walked away, McQueen hoped he had displayed the proper amount of respect without projecting any sarcasm. With McAffey, though, that didn't much matter. He'd worked his way up through the ranks without the virtue of a fast track. He was considered a cop's captain.

McQueen stood back and watched as everyone went about their business. He stuck his hands deep into his pockets again as questions scrolled through his head.

Would this body—this case—stay with them or have to be referred elsewhere?

Also, if the similarities between this one and Thomas Wingate were close enough, what did that mean for the Wingate case?

Did this young man have any connection to the Wingates, or the Deans?

If he didn't, and the circumstances were so similar, did that take Victor Dean off the hook for murder, while he was still on the hook for fraud and conspiracy to commit arson?

137

Did Thomas Wingate die in some other fire?

Could these possibly be two different cases involving bodies that were—even partially—frozen in fresh water ice, but dumped in salt water? That'd be up to the M.E. to determine.

McQueen decided they didn't need him there any longer. Velez and Sommers would be returning to the office soon, and he'd see their reports. At that time he'd have to decide—with Jessup—where the case belonged. It couldn't be decided standing out in the cold, freezing.

The Observer watched from the street with the other onlookers as the body was finally pulled from the water. He'd just been asked by a uniformed if he'd seen or heard anything and he said no. The man moved on, questioning everyone who was craning their necks in the hopes of seeing blood.

Once they loaded the body into a van he turned and made his way through the crowd. His work was done, time to move on to the next one.

The Ice Man was waiting.

26

When Velez and Sommers returned to the office, Mc-Queen was behind his desk, taking care of some squad paperwork. The lieutenant was out, but Mc-Queen decided he wouldn't tell the man about the Sheepshead Bay body. He'd wait for Sommers to type up her report and let the lieutenant read it for himself. If he saw the similarities, let him bring it up.

Velez went to his desk and Sommers walked over to McQueen.

"What do you want to do, Dennis?" she asked.

"About what?"

"About the similarities in these two cases."

"Bailey," he said, "just work your case, don't worry about the other one. You need to ID this body before we can really see a connection between the two that needs to be worked. You also need the M.E.'s report. Get back to me when you have all that."

She stood there for a few seconds, then said, "Yes, sir," and went to her own desk.

There was one other case the squad was working,

which had been caught by the Double Ds the day before. For Sommers, this was the fourth case she had caught in the past two weeks, the seventh she had worked on because Ray Velez caught three. Seven cases in two weeks, but five had turned out not to be homicides, and two had been quickly solved because the perps were family members. That meant that all seven cases had been cleared. The Double Ds had caught a similar number, with almost identical results.

The only real homicide the squad had worked since the Coney Island case *was* the Coney Island case, and McQueen had no idea how that was going over at Brooklyn North. He had called Mrs. Wingate to tell her he was no longer working the case and that was the last contact they'd had. Later, he'd had one call from Lydia Dean, who wanted an explanation of why he was dropping the case. He tried to tell her that he hadn't dropped the case, it had been taken from him as a matter of procedure. She'd told him she didn't care about his procedure, it looked to her like they were burying her brother's murder. Before he could argue she'd hung up on him, and he didn't see the benefit of calling her back.

When Sommers finished her report of the morning's activities she dropped it on his desk for him to approve, and sign.

"We're going to go out and do some canvassing," she told him. "Be back this afternoon in time to clock out."

"Okay."

"Ready, Ray?" she called across the room.

"I'll meet you at the car."

She waved and left the room. As soon as she was gone Velez came over to McQueen.

"What's up, Ray?"

"I can't keep working with her, Dennis."

"Why not? She's good at her job."

'It ain't that."

"What, then?"

Velez looked embarrassed.

"Cookie?" McQueen asked.

Velez nodded.

"She came to pick me up one day last week and saw Bailey," Velez said. "She hit the ceiling, Dennis. I been tryin' to talk to her, but . . . well, you know Cookie."

"Yeah," McQueen said, "I know Cookie."

As long as McQueen had known Velez, his wife had never liked any of his partners. McQueen was probably the one she tolerated the most.

"I never had a female partner before, Dennis," Velez said. "And to top it off, well . . . Bailey's kinda hot, you know? Cookie can't handle it."

"It's not like she's dressed with her tits hangin' out, Ray."

"I know it," Velez said, "but just 'cause they ain't hangin' out don't mean she ain't got 'em, Dennis."

McQueen rubbed his face with one hand.

"What do you want me to do, Ray?"

"Partner with me again," Velez said. "Give Bailey to someone else."

"Like who? Frankie?"

"Why not?" Velez asked.

"Come on, Ray. She'd have him up on sexual harassment charges by the end of the first day."

"Well, better that than I get divorced," Velez said. "Come on, you know how fragile my marriage is."

"Okay, okay," McQueen said, "I'll talk to the boss."

"Thanks, partner. I knew I could count on you."

"It might take a few days, Ray."

141

"As long as I can tell Cookie it's in the works, she should be fine," Velez said.

"Okay," McQueen said. "Get out of here. Your partner's waiting."

"Thanks, Dennis."

As Velez left the room, McQueen sat back in his chair and rubbed his face with both hands. Before he finished his phone rang, so he didn't even have a moment to think over Velez's request, and how it would realign the squad.

"Homicide," he said.

"This is the front desk, Sergeant O'Connor."

"Yeah, Ben, it's McQueen. Whataya got?"

"Dennis, I got a woman down here says she needs to talk to you," the desk sergeant said. Then he lowered his voice and added, "She's a looker."

"What does she want?"

"Won't say," O'Connor replied. "All she says is she's gotta talk to you."

"What's her name?"

"Um . . . Lydia Dean. You know her?"

McQueen closed his eyes and said, "Yeah, I know her. Send her up, Ben."

27

While McQueen was waiting for Lydia Dean to appear, the Double Ds walked in. They were talking about the only two things they liked. For Diver it was golf and for Dolan, tits.

"Hey, guys, do me a favor?" McQueen asked, interrupting what he hoped wasn't a comparison between the two. As far as he could see, the only thing they might have had in common was being dimpled—and in the case of the latter, that was just sometimes.

"Sure, boss," Diver said. "What's up?"

"Go get some coffee?"

"How do you want it?" Dolan asked.

"Not for me," McQueen said, "for you guys."

"Whataya me—" Diver started, but he stopped as a woman appeared in the doorway. She drew the attention of all three men. She was wearing a long, expensive-looking leather coat that was hanging open, revealing a bulky red sweater and a pair of pants that did nothing to hide her curves.

"Sergeant McQueen?" she said, before she spotted him at his desk.

"Oh," Diver said, then he nudged Dolan and said, "He's right there, ma'am."

Lydia Dean came into the room, and when she cleared the doorway Dolan and Diver went out, but not before Dolan looked back at McQueen, bit his knuckle, and then shook his hand.

"Have a seat, Mrs. Dean."

She looked around the office and said, "This is rather . . . cramped, isn't it?"

"It was all they had for us when they formed this squad," he explained.

"You don't have your own office?"

"The lieutenant gets the office," he said, indicating the other door, "but it's even more cramped in there."

"I see." She removed her coat, looked around for a place to hang it, then simply folded it in half and set it down on a nearby chair before seating herself across from him. She crossed her legs and he saw that she was wearing a pair of boots that matched the coat.

"What can I do for you, Mrs. Dean?"

"I'm actually here on behalf of my mother," Lydia said. "She was very disappointed when you withdrew from the case."

"I didn't withdraw, Mrs. Dean," he said. "I was forced—I had to give the case up."

"However it came about, she's very unhappy with the way it's been handled, since."

"How do you mean?"

"Well, nothing's been done," Lydia said.

"No one's been out to talk to your mother?"

"Oh yes, she's been spoken to several times, but it seems to her that the policeman handling the case is

144

more concerned with the fire than with Thomas's . . . death."

"I'm afraid I don't know who the case was assigned to."

That doesn't seem very efficient to me."

"Well . . . it's being handled by a different squad," McQueen said. "In fact, your brother's case is with one detective, while the fire is being investigated by another. As a matter of fact, the fire department also has someone investigating."

"So two people are looking into the fire, and only one into the murder?"

When she put it that way it did sound inefficient.

"Basically, that's it."

She sat back in her chair and stared at him.

"There's nothing you can do to help?" she asked.

"I can make some calls, Mrs. Dean."

"Lydia."

"Lydia," he repeated. "I can call the other investigators and see where they stand, but I can't do much more than that." Then he added: "It's not my case."

"Are you working on a case right now?"

"Well, no . . ."

"Then you have some time on your hands."

"Uh, no," he said, "that's not the way this works. Look, just let me see what I can do, and I'll get back to you."

"All right," she said, getting to her feet. She tugged her sweater down and he found himself staring. He didn't know if they were dimpled, but they were full and firm. "Thank you."

He stood up and came around the desk to help her on with her coat, and then walk her to the door. He wanted the extra time to think about whether or not to tell her about the body that was found that morning in Sheepshead Bay. It wouldn't have done much good, though, without a photo to show her.

"There's something else I have to ask you," she said, at the door.

"What's that?"

"Please don't tell my mother about this. I don't want to get her hopes up."

"Okay, I'll give you a call if I find out anything."

"That's be fine," she said. "When the time comes why don't we have a drink, somewhere?"

"That sounds . . . good."

"Until then," she said, putting out her hand. He shook it, and thought she held onto his a little longer than necessary. As she walked down the hall to the elevator he wondered what was on her mind besides her brother's murder? That she could have been attracted to him never entered his mind as feasible.

28

The next morning, to her surprise, McQueen called Bailey Sommers at home.

"Hello, Dennis," she said. "I was just on my way out. What can I do for you?"

"Bailey, I'd like you to stop and see Dr. G today," he said.

"About what?"

"I want a report on that floater from yesterday," he replied. "And a photo."

"Are you taking the case over?"

"No," he said, "I just want to take a good look at the similarities between the two cases."

"What about having someone from the Wingate family look at this body?" she asked. "Or, at least, a photo. If they know him that might tie the cases together."

"That's a good idea," McQueen told her, not mentioning that he'd decided to show Lydia Dean to see if she could ID it.

"Okay, I'll stop by and see if his report is ready."

"Thanks, Bailey."

She hung up, feeling absurdly pleased that Mc-Queen had called her and not Ray Velez. She thought that her days with Velez were numbered. Just from the conversations they'd had while riding in the car she knew he was a henpecked husband, firmly underneath the thumb of his wife, Cookie. She would have preferred remaining partners with McQueen. She hadn't been with the squad that long, but she knew the Double Ds were joined at the hip. If they broke her and Velez up she'd end up with Frankie Cataldo, or one of the off-shift detectives she never seemed to run into. Left in a car with Cataldo for an afternoon she knew she'd either have to shoot him, or herself.

She got into the used Volvo she'd owned for only three days and drove away from the Brooklyn apartment she'd also been in for three days. She had found a relatively inexpensive one-bedroom on Sackett Street near downtown, and she was pretty happy with it, and with her car. Now all she needed was to find a partner she could be satisfied with.

She pulled away from the curb and headed for the morgue to talk with the handsome medical examiner.

McQueen hung up the phone as the lieutenant walked in. The man had not seemed the worse for wear since forcing McQueen to refer the Coney Island case to Brooklyn North.

" 'Mornin', Loo."

"Dennis."

"Can I talk to you?"

"In my office," Jessup said, without breaking stride.

By the time McQueen had followed him in, Jessup

had seated himself behind his desk. He looked extremely comfortable when he was sitting there. The only time McQueen was comfortable at his desk was when he knew he'd be leaving it to respond to a call. He wasn't in his element while inside.

"What is it, Dennis?"

"I think we need to redesign the squad again, Loo." McQueen sat, holding a file folder on his lap.

"To get you out from behind the desk?" Jessup asked. "Do we have to talk about this again? I thought we had this settled—"

"It's Ray, Loo."

"Velez? What's his problem?"

"Apparently, Cookie is on the warpath."

"Again? What about, this time?"

"She doesn't like Ray being partnered with Bailey."

"Ah, Jesus—"

"Ray thinks his marriage is in trouble if we leave him with Sommers," McQueen added.

The New York City Police Department was a funny place. While many cops felt it was all right for them to have girlfriends on the side because of the dangers of the job, the department itself was a stickler for family.

"What can we do, then?" Jessup demanded. "Put her with Cataldo? She'll end up killin' him—or, at the very least, filing a sexual harassment charge against him."

"I know."

"What about Sherman or Silver?"

"They've got the best clearance rate in the squad," McQueen said. "I don't think we want to mess with that."

"Give me an answer, Dennis."

"There are two possible ways to solve the problem,

sir," McQueen said. "Let me partner with her again—"

"How did I know?"

"—while you put in a request for another detective. When the new guy—or gal—gets here, we'll put them together."

"And the other idea?"

"Put me back with Ray and let Bailey do some clerical work for a while."

"And what do we do with Frankie?" Jessup asked. "However we work it, he's workin' alone, doing whatever shit job we give him."

"Okay, then," McQueen said, "put in the request for another gold shield, and ship Frankie out. Nobody wants to work with him, Loo."

"I've been tryin' for months to get us a civilian clerk," Jessup said. "Now you want me shipping gold shields back and forth."

"I'm tryin' to save Ray's marriage, sir."

"Yeah, right," Jessup said. "It'd be a coincidence that this is working out just the way you want it."

"Well, there is something else."

"What's that?"

McQueen dropped the folder on the man's desk.

"This is the preliminary report on a case Sommers caught yesterday."

"Give me the pocket version."

"Another dead young man in the water, this time in Sheepshead Bay."

Jessup closed his eyes.

"Are you gonna tell me there are similarities to the Coney Island case?"

"I am," McQueen said. "This one still had ice on his hands and feet. Looks like fresh water, Loo."

"What's the M.E. say?"

"I've got Bailey stopping there first on her way to

work," McQueen said, "and I'm gonna put in a call to the Crime Scene Unit."

"Close the door on your way out, Dennis," Jessup said. "Looks like I have a lot to think about."

29

Bailey knocked on the door of Dr. Bannerjee's office and the man looked up from his desk.

"Ah, Detective Sommers."

"Nice of you to remember," she said.

"How could I forget?"

She was impressed. He managed to flirt with her without leering or using a cheesy line. That put him head and shoulders above all the men she'd worked with since joining the department. She'd been hit on by everyone from street cops to bosses, and none of them had the class of the man they all called Dr. G.

"How can I help you?"

"The Sheepshead Bay floater from yesterday?" she said. "I'm afraid it's mine."

"And you want your report."

"Sergeant McQueen wanted me to stop by—"

"Say no more," he said, holding his hand up. "I already know how impatient and demanding Sergeant McQueen can be."

"If you haven't had a chance—"

"Ah, but I have," he said. "I did it first thing this morning. Moved it up ahead of some others who were here first."

"You did? Why?"

"Because I, too, was curious to see how similar this body was to the one found in Coney Island last month."

"And?"

He picked a folder up off his desk and held it out to her. She took several steps into the room to accept it.

"Blunt trauma to the back of the head," he said, "and ice in the lungs."

"Jesus . . ." she said.

"It's not similar," he said, "in many ways it's identical, right down to the freshwater ice."

When Detective Sommers walked into the Homicide office, McQueen was hanging up his phone.

"Took you long enough," he said.

"Ethan wanted me to have a cup of coffee with him."

"Ethan?" he asked. "You mean Dr. G?"

"He doesn't like to be called that."

"Well, excuse me," he said. "What did *Ethan* tell you?"

"He told me lots of things, and none of them came out sounding smarmy or cheap," she said. "He's a gentleman."

"Okay," McQueen replied, "What did the gentleman tell you about our case?"

She put the M.E.'s report on his desk.

"In a nutshell," she said, "it's almost identical to the Wingate case."

"Almost?"

"Well, the head trauma and ice in the lungs are there. No smoke inhalation, though."

"What killed him?"

"An ice pick in the ear."

"Ice pick? Where did that come from?"

"Maybe it's not the same killer."

"There are a few ways to find out. Is there a photo in here?" he asked, picking up the file.

"Yes."

"Good. I'm going to take it over to Mrs. Dean and show it to her."

"I was hoping you wouldn't say you were going to show it to Thomas Wingate's mother," she said. "I don't think that nice lady needs to see another dead body."

"I agree. Actually, Mrs. Dean came here last night, before I left, to ask me for help."

"With what?"

"The investigation into her brother's case," he said. "Apparently her mother is not satisfied with the way it's going. She says they're concentrating more on the fire."

"She says her mother's not satisfied?"

"That's right."

Sommers shook her head.

"What's wrong?"

"This broad doesn't sound like the type who cares about Mom," Sommers said.

"Broad?"

She smiled.

"I've been here over two weeks," she said. "I can stop tryin' to impress you now."

"You mean I'm gonna start seein' the real you from now on?" he asked.

"From head to toe."

McQueen made no comment, which impressed her. All along since they'd met, he never took the opportunity for a cheap shot. Dennis McQueen was as much a gentleman as Ethan Bannerjee, just not as smooth or good-looking.

At that moment his phone rang. Sommers went back to her own desk as he answered it.

"McQueen."

"I heard you got another body," Fire Marshal Mason Willis said.

"Where'd you hear that?"

"Word gets around. Listen, I want to have a chat with Lydia Dean. You want to go with me?"

She wasn't fooling him. Lydia Dean would feel more compelled to talk to a cop than a fire marshal. Still, he was going over there, anyway.

"Why not?" he asked. "I have a few questions myself. Meet you there?"

"Half an hour?"

"See you then."

He hung up and looked around the office. No one was looking at him. He wondered if Willis just had very good contacts, or if there was a leak right there in the office.

He hoped it was the former.

30

McQueen found Mason Willis waiting for him in front of Lydia Dean's house.

"You got here quick."

"I tend to move quickly when I smell smoke."

"And you smell it now?"

"I think she and her husband burned down their own business," Willis said. "I can't prove it."

"What do you hope to accomplish today?"

"I'm guessing you want to find out if she knows the second victim."

"You're guessing right."

"I just want to ride your coattails, maybe ask a question or two. I want her to know I'm around."

"Okay," McQueen said. "I'll introduce you."

Lydia Dean smiled when she saw McQueen on her doorstep, but the smile faded when she noticed Mason Willis standing next to him. She had apparently been expecting him to come alone.

"Mrs. Dean," he said, then, "Lydia."

"When you called," she said, "you didn't say anything about bringing someone with you."

"This is Fire Marshal Mason Willis."

"Fire marshal?"

"She's investigating the fire in your building."

"I thought your Arson Squad—"

"The fire department tends to conduct their own investigations into . . . suspicious fires," Willis said.

"May we come in?" McQueen asked.

Lydia hesitated, then said, "Of course." From the look in her eyes McQueen figured Willis's presence had created the desired effect.

They entered and she led them into the living room. For Willis it was the first time she'd seen the place, and she was impressed.

"You have a beautiful home."

"Thank you," Lydia said. "Well, I suspect it's too early for a drink. Can I get you coffee, or tea?"

"No, nothing, Lydia," McQueen said. "I don't think this is going to be a pleasant visit."

"Oh," she said. "Have you . . . found out who killed my brother? Have you found Victor?"

"No, neither of those things," he said. "We . . . there was another body found yesterday, and the condition of it is . . . similar to that of your brother."

"All right," she said, staring at them, expectantly. "What does that mean to me . . . exactly?"

"This isn't pleasant, Lydia," McQueen said, "but I was wondering if you would be willing to take a look at a photo of the man."

"A photo of a dead man?"

"Yes."

"Why?"

"To see if you know him," he said.

"And if I do?"

"Then it connects his death with your brother's," McQueen explained.

"And this new case?" she asked McQueen, flicking a finger at the file he was holding. "You're investigating it?"

"No," he said, "this is another detective's case. I'm just helping out."

She thought a moment, her arms folded in front of her. "After seeing my brother dead, I don't see how this could be any worse."

McQueen opened the file just enough to be able to slide the black-and-white photo out. He handed it to her and watched while she examined it. He caught nothing in her face, no flicker of recognition as she handed it back.

"He looks like he's sleeping," she said.

"Yes," McQueen replied, "his face was not marked."

"How was he killed?"

"Lydia—"

"I'd like to know," she said. "I assume not in a fire."

"No," McQueen said. "He was stabbed, uh, in the ear with an, uh, ice pick."

"I see."

She looked at the photo again.

"I don't know him." She handed it back.

"Are you sure?" McQueen asked.

"I never saw him before in my life."

"All right," McQueen said, returning the photo to the folder, "that's clear enough. Thank you, Lydia."

"That's all?"

"Yes," he said. "That's it . . . for me. Fire Marshal Willis may have some questions of her own."

"Mrs. Dean," Willis said, "do you know any reason

why your brother may have wanted to burn down your business?"

"My . . . my brother?"

"Yes."

"Why, no, not at all. Is that what you think? Thomas was there to set the fire?"

"Somebody set it," Willis said. "He's just one suspect."

The implication was plain. McQueen was impressed that Lydia Dean did not rise to the bait.

"Do you think the same person who killed this man killed my brother?" she asked McQueen.

"It's too early to tell," he said, "but we're working on it."

"If that's the case," she went on, "then my husband didn't kill Thomas, did he?"

"Well," McQueen said, "if you didn't know this man, and your husband didn't either, then I don't see where there would have been a motive for your husband to kill him. As for your brother, there's still the very real possibility that your brother was killed by the fire. The question is, who set it? And then we have to ask did that person kill this second victim?"

"Then again," Willis added, "both cases could be very separate."

"But—that confuses things, doesn't it?"

"Quite a lot," McQueen said. "Have you heard from your husband?"

"No," she said, "no, I haven't."

"If you do hear from him," McQueen said, "maybe you can tell him about this new development. Maybe you can tell him to give himself up? It might help us with the investigation."

"What about . . . the fire? Won't he still be arrested for that if he gives himself up?'

"That would be up to the Arson Task Force," he said, "and the fire marshal's office. We're only working the homicide angle."

"I see."

"We should be going," Willis said to McQueen.

"Right."

As they turned, Lydia Dean reached out and put her hand on McQueen's arm.

"Can I speak to you before you go?" She looked pointedly at Willis. "Alone?"

"Sure," he said. "I'll be right out, Marshal."

"Sure."

As Willis went through the front door and pulled it closed behind her, McQueen turned to Lydia Dean.

"What is it, Lydia?"

"You're not going to show that photo to my mother, are you?" she asked.

"Why? Do you think she'll know the man?"

"No!" she said, sharply, then lowered her tone and said again, "No. It's just . . . she's been traumatized enough, don't you think?"

"If you assure us that no one in your family knew this dead man," he said, "I don't see any reason why I should have to bother your mother with this."

"Good," Lydia said, "good . . . Dennis?"

"Yes?"

"How about coming back for that drink, sometime . . . alone?" She hugged herself and rocked a bit when she asked.

"I'll . . . have to see about that, Lydia," he said.

"Well . . . just let me know."

He nodded and went out the front door.

"What'd she want?" Willis asked outside.

He told her.

"Sounds like she's after you."

Now she sounded like Bailey Sommers.

"She's after something, that's for sure."

"And it couldn't be you?"

"No," he said, "it couldn't."

His tone put an end to that part of the conversation.

"You think she knows where her husband is?" she asked.

"She's lying about something," he said. "Either she knows where he is or he's been in touch with her."

"And what about that crap about worrying about her mother being traumatized?"

"You think that was crap?"

"She doesn't strike me as the caring type."

"She is kind of . . . cold."

"Does the mother have enough money to bail out the business?" she asked.

"Probably."

"Would her mother help her?"

"That I don't know."

"You think the husband did the brother?"

"It looked that way, for a while."

"And now?"

"If the family really doesn't know the second dead man . . ." He let it trail off.

"And how are you going to be sure of that?"

"I guess," he said, "I'll have to go ahead and ask the last member of the family."

31

McQueen and Willis split up in front of Lydia Dean's house. He got in his car and put in a call to Sommers. He told her he was going to the mother's house, and asked her to meet him there. It was her opinion that when they saw Mrs. Wingate she should do the talking.

"Fine," McQueen said. "It's your case, anyway."

But he also told her that she was now partnering with him again, and not Ray Velez.

"Why?" she'd asked. When he didn't answer immediately she added, "Let me guess. Cookie?"

"Uh, yeah."

"What a bitch," she said, "and before you tell me I've never met her, I've heard you and Ray talk about her. How could anybody stay married to her?"

"Well," McQueen said, "obviously you've never seen her."

That, she'd thought, was the first typical man thing she'd heard McQueen say since she'd met him . . .

* * *

When Mrs. Wingate answered the door, she looked to McQueen like a woman who had aged a year in a couple of weeks. She smiled weakly at Sommers.

"Hello, dear," she said.

"Do you remember me from the hospital, Mrs. Wingate?" Sommers asked.

"Of course I do," the woman said, "but not by name, I'm afraid."

"I'm Detective Sommers," she said, "and this is Sergeant McQueen. May we come in?"

"Of course."

The inside was not as expensively furnished as her daughter's home, but it felt warmer, more welcoming.

"Can I offer you something? Some tea, perhaps?"

Before McQueen could speak Sommers said, "We'd love some tea, ma'am."

"We can have it in the kitchen," the older woman said. "You can come with me while I prepare it."

In the kitchen there was more tea talk—sugar? lemon? milk?—before they all sat down at the table with a cup each. Sommers and McQueen took it plain, but Mrs. Wingate added sugar and milk to hers, then stirred it for a long time—long enough for the sound to start to get on Dennis McQueen's nerves. He gave Sommers a look that said, "Well, go ahead, already!"

"Mrs. Wingate—"

"Is this about my Thomas?" the woman asked.

"In a way, ma'am," Sommers said. "You see, the body of another young man has been found, in much the same condition as your son's."

"Oh, no," she said, sincerely. "That's too bad. I feel so sorry for that mother."

"We were wondering if you could tell us if he was a friend of your son's?" Sommers asked. "Or perhaps someone your family knew?"

"I'll certainly try," the woman said. "What's your boy's name?"

"We don't have a name yet, Mrs. Wingate," Sommers said. "We haven't identified the body, yet. But we do . . . have a photo."

"A photo?"

"Of the . . . dead man."

"Oh," Mrs. Wingate said, "I see."

"We can't compel you to look at it," Sommers told her, "but it would certainly help us if you would."

She stared at them across the table for a few moments. She was wearing no makeup and her hair was grayer than he remembered. And where she'd been well-dressed the first time he saw her, she was now wearing a housedress. He saw now that she was older than he'd first thought because—like her daughter—the first time they'd met she'd had some defense against aging. The woman sitting across from him now, at her kitchen table, was totally defenseless against it.

"I suppose I could look at it," she said. "Is it—is he . . ."

"He died the same way your son did," Sommers said. "There's no . . . trauma."

"Very well."

Sommers looked at McQueen, who once again eased the photo out of the folder. He set it down on the table, face up, and passed it across the table.

Mrs. Wingate moved the photo close to herself. At first she examined it without picking it up, but finally she took it in her hands and brought it up closer to her face.

"He looks very peaceful," she commented. "It's as if he's just . . . sleeping."

Sommers leaned forward.

"Do you know him, Mrs. Wingate?" she asked. "Do you recognize him?"

The older woman stared at the photo for a few moments, then released it. It fell to the table in front of her.

"I don't know him," she said. "He somebody else's son, but I don't know whose."

"What about your daughter?" McQueen asked. "Do you think she'd know him?"

She looked at him.

"My daughter? I'm sure I don't know who my daughter's friends are. You see, we don't speak."

"When was the last time you did speak?" he asked.

"That day," she said, "that day . . . I called and left her a message that her brother was dead. I thought she should know. We spoke at the hospital, but not since, and not for a long time before."

"Wait a minute," McQueen said. "You and your daughter have not spoken since that day at the morgue?"

"That's right."

He looked at Sommers, who frowned at him questioningly. He shook his head.

"All right, Mrs. Wingate," Sommers said. "We won't hold you up any longer."

She looked at their cups of tea, which had hardly been touched.

"But . . . your tea . . ."

"Yes," Sommers said. "It was delicious."

Outside the house, even before they reached the car, she asked McQueen, "What's wrong?"

"I told you the daughter came to see me," he said, "told me that her mother was concerned the case wasn't being handled properly."

"But the mother just said they hadn't spoken since the hospital," Sommers finished. "So, one of them was lying."

"Yes."

"But why? And which one?"

"That I don't know," McQueen said.

"Well, for the daughter . . . just an excuse to come and see you, maybe?" she asked.

"Bailey . . ."

"Couldn't be, Dennis?"

"No."

"You're selling yourself short—"

"Stop!" he told her. "I'm not a fool, Bailey. I think Lydia's the one lying, and I think she's up to . . . something."

"Like what?"

"That's what we're gonna to find out."

32

It was late for lunch and early for dinner, but they were both hungry so they drove to Sheepshead Bay and stopped in a diner. McQueen grabbed a booth in the front, next to a window.

"Why here?" Sommers asked.

"I like to look out the window at the water while I eat," McQueen said. He turned his head and pointed outside. "See?"

A waitress came over. McQueen ordered a pizza burger and fries, Sommers a salad and, at the last minute, garlic dressing. Both of them took iced tea to go with it.

"Tell me the real reason we're eating here," Sommers said.

"It's close to the crime scene," McQueen said. "I just wanted to be close while we ate, and talked."

"Expecting to . . . absorb something from the cosmos?"

"My methods are not New Age, Bailey."

"I'm impressed."

"With what?"

"The fact that you know the term 'New Age,'" she said.

"Sorry I'm not the Neanderthal you're used to working with," he responded.

"I'm not. Are we going to talk about the case, or personal stuff?" she asked.

"The case," he said, then asked, "What personal stuff?"

"Do you go out much, Dennis?"

"Out?"

"You know, to have fun."

"Oh, sure," he said, "I go to ball games, the track, sometimes Atlantic City."

"No," she said, "I mean out with women?"

"Oh," he said, "you just want to get nosy."

"I'm just wondering—"

"Bailey," he said, "I've been out with women. I know when a woman is interested in me."

"You do?"

"Yes," he said. "I'm not a total idiot."

"When's the last time you were on a date?"

"I don't know," he said. "Weeks . . . maybe months . . . what's the difference?"

"If you don't use it," she said, "it—"

"I don't think I want to hear the rest of that," he said, holding up his hand.

"Okay, let's talk about something else."

They both leaned back so the waitress could set down their drinks.

"The case?" he asked, hopefully.

"First," she said, "let's talk about why there's so much tension in the squad."

"Tension?"

"Yes," she said. "Don't tell me you don't notice it."

"Well . . ."

"You and Ray get along, you joke around with each other. So do the Double Ds," she said. "Everybody else seems to have sticks up their asses. Even Sherman and Silverman, and they work pretty good together. What gives?"

"There's only one Manhattan North, Bailey."

"Manhattan North," she repeated. "Best squad in the department, right?"

"Right," he said, "and there's only one. Brooklyn South is not Manhattan North. In fact, there aren't many of guys who actually want to be there."

"Why not?"

"Did you want to be there?" he asked. "Did you ask for Brooklyn South?"

"I asked for a homicide squad," she said. "This is the opening that came up."

"Not your first choice, though, right?"

She hesitated, then said, "Right."

"So nobody's where they really want to be," he said, "and nobody really likes anybody."

"Does that include Jessup?"

"He's stuck in rank, like a lot of lieutenants and captains on this job who were once on the fast track," McQueen said.

The waitress came with their food and they suspended the conversation again.

"And what about you?" she asked, mixing her dressing into her salad.

"What about me?"

"Are you where you want to be?" she asked. "Are you stuck in rank?"

She didn't know where she got the nerve to talk to him this way, except that she felt really comfortable with him. Maybe nobody in the squad liked anybody else, but that wasn't true in this case. She liked Dennis McQueen, and she wanted to know more about him. And there was nothing romantic about her interest.

"First," he said, "I'm doin' what I want to be doin', where I want to do it. I live in Brooklyn, and I want to keep it clean—or, as clean as we can keep it."

She looked out at the street in front of the diner and said, "That seems to be a losing battle."

"That may be so," he said, "but that doesn't mean I'm gonna stop tryin'."

"Okay."

"As for my rank," he said, "I never even wanted to be a sergeant. I was very happy as a first-grade detective. So no, I'm not stuck in rank. I don't really have much ambition, Bailey. I'm a simple man, happy with simple things."

"But are you a happy man?"

"Who's happy?" he asked. "Are you? I'm divorced, my grown daughter doesn't have much use for me."

"What about your ex-wife?"

"We don't talk," he said. "To tell you the truth, I don't have much use for her."

He bit into his pizza burger, grabbed a napkin to keep the sauce from running down his chin.

"What about you?" he asked. "Are you happy with your life? Your assignment? Your rank?"

"Well," she said, "the easiest way to answer that would probably be no, no, and no—but that's not really true."

"Which 'no' isn't true?"

"I'm not happy with my life, but I'm kinda all right with it, you know? I mean, I live alone—which is fine—and I feel like I'm heading in the right direction."

"And what direction is that?" he asked. "You wanna be the first female police commissioner?"

"It's not on my list," she said, "but if the job was offered to me I'd take it. As for my rank, it's fine, right now. I know I'm going to move up. It's just a matter of time."

He didn't comment on that, let her believe it, but he knew lots of men and women who thought the way she did. One misstep, though, and plans changed.

"And your assignment?" he said. "The one you didn't ask for?"

She sat back, chewed what she had in her mouth, washed it down with some tea, and then said, "That I'm happy with."

"You are?"

"Well, I'm happy to be partnering with you," she said. "Ray was okay, but he was tense all the time—and now I know why. And I admit I was afraid you were going to partner me with Cataldo."

"I wouldn't do that to you."

"I've already heard his fat girl jokes."

"Both of them?"

"He only has the two?"

" 'How do you fuck a fat girl? Roll her in dough and aim for the wet spot,' " McQueen quoted.

"Oh yeah, and . . . 'gimme a hint, pee a little.' "

They both laughed, not at the jokes, but at the man.

"I'm learning a lot, Dennis," she said, "and mostly from you. So when you told me today we were partners again . . . that's when I got happy with my assignment."

"Well," he said, picking up a couple of French fries, "I'm flattered."

"Don't be," she said. "I'm not trying to flatter you. I respect you as a detective and I think I can learn a lot from you, so there's no flattery intended."

He chewed his French fries, said, "Okay," and took another huge bite out of his burger.

* * *

Later, over coffee, they discussed the case.

"Are you going to talk to the boss about getting the Wingate case back?"

"That's not gonna happen," he said.

"Why not?"

"The ice pick," he said. "It throws a monkey wrench into the works."

"But the similarities—"

"Are not enough," he said. "Not with the different ways they were killed."

"Smoke inhalation," she said, "and an ice pick. What about the ice in the lungs? Well, actually Ethan—Dr. Bannerjee—called it 'frozen condensation.' And what about finding them both in the water?"

"Maybe," he said, thoughtfully, "what we have are two different killers, but the same person disposing of the bodies."

"You mean, somebody's making a living getting rid of bodies? A serial disposer?"

He shrugged.

"Could be. It's just a thought."

She sat back and said, "Wow. It is a thought, isn't it?"

"We have to get an ID on this body," he said, "see if we can find out when he died. If he's been in storage someplace for weeks, like Thomas Wingate, then maybe we'll have something."

"A real serial?" she asked, eagerly.

"Don't be so eager to work on a serial case, Bailey," he said. "It's a pain in the ass, and the pressure is murder."

"But if the cases are enough alike they'll put together a task force, won't they?"

"Possibly."

"And since we caught both of these, we'd be included, wouldn't we?"

"Maybe," he said, "but we've got a long way to go before that happens. You done?"

"Yes."

"Let's go, then."

She reached for her purse and he said, "On me."

"Like a date?" she asked, with a smile.

"Bailey," he said, as they stood up, "don't be such a wise guy all the time, huh?"

"Can't help it," she said. "I'm starting to feel real comfortable around you."

"God help me . . ." he said.

33

The Ice Man sliced the veal extra thin, the way he knew Mrs. O'Brien liked it. You could almost see right through it.

"Is that okay, Mrs. O'Brien?" he asked, showing it to her.

The old lady—eighty if she was a day—smiled at him and said, "Your father would be very proud, Owen."

"Yes, ma'am." He wrapped the bloody veal up in brown paper, taped it and handed it to her. She paid him and told him to have a nice day.

He walked to the window and watched as she walked down the street—a street that had changed a lot since the day his father first opened the butcher shop. There were few businesses on this street that were as old as Harry's Butcher Shop. In fact, last month a new coffee bar opened up on the corner, a sure sign that the end might be near.

Owen had taken over the butcher shop when his father died ten years ago. Tempted to close it after his mother died eight years back, he decided to fight the neighborhood change as long as he could. This was his family business, after all.

Besides, he had very special use for the big freezers in the back room.

34

Over the next few days, Dennis McQueen and Bailey Sommers were unable to identify the Sheepshead Bay body. AFIS, LEADS, NCIC, VICAP, WXY & Z and every other anagramed identification program he could think of all came up with a big fat zero. Without the young man's identity, it was impossible to come up with any suspects.

Sommers decided to do a computer search in an attempt to find any other bodies with similarities to the Coney Island and Sheepshead Bay bodies. Each search came up empty. She also checked with Missing Persons, but they had nothing matching the dead man's description. If he was missing, nobody cared enough to report it.

McQueen, on the other hand, simply called Dr. Bannerjee to ask if he'd done any postmortems on bodies with similarities. Dr. G told him he doubted he'd seen anything to match those two. The presence of the iced condensation in the lungs would have stood out, he explained. Nevertheless, McQueen asked Dr. G to go back in his files to previous winters to see if he could find anything.

McQueen also spent that time talking to the other investigators who were looking into the murder of Thomas Wingate, and the arson connected to it . . .

Detective Jack Orson of the Arson Task Force said he was still looking for Vincent Dean and the man he hired to torch his building. They had checked all of the known arsonists in Brooklyn, in the five boroughs, in New York State, and then on the East Coast.

They might have flown somebody in from the Midwest, or the West, Orson said. "Guess that'll be our next move."

Or maybe, McQueen had thought, the person who torched the building was just a talented amateur who had no record . . .

He didn't voice his thoughts to Detective Orson, but he did to the fire marshal.

"You could be right," she said. "In fact, you probably are. The more I look at this the more I think it wasn't a pro."

"You know any amateurs who could have done this?"

"Lots of people can burn down a building, Sergeant," she said. "All you really need is a match."

She promised to keep him informed as her investigation proceeded.

And she told him to call her Mace . . .

Finally, he talked with the detective who had taken over his homicide case for Brooklyn North, Detective Hal Northrop.

"I got nothin'," Northrop told him on the phone.

"I'm thinkin' when the Arson Task Force finds their guy, they'll find my guy, too."

"But you're still workin' the case, right?" McQueen asked.

"It's still an open case, Sarge," Northrop said, "but you know how that is. I got two other cases I'm workin' on at the same time."

"Yeah, Northrop," McQueen replied, "I know what it's like . . ."

McQueen had also caught another case, but he and Sommers had been able to clear it within twenty-four hours, enabling him to go back over both the Coney Island and the Sheepshead Bay cases.

He had copies of both reports on his desk when Sommers came up from downstairs, where she had continued to labor on the computer.

"You know," she complained, "if we had a computer of our own I wouldn't have to keep going up and down those stairs."

"Try using the elevator," McQueen said.

"Not exactly my point."

"I know . . ."

She leaned over his desk to see what he was looking at.

"Don't let the lieutenant catch you looking at that Coney Island file," she said.

"Just for reference."

"Right."

She perched a hip on his desk.

"You know what I think is the only thing that can jump-start this investigation?"

"Yes, I do."

She raised her eyebrows.

"You do?"

He looked up at her.

"Another body."

"What are you, a mind reader?"

"We've just been thinkin' along the same lines, Bailey."

"That would give us a serial," she said.

"Still eager to work a serial case, huh?"

She shrugged.

"I want to experience everything I can on this job."

"Well, we'd need more than just the freshwater ice to get the department to form a serial killer task force," he told her. "We're also short on one other thing."

"What's that?"

"Time," he said. "It's February. It's not gonna stay winter forever. If preserving the bodies and then dumping them in freezing cold water has any significance, what's gonna happen when the temperature starts going up?"

She shrugged helplessly. He pushed his chair back from his desk and regarded her.

"How about this? He wants us to find the bodies, that's why he's dumping them in or near the cold water. But maybe he doesn't realize that he's preserving the evidence in their lungs by doing so."

"Okay, say you're right," she said. "If he's keeping the bodies on ice someplace, the weather isn't going to affect that. He's got to have a man-sized freezer someplace."

"And who has access to freezers that size?" he asked.

"Lots of people," she said. "There are lots of business that require freezers."

"Okay then," he said, "that's your next job."

"What is?"

"Prepare a list of the types of businesses that need freezers," he said. "Large, industrial-type freezers,

179

not the kind people keep in their basement to hold extra meat."

"And why not that kind?"

"They'll be harder to track," he said. "Let's start with industrial types that would be ordered by businesses."

"That could be a long list."

"Then you better get started."

35

The more McQueen thought about it, the more convinced he became that the killer of the two young men was the same. And for him the stronger link was not how the bodies were disposed of, or the frozen condition of the lungs. For him it was the scratch at the small of the back of both men.

"That's the most unusual aspect of this case," he told Sommers. "Your buddy Ethan is gonna have to come up with something from those scratches."

"He's not my buddy," she said. "He's just a rarity in law enforcement—a gentleman."

"A rarity, huh?"

"If you're a woman in law enforcement, yes."

"Uh-huh."

"Would you like me to go and see Eth—Dr. Bannerjee and see what he has?"

McQueen grinned at her across his desk and said, "No, I think we should go together."

"I don't need protection, you know," she said.

"It wasn't you I was thinking about protecting . . ."

181

* * *

It was several days after the discovery of the second body and, somehow, the M.E. had gotten bust while McQueen and his squad were not.

"Sergeant McQueen," Bannerjee said, when McQueen and Sommers appeared in his doorway, "and your lovely partner, Detective Sommers. Please, come in."

"Thanks, Doc," McQueen said. He allowed Sommers to precede him into the doctor's office. He'd show her there were some other gentlemen out there, as well.

"I'm surprised you responded so quickly to my message," Bannerjee said.

"What message was that?"

I called your office just a little while ago," the M.E. said. "I thought you were in response to that."

"I never got your message," McQueen said. "I just thought we'd stop in and see where you were on Detective Sommers's case."

"The Sheepshead Bay victim," Bannerjee said. "Actually, that's why I called you, about that and about last month's case, from Coney Island."

"Did you get something on those scratches?"

"I did, indeed," Bannerjee said, "and knowing your preference for getting straight to the point, I'll tell you that the blood found in the wounds did not belong to either of the victims. In fact, it was not even human blood."

Bannerjee paused and McQueen said, "Doc . . ."

"Yes, yes, all right," Bannerjee said. "You will not even allow me to build the suspense. Very well, it was bovine blood."

"Bovine?"

Bannerjee sighed and said, "Cows."

Sommers slapped McQueen on the arm and said, "Beef."

"Exactly."

"In both cases?"

"Yes."

"Slabs of beef," Sommers said, "hanging from hooks."

"Excuse me?" the doctor asked.

"Doc, could the scratches have been made by metal hooks?" McQueen asked.

"Hooks?"

"The kinds slabs of beef hang from, Doctor," Sommers said.

"Ah, I see what you're getting at," Bannerjee said. "Both bodies were preserved in freezers, apparently, and so now you think they were . . . hung from hooks?"

"That's what we're thinking," McQueen said.

"Well," Bannerjee said, "it's not exactly my area of expertise, but I imagine the scratches could have been made by metal hooks, but . . ."

"But what?"

"Wouldn't that mean they would have had to be hung up by the back of their belts?"

"Exactly," Sommers said.

"That would have to be done by someone with very little regard for . . . for personal dignity."

"I think murder would be an indication of that, Doctor," Sommers said.

"The blood could have been transferred to their bodies by the point of the hooks, couldn't it?" McQueen asked, still following the train of thought.

"Definitely," Bannerjee said, "especially the way this blood was imbedded into the scratches."

"You still have one of the victims here, don't you, Doc?" McQueen asked.

"Yes, your unknown man from Sheepshead Bay. Why?"

"I'm gonna ask the lab to send someone over to look at that scratch," McQueen said.

"Looking for what?" Bannerjee asked.

"Something you wouldn't be lookin' for," McQueen said. "Traces of metal."

"Which would confirm your hook theory."

"And give us someplace definite to look for," McQueen said.

Bannerjee looked at Sommers, who said, "Butcher shops, slaughter houses, like that."

"Ah . . ."

McQueen put in a call to the lab and actually reached the technician from the first case, Marty Cahill. He told McQueen he'd be glad to take a look, but couldn't get down there until the next morning. McQueen figured that would have to do and thanked the man. He then told Bannerjee to expect Cahill in the morning and give him access to the body.

"Of course."

The doctor then offered them coffee or tea, choosing to look directly at Bailey Sommers while he made the offer.

"I don't have time to stay for coffee, Doc," McQueen said, "but Bailey might—"

"Sergeant McQueen is my ride," she said, cutting him off. "Maybe another time?"

"Of course," Bannerjee said, with a charming smile, "another time." He shook hands with Sommers, holding her hand a little longer than was necessary.

Outside McQueen said, "I thought you were stuck on the doc. Why didn't you stay?"

"I never said I was stuck on him," she argued, "all I said was that he was a gentleman."

"Don't tell me you're the type who likes bad boys?"

"No, I'm not," she said.

"So your type lies somewhere in the middle?"

"Why are we discussing my type?" she demanded.

"I'm just trying to—"

"You don't like it when I try to discuss this kind of thing with you, do you?" she asked.

"Point taken."

They got in the car and she headed them back to the office.

"You'll have to modify your list," he told her.

"I've already thought of that," she said. "We need to look for large, walk-in freezers used by commercial meat-packing plants and—like I told the doc—butcher shops, slaughter houses . . . anyone who deals with huge slabs of meat hung on hooks."

"Rocky."

"What?" she asked.

"Puts me in mind of the first *Rocky* movie, where he trained on slabs of meat."

"Oh, right."

"You have seen *Rocky*, haven't you?"

"Are we going to discuss my taste in movies now?"

"Jesus, Sommers," he said, "you haven't seen *Rocky*? Any of the *Rocky* movies?"

"Boxing is not my thing."

"They're about more than just boxing."

"Dennis, let's not get into a discussion about movies, now," she said.

"Yeah, but *Rocky* . . . next thing you'll tell me is you've never seen the *Star Wars* movies."

When this comment was greeted by silence he said, "Jesus Christ, Bailey—"

"Have you ever seen *The First Wives Club*?"

"Uh, no . . ."

"*The Banger Sisters*?"

"No . . ."

"How about *Same Time, Next Year*?"

"Okay, okay, I get your point."

They drove along in silence for a few moments, then McQueen said, *"Thelma and Louise."*

"What about it."

"I saw that one."

She shook her head.

"Jesus, Dennis . . ."

"What?"

36

The next morning McQueen was in the squad room alone when the phone rang.

"Brooklyn South Homicide," he said.

"Sergeant McQueen?"

"Speaking."

"This is Marty Cahill, from the lab?"

"Hey, Marty," McQueen said. "You got somethin' for me already?"

"I got a little chip of metal, if you call that something," Cahill said.

"Dug it out of the deepest part of the scratch," Cahill said. "I was gonna call it a wound, but it ain't hardly much more than a scratch."

"Did the doc tell you my theory?"

"About the metal hook? Sure did. Makes more sense then mine did, about the ice blocks?"

"Just a bit more, yeah."

"Well, I'd say you're on the right track, Sarge," Cahill said.

"Can't thank you enough, Marty," McQueen said. "You'll get me that report in writing?"

"Soon as I can."

"Thanks, I owe you."

"I'll collect," Cahill said, "some time."

As McQueen hung up Sommers came walking in, deposited her purse and attaché case on her desk. She'd started carrying case files in the case so she could take them home and study them.

"News?" she asked.

"Cahill," he said. "Looks like we're right about the hooks."

"So what do we do now?" she asked. "Start hitting all the places on my list?"

McQueen sat back and rubbed his eyes. He hadn't slept much the night before. His stomach had been upset. He'd blamed it on the frozen dinner he'd eaten for dinner, but maybe it was these cases.

"Your list is too long."

"I cut it down last night," she said.

"To what?"

"Sixty-six."

"Sixty-six places in . . . what? Manhattan? Brooklyn?"

"The five boroughs," she said, with a shrug. "That seemed to make sense."

"So if he lives or works in Jersey, we're fucked."

She perched her hip on his desk and said, "Pretty much."

"Okay," he said, "procedure. We'll take your list and split it in half."

"We're gonna work separately?"

"No," he said, "we'll give the other half to one of the other teams. The Double Ds when they're working, Sherman and Silver when they are."

"Sounds good to me," she said, "but you have to clear it with the Looie, don't you?"

"Yeah, I do," he said. "I'll talk to him when he comes in. Meanwhile, see if you can split the list up geographically, so we're not tripping over each other."

"Will do," she said. "I'll have to go downstairs and use the computer."

"They don't mind when you do that?"

She smiled and said, "I use my considerable charm to overcome any objections."

"And that works?"

"Almost every time."

She grabbed her purse and case from her desk and headed out the door, almost colliding with Frankie Cataldo. He let her by, but turned to look at her ass as she went by.

"You tappin' that yet, Sarge?" he asked, with a wicked grin.

"Go fuck yourself, Frankie," McQueen said.

"I don't have to," Cataldo said. "They're standin' in line ta do it for me."

McQueen ignored the man as he went to his own desk across the room. Cataldo seemed satisfied with the grunt work they gave him in the office. He apparently had no desire to go out on the streets again. McQueen knew that Frankie had worked for years undercover and was only a few years from pulling the pin, so maybe he was entitled to skate, but he didn't have to be such a monumental asshole while he was doing it.

He was still going through his pitch in his head when Lieutenant Jessup walked in. He decided to allow the man to settle in, have his coffee and whatever else was in the paper bag he was carrying before he hit him with this.

189

Several minutes later the Double Ds walked in, debating something as they usually were.

"Hey, Sarge," Diver said, "can we ask you somethin'?"

"Sure, why not?" McQueen said.

"Come on . . ." Dolan said.

"Naw, naw," Diver said, "the Sarge is pretty smart. He'll know the answer."

"I know the answer already," Dolan said.

"Sarge, is it 'orient,'" Diver asked McQueen, "or 'orient*ate*'?"

McQueen knew this was important to them. He had no doubt that they'd been debating this as hotly as they would have debated a presidential election.

He didn't know which side they had each taken, but it didn't matter to him. They were pretty much an interchangeable pair to him.

"It's orient," he said. "There's no such word as orientate."

"See?" Diver said to Dolan. "See? I told you." He looked at McQueen. "We even looked it up in the dictionary and he said *Webster* was wrong."

"Well," McQueen said, "if he won't believe Webster why would he believe me?"

"I'll have to give it some thought," Dolan said. He turned to go to his desk, then turned back to McQueen. "What about supposedly?"

"What about it?" McQueen asked.

"Is it 'supposedly,'" the man asked, "or 'suppos*ably*'?"

"Oh, jeez," Diver said, rolling his eyes, "I thought we had that one settled."

"Naw, naw, let the Sarge answer that one."

They both stared at McQueen expectantly.

"Okay," he said, "but this is the last one."

They waited patiently.

"It's supposedly," McQueen told them. "There's no such word as supposably."

"I knew it!" Dolan said.

"So, you believe him on that one?" Diver demanded, as they both walked to their desks. "How about nuc*lear* and nuc*ular* . . ."

McQueen stood up and hurried to the lieutenant's office.

37

"Loo, got a minute?"

"Those two getting you involved in their insane debates?" Jessup asked.

"Pretty much, yeah."

"Good," the lieutenant said. "They were buggin' me, and I told them to find somebody else."

"Thanks."

"What can I do for you, Dennis?"

"It's this case of Sommers's, Loo."

"The stiff in Sheepshead Bay?"

"Yeah."

"What about it?"

"Well . . . there are a lot of similarities to the one we found on Coney Island last month."

"Not that again, Dennis," Jessup said. "That's Brooklyn North's case."

"I know it is, I know it," McQueen said, quickly, "but hear me out."

Jessup looked forlornly at his half-eaten danish, then sat back in his chair and said, "All right."

McQueen laid out the theory he and Sommers had come up with about the hooks and the meat, then reiterated the other things that were the similar.

"You're tellin' me what's the same, Dennis," Jessup said. "What about what's different? Like what way they were killed?"

"But that's about the only thing that's different, boss," McQueen argued.

"Look at the difference, Sergeant," Jessup said. "One died in a fire, one had an ice pick stuck in his ear. Do you even have a link between the victims?"

"No . . ."

"What about the scratch on the back of the first victim?" Jessup asked. "Cow's blood there, too?"

"Yes," McQueen said, triumphantly. "Yes, the M.E. says there was."

"And what's the crime lab say about it?"

"I . . . they didn't check that on the first body, and now it's too late. It's been interred."

"Do you want to dig it up?"

"Um, no, not at this point, but . . ."

"Dennis, are you trying to make a case here for a serial killer?" Jessup asked. "Is that what you're trying to do?"

"No, sir."

"Then what do you want?"

"I want to check out meat-packing plants, slaughterhouses, butcher shops, pretty much anywhere in the five boroughs where they hang meat up on hooks."

"What do you expect to find?"

"More than I'd expect to find if we didn't do it."

"You and Sommers are gonna do this?"

"I thought we'd bring in another team," McQueen said. "That is, if they're available."

Jessup studied his sergeant, then picked up his

cardboard cup of coffee. He sipped it, made a face as he realized most of the warmth had gone from it. He had a microwave in his office, a small one right behind him on a table. He swiveled around, stuck the coffee inside, set the timer for a minute and then turned back.

"I can't let you do that, Dennis."

"It's Sommers's case, boss," McQueen said. "She's got a right to run down leads."

"Then let her run them down, but don't drag anyone else into it," the man said.

"Loo—"

The timer went off behind him and the man said, "That's all, Sergeant."

McQueen hesitated, then said, "Yes, sir."

As he got up to leave Jessup removed his coffee and swiveled back around.

"Dennis, come up with a third body that has that scratch, and some of the other similarities, and maybe you'll have something to hang your hat on."

"Yes, sir."

"Although if that one is killed in still a different way . . ."

38

McQueen and Sommers spent the final week of February checking out places that hung meat on hooks whenever they could. They kept the list in the car with them so that if they found themselves near one they could stop in. If they weren't working a case, then they went out specifically to check places out. They managed to get through Brooklyn that way, but they also knew there were bound to be places that weren't on their list. This was a real long shot, but McQueen had followed long shots before and had them pay off.

Of course, usually they didn't pay off, and that's pretty much why they were called long shots.

McQueen also got another call from Lydia Dean during that past week.

"Sergeant, I was just checking in with you to see if there's been any progress in finding my brother's killer."

"I'm afraid not, Mrs. Dean," he said. "Have you spoken to Detective Northrop about it?"

"I'm afraid if I'm not standing directly in front of

Detective Northrop so he can look at my tits he doesn't want to have anything to do with me," she said, frankly.

McQueen promised to call her if he found out anything. "Or even if you haven't," she said, before she hung up.

He decided not to tell Sommers about the call. She always managed to make him feel silly after a call from Lydia. He still thought the woman had her own agenda, but the murder of her brother was not officially his case. All he could do was work it with Sommers from the Sheepshead Bay angle, but without identification of the victim there wasn't much to work on, there. All they could do was run down their meat hook theory whenever they could.

"This is hopeless," Sommers said. "At this rate there's no way we can check all these places before spring."

"Not as hopeless as you think," McQueen said.

"What do you mean?"

"Leap year," he said. He pointed to the calendar on the wall behind his desk. "We've got one extra day of February, tomorrow."

"Oh great," she said. "With our luck February twenty-ninth will only serve to muddle things up even more."

When she went home that night, she had no idea how right she was going to turn out to be.

The call came in to McQueen at home the next morning, before he even had a chance to get dressed.

"What?" he said into the phone, which rang five minutes before his alarm was due to.

"Sergeant McQueen?"

"That's me."

"This is Detective Stamp, from the six-nine squad?"

"There's gotta be a good reason you're callin' me at home, Stamp."

"Yes, sir," the man said. "I got the word you're interested in bodies found in the water?"

"Where'd you hear that?"

"It's on our bulletin board," Stamp said. "A Detective Sommers was calling around askin' about it a few weeks back."

"So?"

"So, uh, we got one."

"Who gave you my home number, Detective?"

"Somebody workin' the night watch in your squad," Stamp said. "A detective named ... uh, Catalano?"

"Cataldo."

"Right, that's it."

McQueen knew that Frankie would have delighted in giving out his home number.

"All right," he said, swinging his legs to the floor and hitting his alarm button before it could go off, "give me the location."

He wasn't about to be the only one awakened early, so he put in a call to Sommers and gave her the information, as well. After all, it was her calls that resulted in this early morning wake-up.

They arrived on the scene at just about the same time. The body had been found half in and half out of the water beneath a Belt Parkway overpass between the Rockaway Parkway and Pennsylvania Avenue exits, technically still in the Canarsie section of Brooklyn, and within the confines of the 69th Precinct.

They pulled off the highway onto the shoulder amid all the other emergency vehicles and got out of their cars.

"Happy Leap Year," Sommers said. "You didn't know about this when you made that comment yesterday, did you?"

"Hardly."

They walked down the embankment together and joined the party.

"Sergeant McQueen?" a man in his thirties asked.

"That's right."

"Detective Stamp."

The two men shook hands.

"This is Detective Sommers, from Brooklyn South Homicide," McQueen said.

"A pleasure, Detective," Stamp said, shaking her hand.

Sommers was surprised. No leer, and he didn't look her up and down.

"Detective," she said. "What have we got?"

Stamp's words came out amid the cold mist of his breath. His eyes were shiny and his nose red. He quickly replaced his glove after shaking hands with both of them.

"Female DOA, half in, half out of the water," he said.

"She wash up?" Sommers asked.

"Unlikely," Stamp said. "The water level's real low here. No, judging from the indentation she made in the mud seems like she was dumped from the overpass."

McQueen involuntarily looked up, caught sight of a few dozen onlookers peering down. He brought his eyes back down to the shoreline, where men and women were milling about, each waiting for the opportunity to do their job.

"Let's take a look," he said to Sommers, "then we can let everybody get to work."

"Right over here," Stamp said.

When they reached the body there was another detective standing there. Stamp introduced his partner, Feinstein, a sad-faced man in his forties.

The woman was naked, a slender woman who looked even thinner in death. At certain points of her body, her bones seemed ready to poke through her skin.

"Looks to be in her twenties," Feinstein said. "Can't see any marks on her, and no blood. She was probably dead when they dropped her from up above."

"We'll leave it to the M.E. to figure out how she died," McQueen said. "I'm only interested in one thing."

"What's that?" Stamp asked.

The woman was facing McQueen, so he had to walk around to get a look at her back.

"Bailey."

Sommers walked around to join McQueen and stare down at the woman. The first place she looked was down around the small of the woman's back, but the flesh there was unmarked—pale, and unmarked. But then she brought her eyes farther up and stopped when she saw the scratch between the woman's shoulder blades.

"My God . . ." she said.

McQueen put his hand on her arm to quiet her, and she caught on quickly.

He walked back around the body and saw that, for a slender girl she had very large breasts.

"Are those real?" he asked Sommers.

"What?"

Stamp and Feinstein smirked at one another, as did some of the Crime Scene and M.E.'s men who were within earshot.

"Are her breasts real, or implants?"

199

Sommers knew McQueen well enough by now to know that he didn't ask frivolous questions. She actually squatted down to take a better look.

"I'd say they're real," she said, "although, real or not she'd need a support bra to carry them."

"Okay," he said, and that was it. They didn't discuss it any further in front of the others.

It took some time to go through the proper procedures of M.E., Crime Scene Unit and duty captain and finally the body was carried up the embankment to an ambulance and removed to the morgue. The M.E. was not Doctor Bannerjee, but McQueen still extracted a promise of a written report as soon as possible. He also told the 69th Precinct squad detectives to go ahead and D.D. 5 the case over to him at Brooklyn South Homicide. After that he and Sommers went back to their cars. Around them emergency vehicles were backing out and pulling onto the highway to leave. Eventually, they were left alone.

"This sick bastard hung her up by her bra?" Sommers demanded.

"Same scratch, higher up," McQueen said. "That's what it looks like he did."

"Arrogant prick!" she snapped.

"We need to get an ID on this woman, Bailey," McQueen said. "This is our chance to link all three cases and get the third one back."

"And how do we do that, Dennis?" she asked.

"By the numbers, Bailey," McQueen said. "By the numbers."

PART THREE

39

December . . . nine months later

McQueen looked down at the body and had a feeling that it had finally started again.

It was the middle of December and there was snow on the ground. The forecast was for a terrible winter, and it had already begun. The temperature was close to zero and he could see just how unhappy this was making his partner, Bailey Sommers.

This time the body had washed up underneath the Verazzano Bridge, which connected Brooklyn to Staten Island. McQueen and Sommers were the last to arrive this time—even after the duty captain and M.E.—and now they were waiting for the body to be brought up the steep, craggy hill that led down to the water's edge.

While McQueen watched the men struggle with the bagged body, losing their footing several times, he thought back to the previous winter, and the third body that had been found at the end of February. After Thomas Wingate and the second male had been found, the woman's body was discovered in Canarsie, in the 69th precinct. McQueen and Sommers had responded, and the M.E. had confirmed the similarities with the other two bodies. However, since the woman had been strangled, the question of a serial killer had never been raised. They had successfully identified the woman because a missing persons report had been filed. She was Melanie Edwards, wife, mother of two small children, an attractive woman who had gone out with some friends and never returned home.

They had never identified the second male, and both his and Melanie Edwards's murders remained unsolved, as did the murder of Thomas Wingate. The cases were still open—technically. It was as Detective Northrop had told McQueen almost a year before on the phone. "You know how it is."

Yes, he did.

During the course of the year several other changes had occurred. First, Lieutenant Jessup had been replaced as head of the Brooklyn South Homicide Squad. He'd been laterally promoted, which meant he was still stuck in rank.

The new boss was Lieutenant Bautista. He was the first Hispanic head of a specialty squad in the NYPD. All eyes were on him to see how he performed and, consequently, on the squad. For that reason Bautista made some immediate changes. So the second major change was in squad personnel. Cataldo was out, shipped to a Staten Island Precinct, and Detective Second Grade Andrew Tolliver was in. In addition, Tolliver was teamed with Bailey Sommers, and McQueen went back to a supervisory position.

Also, Ray Velez was out on extended leave due to an injury. He'd fallen through a rooftop while in pursuit of a suspect, and nobody was sure when he'd be back. In fact, there was a possibility he might go out on disability, which would make him eligible to collect a three-quarters pension.

This was not all bad news—except for Velez. In his position McQueen was not catching cases, so he was free to continue to work on the three murders from the previous winter in his spare—and not so spare—time. He was also able to continue to work the list Bailey Sommers had prepared in order to pursue their meat-hook theory, but the going on that was very slow and so far had yielded nothing.

Now, as they loaded this new body onto the ambulance, McQueen approached and called out, "Hold on!" Sommers and Tolliver moved in behind him.

"What's goin' on, boss?" Tolliver asked.

"I just want to take a look at the body."

Tolliver turned and looked at Sommers.

"I don't even know why you called him," he complained. "We had this under control."

"History, Andy," she said. "History."

Tolliver lowered his voice.

"You told me nothing went on—"

"Not that kind of history," she hissed. "Now keep still."

McQueen heard them bickering behind him. After only four months together they had coalesced into a good team. The bickering was just proof of that.

"Excuse me," McQueen said to the M.E.'s staff and stepped up into the ambulance. He unzipped the body bag and got a look at the back of the dead man.

"Okay, thanks," he said, stepping down.

The two men exchanged a look, shrugged and then got into the vehicle and drove off to the morgue.

"The scratch?" Sommers asked.

"It's there."

"What scratch?" Tolliver asked.

"I'll tell you later," she said. "Dennis, what now?"

"Finish up here," he said. "I'll see you both back at the house."

"Okay," she said.

"Andy," McQueen said, "I don't mean to step on your toes. Bailey will explain."

"Okay, boss," Tolliver said. "Whatever you say."

Back behind his desk, McQueen started to open the drawer in which he kept the three case files, but then resisted. The lieutenant's door was closed, which usually meant he was in. When he went home he had a habit of leaving the door open. McQueen quickly realized this was because the man kept nothing personal in the office.

He decided he couldn't go the man until he had the report from Sommers and Tolliver, and from the Crime Scene Unit and the M.E. He didn't want to blow his request out of impatience.

He knew that no progress had been made on the Wingate case by Brooklyn North. The original detective assigned, Northrop, had moved on and typically, in a situation like that, a case—if it's not fresh—can end up orphaned. He would probably meet no resistance in trying to get that case back from them, but he'd need his supervisor's okay. Bautista had been his boss for almost six months, but during that time the two men had not come to know each other well. He couldn't predict what Bautista would say when he made his request, so he decided he had to be well armed when he went in.

He took his hand away from the desk drawer and reached, instead, into his in-basket.

40

He was deaf to the child's screams as he held her by the elbows and pushed her hands down into the scalding water. Children had to be taught that you meant what you said, or they'd walk all over you. He'd learned that from his own father. Never had a beating been promised and not delivered. That was how he was going to be with his kids.

Granted, this wasn't his kid, it was Kathy's, but the principle was the same. Kathy had left the little girl in his care, and it was up to him to discipline her.

Miranda was screaming and crying now. When he thought she'd had enough he pulled her from the hot water and walked her over to the kitchen sink, where he ran cold water over her already reddening hands and forearms. That done he sent her to her room, where she settled into a low wail, and he pulled the plug out of the tub to let the hot water drain out. That done he went downstairs to the living room to read the *T.V. Guide* to see what was on tonight. He didn't hear a sound out of Miranda for the rest of the afternoon.

Children should be unseen, and unheard.

Kathy returned home from work at six and came over to kiss him hello. She stood in front of the TV to do it, so he put his hands on her hips and moved her.

"What's for dinner?" she asked.

"I don't know," he said. "Whatever you wanna make."

Kathy stared at him. The price you had to pay to keep a young stud around, she thought. Here she was, almost forty, the mother of a four-year-old, trying to hold onto a twenty-seven-year-old boyfriend who didn't work, didn't clean, and didn't cook. He fucked like a machine, though, and ate pussy like a starving man, but now she was starting to wonder if that was enough.

Oh well, at least he was starting to watch Miranda, since she couldn't afford day care anymore.

"Where's the baby?" she asked.

"Upstairs, in her room," he said, without taking his eyes from the *Seinfeld* rerun. Now the broad on that show, she was something, not a washed-out, middle-aged mother like Kathy. Lately he was considering when to move on. He'd been seeing Kathy for four months, living with her almost from the beginning, but she was boring in bed and getting thick around the middle. The stretch marks on her stomach were starting to gross him out so much that he only fucked her in the dark the past few weeks.

"Was she any trouble?" she asked.

"Not much," he said, and as she went upstairs he

added to himself, "not after I showed her who was boss."

Moments later he heard Kathy shout and then she was back downstairs with the kid in her arms. Miranda was soaked with tears, but too tired to cry anymore, even though the pain had hardly subsided. Her hands and forearms were an angry red, and swollen with puss-filled blisters.

"What happened?" Kathy demanded. "What did you do to her?"

Wearily, he pulled his eyes from the TV and looked at her.

"If you're gonna leave her with me you can't question how I discipline her."

"Discipline her?"

"She wouldn't shut up," he said, "so I stuck her hands in some hot water—"

"You what?"

"I—"

"How could you do that to a child?"

"Hey, she'll live," he said. "My old man did worse than that to me plenty of times, and look how I turned out."

Kathy stared at him for a few moments, feeling totally amazed by the fact that she could have been fooled by this monster, fooled not only into letting him move in with her, but ultimately leaving her daughter in his care, all because he paid attention to her every now and then.

"You're crazy," she said, "you know that? Crazy!"

She started for the door, but he got there first, barring the way.

"Where do you think you're going?"

"I've got to get her to the hospital," Kathy said. "Look at her hands, her arms . . . Jesus—"

"No hospital," he said, shaking his head emphatically.

"Why not?"

"Because they'll ask questions."

"So what? You don't think you did anything wrong, so what do you care?"

"No hospital," he shouted. "I mean it."

"Get out of my way. I'm taking my child to the hospital."

"No, you're not."

"You sick fuck," she screamed, "get out of my way!"

Maybe things would have gone differently if Miranda hadn't started to cry again at that moment, but he couldn't take Kathy's screaming and Miranda's crying, not at the same time.

He backhanded Kathy across the face, a stinging blow that sent her staggering back. She tripped on the throw rug behind her and fell. The sound that her head made striking the coffee table was a loud crack, like a bone breaking. He'd heard a similar sound when he was a child, the time his father snapped his arm. There was also the sound of the cheap coffee table splintering.

Miranda flew from her mother's arms, landed on the floor and began to scream.

"Shut up!" he snapped. He took two quick steps and kicked out at her blindly. His foot caught her in the ribs, snapping two of them and quieting her.

He leaned over Kathy and shook her, but he already knew she was dead.

"Stupid cunt," he said, and kicked her, too.

Then he turned and walked toward Miranda. She was lying in a crumpled heap, trying desperately to get her breath back. He had to take care of her before she started screaming again. After all, he couldn't let her be the only witness who could link him to Kathy's death . . . even though it was her own damned fault!

He moved toward the child, drawing back his foot for another kick . . .

41

The next day both Sommers and Tolliver came into the office just after noon, both obviously excited about something.

"You got it, boss," Tolliver said.

"Got what?"

"This is the M.E.'s report," Sommers said. "I went down and got it personally."

"And?"

"The lungs are the same," she said.

"And means?"

"His neck was broken."

"You got yourself a serial killer, boss," Tolliver said.

"It's hard to get this department to go that way, Detective, when we have four different MOs."

"Yeah, but from what Bailey's been tellin' me I bet you got enough," the younger man said. He was about Bailey's age, which also made them a good fit.

"It won't be up to me," McQueen said, "but this helps."

"Just remember us when you've got to put together your task force," Tolliver said.

"I've got dibs," Sommers said, "I was there at the beginning."

"Don't worry," McQueen said, "I'll remember. Look, until I've got some word on this, keep working the case. Get an ID on this guy."

"Already did," Tolliver said. He slapped another folder down on the desk. "John Bennett. His prints were on file."

"Rap sheet?"

"No," Tolliver said. "Get this. He took the test for P.A.A. a few years ago. He got called for the job, went as far as getting fingerprinted, and then suddenly withdrew."

"So we got his prints because he almost got a job with the department?"

"Ain't that a kick in the head?" Tolliver asked.

"The only problem is, the address we've got on file is old," Sommers said.

"Well, you've got his name," McQueen said. "Find out where he lives now and find somebody to ID the body."

"Are you gonna talk to the Loo today?" Tolliver asked.

McQueen looked over at Lieutenant Bautista's door, which was wide open.

"As soon as he comes in," he said. "Now you two get back to work."

"Yes, sir," Sommers said.

McQueen collected the folders off his desk, opened his drawer and added them to the three cases there. As soon as Bautista put in an appearance, he'd make his pitch.

* * *

213

Around three P.M. the lieutenant arrived. He was, as usual, impeccably dressed, today in a dark blue suit, powder blue shirt and red tie. He went directly to his office without speaking to McQueen and the Double Ds, who were seated at their desks, and closed the door behind him.

"One day he'll say hello, or good afternoon," Diver said, "and I'll faint."

"Quiet, Jimmy," McQueen said.

"Sorry, boss," Diver said, "but it wouldn't hurt him one time to act like we're here."

"This is just a pit stop for him, Jimmy," McQueen said. "He'll be gone inside of a year."

"They should give the squad to you then, Sarge," Dolan said.

"Forget it, Artie," McQueen said. "I got enough problems."

"Let's go, Jimmy," Dolan said. "We got that interview to do."

Both men stood up and Diver said, "See ya later, Sarge," as they went out the door.

McQueen was actually glad they were gone. Now nobody would see him going into the boss's office. He grabbed his files, went to the door and knocked.

"Come!"

He opened the door and entered.

"Afternoon, boss," he said.

"Sergeant," Bautista said. "Something I can do for you?"

Bautista was an extremely handsome Latino in his late thirties, lots of black hair, broad shoulders. In fact, he reminded McQueen a lot of the actor who played in the movie *Desperado*, and also *Zorro*. The kind women creamed in their pants over.

"I've got a request, Loo," McQueen said, "and it may take me a few minutes to lay it out."

"Really," Bautista said. "Is it important?" Bautista spoke with a slight accent.

McQueen was about to answer when he replayed the question in his mind. At first he'd heard the man say, *"Is it important?"* but then he heard, *"Is it important to the squad?"* which meant, of course, *"Is it important to me?"*

"Well, sir," he answered, finally, "to tell you the truth I not only think it's important, I think it would be quite a feather in our caps—all of us . . . but especially you, sir, as squad commander."

"Is that a fact?" The man sat back in his chair and regarded McQueen with interest for the first time. "Then perhaps I'd better hear all about it."

42

McQueen was still making his case to Lieutenant Bautista when Sommers stuck her head in the door.

"Excuse me, boss."

"Yes, Detective?"

"Dennis, we caught one. Sounds bad. A mother and a child."

McQueen closed his eyes; dead kids were the worst.

"Go ahead," Bautista said, reaching for McQueen's files. "Leave those with me and I'll review them. I'll have something for you by the end of the day."

"Yes, sir."

He handed them over and left the office. Sommers tossed him his jacket. He caught it and followed her and Tolliver out the door.

A couple radio cars were parked out front with their headlights on, but not the turret lights. There were people in the sidewalk, looking at the house. Some were dressed, some were in robes. McQueen thought they must be freezing, but apparently morbid curiosity was enough to keep them warm. He pulled his car to a stop right behind Sommers and Tolliver's car.

A uniform stepped up to intercept them, the 70 numerals on his shirt collar catching the sun. His name tag said "Daniels."

"Who do we have?" McQueen asked, showing the cop his ID. Sommers and Tolliver had their shields out, as well. Once they'd showed their shields, McQueen and Tolliver hung them from their jacket pockets. Sommers took a stretch cord from her purse and hung her detective's gold shield around her neck.

"Mother and daughter," the cop said. "Kathy and Miranda Richards."

"Who found them?"

"A neighbor," the man said. "She said she and the victim were supposed to have tea together. When she didn't show up she came over, found the door unlocked, and walked in on . . . them."

McQueen nodded to the uniforms outside the door and he, Sommers and Tolliver went inside.

It was a small house, an A-frame in need of repair. These homes on Albemarle Road were not the cream of the crop, McQueen had noticed as he drove up.

Inside, however, despite the current state of the place, he could see it was a neatly kept house. Neatly kept, probably by the woman who was now lying on her living room floor, about five feet away from a small girl who appeared to be—to *have* been—three or four years old. The first thing McQueen noticed was the child's arms. From fingers to forearm, her arms were red and blistered.

"What happened here?" he said aloud, to no one in particular.

He took in the scene, the woman lying on the floor near a splintered coffee table with the child five feet away.

"Could it be an accident?" Sommers asked.

"Lay it out for me."

"She's carrying the child, trips and falls, hits her head, maybe snaps her neck."

"And the child?"

"Is thrown across the room."

"And lands with enough force to kill her?"

"Kids are fragile," Tolliver said.

"You have any kids, Tolliver?" McQueen asked.

"No, but—"

"Kids are resilient."

McQueen walked to the child and crouched down next to her to examine her.

"Look at this."

Sommers crouched next to him. Tolliver came up behind them and leaned over.

"This side of her head," McQueen said, pointing with his right index finger. "Can you see it?"

"It looks like . . . Jesus, is that an indentation?" Sommers looked around. "What did she hit her head on? Not the floor. The floor wouldn't do that."

"She didn't hit her head," McQueen said. "I've seen that mark once before, on an adult."

"So what is it?"

McQueen looked at Sommers and her partner and said, "She was kicked."

Sommers winced.

"Somebody kicked her in the head?" Tolliver asked. "Man, that's cold."

"Looks like it," McQueen said, standing up. Sommers followed, and Tolliver backed off to give them room.

"What about her arms?" Sommers asked. "Those blisters look fresh."

"Yeah."

McQueen went to the mother now, and as he crouched down he asked. "The M.E.?"

"Officer Daniels says he's on his way," Tolliver said.

McQueen examined the mother as well as he could without touching her. At the same time he slipped a pair of rubber gloves from the pocket of his jacket and donned them. You had to figure crime scene contamination into outside scenes, but inside McQueen always wore gloves, and insisted others wear them as well. Bailey knew that, so she pulled two pairs of gloves from her pocket and handed one to her partner.

"Was she kicked, too?" Sommers asked, peering past McQueen at the mother's body.

McQueen leaned over the body for a close look at the woman's face and head.

"There was no need," he said. "She was killed instantly when her head hit this coffee table."

"God, with enough force to splinter the thing?"

"It's a cheap table," McQueen said, "but it was sturdy enough to do the trick."

McQueen examined her arms.

"Looks like there might be bruises on her upper arms," he said. "They can tell us better when they examine her closer."

"So she was grabbed, and pushed," Sommers recited. "She falls, dropping the baby, hitting her head. Then, whoever did this walks to the kid and . . ."

"Right," McQueen said.

"Sonofabitch," Tolliver said.

"M.E.'s here," one of the uniforms said from the door.

"Let him in," McQueen said. "Bailey, I'm going to have a look around."

"We'll talk to him."

Sommers knew that McQueen liked to walk a crime scene, and she left her boss to it.

43

McQueen went upstairs.

The downstairs had a small living room and an eat-in kitchen. Upstairs there were two bedrooms, one very small—the child's—and one master. He went into the larger one first and was immediately aware of a male presence. Husband or boyfriend? The neighbor would be able to tell them, but he snooped around, anyway.

Most of the dresser drawers were filled with a woman's things, as was the night table by the bed. When he opened the closet it was crammed with dresses, sweaters and other feminine garments. All the way on the right side he found a few men's shirts and a pair of trousers. On the floor, among the jumble of shoes, were a pair of men's loafers. Just enough essentials to show a man made himself at home here, occasionally.

Next he went into the bathroom. Again, most of the things were feminine, but in the medicine cabinet was a man's razor. There were three toothbrushes on the sink, two adult size and one tiny one.

Just for good measure he went through the child's room, but found nothing of interest, except that the child apparently was still sleeping in a crib. He did not know for sure if this was normal, or if the mother simply didn't have enough money to buy the child her first grown-up bed. Now she wouldn't have to worry about it.

As unsettling as the burn victim that afternoon had been, this kind of crime sickened McQueen more. The death of the woman was a crime and a shame, but the death of the child . . . that was a catastrophe.

He went back downstairs, where Sommers and the M.E. were talking.

"Here he is," Sommers said.

"You called it right, Sergeant," Dr. Bannerjee said. "It looks like the kick to the head probably killed the child, and your supposition concerning the woman appears correct, as well." Without rancor he added, "You're going to put me out of a job, if I'm not careful."

"I don't think that's likely, Doctor," McQueen said. "What about the child's arms?"

"Looks like she was scalded, all right, probably with hot water—extremely hot water."

"I haven't been in the kitchen yet," McQueen said. "I don't suppose there's a big pot on the stove?"

"No, there's not," Sommers said.

"Wouldn't have to be boiling water," the doctor said. "Tap water in the tub would blister a child like that, especially if she was in it long enough."

"Could that have been a cause of death?" McQueen asked.

"Water that comes out of the tap can reach a hundred and forty degrees," the M.E. said, "and a child's skin is very soft. If he'd immersed her for, say, thirty seconds or more, it could have killed her."

"Jesus," Sommers said. She looked pale. It was the first reaction McQueen had seen from her since they had arrived on the scene.

"You okay?"

"Fine."

"Where's the neighbor?"

"In the house across the street."

"Let's go and talk to her."

"Can I have them?" the M.E. asked, motioning to the bodies.

"As soon as a supervisor shows up, you can take them," McQueen said.

"Great," the doctor said. He seemed to spend a lot of his time waiting for patrol supervisors to finally reach the scene of a crime.

"Tolliver, why don't you wait here for the duty captain?"

"Sure, boss."

"What did you find upstairs?" Sommers asked.

"I'll tell you on the way."

44

The floor plan of Cynthia Hathaway's house was almost identical to the one they had just come from.

"It's too big for me," she said, as they all sat at the kitchen table, "since my Caleb died. But I don't have the heart to move."

She had insisted on making tea for all three of them and neither McQueen or Sommers had the heart to say no.

"When did Mr. Hathaway die?" Sommers asked.

"About twenty years ago."

From the looks of Mrs. Hathaway she could have been anywhere from fifty to seventy.

"Kathy was so sweet," she said. "She'd come over here three times a week just to have tea with me in the evenings. She knows—knew—how lonely I was. And Miranda, that child was just a delight."

"Mrs. Hathaway," McQueen said, "I found some things in the house that indicate there was a man in the picture?"

"The picture? Oh, you mean that . . . boyfriend of hers."

She made a face when she said it.

"I take it you didn't like him."

"My Caleb would have called him a bum," she said. "I called him a no-account."

"Was there any particular reason you didn't like him?" McQueen asked.

"The bruises."

"What bruises?"

"She'd come over here to have tea with me and she'd have bruises on her arms, or on her face. Tried to tell me she fell down, but I knew different."

"He hit her?" McQueen asked.

"A lot. I wouldn't be surprised if he's the one that killed her tonight." Suddenly the old woman took a wad of damp tissues from the pocket of her housecoat and pressed them to her nose. Her eyes moistened and tears trickled down her face. "That poor child. He killed them both, I just know he did."

"Mrs. Hathaway, Miranda had burns on her arms," McQueen said. "Had you ever noticed anything like that on her before?"

"Burns? No, but on occasion I saw bruises on the child, as well. I told Kathy I'd take care of Miranda, but she insisted on letting that . . . that boyfriend babysit for her."

"Do you know the boyfriend's name, ma'am?" Sommers asked.

"Yes, I do," she said. "His name was Allan Hansen."

"And would you happen to know where he lives?"

"No, but I'm sure it's in Kathy's phone book."

"Do we have a phone book?" McQueen asked Sommers.

225

"I think they got it from the kitchen and bagged it as evidence," she said.

"We'll check on that, Mrs. Hathaway. Now, if we sent over a police sketch artist would you be able to describe him well enough for us to get a drawing?"

"You mean like on TV? Yes, I believe I could."

"That's good, ma'am. We'll call you to make an appointment."

"You have to get that . . . that monster for what he did to those . . . those sweet, dear people . . . that poor child . . ."

"We'll get him, Mrs. Hathaway," McQueen said, patting her hand, "we'll get him."

Outside the house Sommers said to McQueen, "I thought you said you didn't make promises?"

"I said I didn't make promises to suspects," he corrected. "That old lady is not suspected of anything."

"I stand corrected," she said, contritely. "What do you want to do now?"

"Let's go back to the scene and look it over," he suggested. "I'd also like to get a gander at that phone book."

"We'll have to send it in as evidence, Dennis."

"Maybe," he said, "I'll give you a little lesson in bending the rules, Detective Sommers."

45

By the time they all returned to the office Lieutenant Bautista was out. McQueen had wanted to finish their discussion, but that was going to have to wait.

McQueen sat at his desk and dropped the plastic bag containing the phone book on top of his desk. Tolliver, who had been parking the car, came in just as he dumped the book out. He joined Sommers in staring down at it.

"That's evidence, Dennis," she reminded him again, as he picked it up. "We're supposed to log that in."

"What's it really evidence of, Bailey?" he asked. "That the woman had friends and family? The only thing we need this book to tell us right now is Allan Hansen's phone number and/or address."

He opened the book and flipped to the page that had the Hs, only there wasn't one. It went right from G to I.

"He tore it out," he said.

"Then his prints are on that book," she said.

"They'd be there, anyway," he replied. "He was all over that house, Bailey. We'd have to expect to find his prints."

"So what do we do now?" she asked. "Check all the utilities? Look for his bills?"

"Can you do that on the computer?"

"I can try."

She walked to her desk and sat down. To her right was the first change Lieutenant Bautista made when he took over the squad. Somehow he had managed to get them a computer. McQueen had walked in one morning and found it next to Sommers's desk. The fact that it had no brand name led him to believe that the lieutenant had probably made the arrangements himself, without going through the department.

According to Sommers it had everything a computer needed, and then some. To her it looked home-built, she said, by somebody who knew what he was doing. So that was either the lieutenant himself, or somebody he knew.

However they'd managed to get it, Sommers was glad it was there. She no longer had to run down to the precinct to use theirs every time she wanted to Google something.

While her fingers danced over the keyboard and the thing clicked and whirred into life, McQueen began to leaf through the book. If he called every number in it there was a possibility he'd come across someone who knew Allan Hansen. But he also knew from experience how outdated numbers and addresses in a phone book could become, so the entire exercise could turn out to be counterproductive—maximum time expenditure for minimum return. Christ, he was starting to think like a desk jockey.

McQueen sat back in his chair and sighed. He hated child killers, even more than he hated serial killers. There, he'd thought it. It was almost as good as saying it out loud. They had a serial killer, and he was playing games. He was killing in a different manner each time, but disposing of the body the same way. He knew he wouldn't get a lot of support from profilers on this one. Serial killers usually used the same methodology, their victims tended to have great similarities, and they usually took some kind of a token, a "momento" of their kill.

But this one—Christ. The only real similarity they had was the scratch on the victim's back, and for all he knew the killer was putting those there to throw the police off. Maybe they had no meaning at all, but McQueen doubted that. He thought he was on the right track, but if he was he was traveling it alone.

He was still wondering which case to give priority to when Lieutenant Bautista walked in.

"Sergeant, can I see you in my office, please?" he said loudly as he passed McQueen's desk.

Sommers looked over her computer screen at McQueen, who stood up and gave her a shrug before following his leader.

"Close the door and have a seat," Bautista said as McQueen entered.

McQueen obeyed. He saw the files he'd given the man sitting on his desk.

"You think we have a serial killer at work, stretching from last year to this latest victim."

"Three last winter," McQueen said, "and so far, one this winter. Yes, sir, that's correct."

"What did your last commanding officer think of your theory?"

"Not much," McQueen said, "but Lieutenant Jessup wasn't—"

"Wasn't what?" Bautista asked. "I like a man who speaks frankly, Sergeant."

"He wasn't like you, sir," McQueen said.

"And how is that?"

"Ambitious," McQueen said. "Also, we have this new case, which he didn't have."

Bautista put his hand on top of the case files and tapped his index finger.

"You're saying you believe that it would be advantageous to my career to allow you to pursue this."

McQueen shrugged and said, "Couldn't hurt."

"Oh yes," Bautista said, "yes, it could hurt, Sergeant. That is why I'm hesitating."

"How about this?" McQueen asked. "If it helps, it helps you, and if it hurts, it hurts me?"

"You are willing to put your career on the line for this?"

"With all due respect, sir," McQueen said, "you have a career. I have a job, and I'd like to do it."

"And that job is?"

"Puttin' this sick sonofabitch out of business," McQueen said. "I do that and I don't care who takes the credit."

"You are not looking at this case as a way to advance in the department?"

"I'm happy where I am, Lieutenant," McQueen said. "You might want to be commissioner, but I'm happy being a detective."

"And you're a good detective, aren't you?"

"I think so."

Bautista pulled a file folder from beneath the stack on the desk. He put it on top, then placed his hand on it.

"This is your personnel file, Sergeant," he said. "From what I see in here, you are, indeed, a good detective."

"Thank you, sir."

"And your offer is intriguing, to say the least. But

it's not quite accurate. You see, if I let you work on this as a serial killer case and it blows up in your face, I won't get off scott-free. I'll take some shrapnel from it. Whether or not it's enough to hurt my career advancement would remain to be seen."

So the man was on the fence. All he needed to go one way or the other was a good push. But Bautista went on before McQueen could react.

"These scratches you've pointed out on the victim's backs," he said. "The first victim had one, as well?"

"Yes, sir."

"I don't see a photo of that in here, anywhere. If I'm going to go to my superiors with this I need as much ammunition as you can give me."

"There must be a photo . . . somewhere, sir."

"Find it." Bautista sat back in his chair, took his hand off the stack of folders. "And bring it back to me."

McQueen sat forward.

"That's all you need?"

"No," Bautista said. "Come back with a proposal for what you'll need to catch this guy. How many detectives, who you want, what size task force—"

"I don't want a task force, Lieutenant," McQueen said. "I'd like to handle it right here in the squad."

"Lay it out for me, Dennis," Bautista said. "Convince me so I can convince them."

McQueen wasn't sure who "them" was, but apparently his only task was to convince his lieutenant, give him that final push to get him off the fence.

He leaned forward, collected the files from the desk, and stood up.

"I'll get right on it, sir."

"I understand the Albemarle Road murder was a pretty bad one?" he asked.

"Yes, sir," McQueen said. "A mother and child

231

were killed. I'll have a report on your desk by the end of the day."

"Can you give that case to someone else?"

"I'd . . . really rather handle that one myself, sir."

"In addition to—well, never mind. Bring it all to me and we'll see what happens."

"Yes, sir."

As McQueen turned to leave Bautista said, "And Sergeant?"

"Sir?"

Bautista put his hand out.

"Leave your file here with me."

McQueen hesitated, then took it off the top and handed it back to the man.

"Yes, sir."

"That's all," the lieutenant said. "Close the door on the way out, please."

McQueen left the office and pulled the door closed behind him. He caught a glimpse of Bautista picking up the phone just before the door closed.

46

Later that afternoon, Sommers came over to McQueen's desk and looked at him.

"You don't look happy," he said to her.

"I spoke with the M.E.," she said. "He's very sorry, but he doesn't seem to have any photos of the scratch on the first victim's body."

"How could that be?"

She shrugged.

"Doctor G said to tell you he can't explain it," she said. "It was a busy time—"

"Yeah, yeah," McQueen said, "yadda, yadda, yadda, that doesn't help me any."

"You don't think the lieutenant would bail out just because we don't have a photo of Thomas Wingate's back, do you?"

"He's not goin' anywhere if he thinks he's short of ammo, Bailey," McQueen said.

She folded her arms and said, "I find it hard to believe no one took a picture of Wingate's back."

"Wait a minute," he said. "Somebody did."

"Who?"

"Me." He dug his cell phone out of his pocket. "How long do photos stay in this thing?"

"I'm not sure," she said, "but I can hook it to the computer and check."

He handed the phone over and said, "Do it."

"What are you going to do in the meantime?" she asked.

"Work on logistics," he said. "I'm a boss. That's what I do."

"Right."

As she returned to her desk he grabbed his phone and called the crime lab. He asked for Marty Cahill. He'd had a few more cases with that particular tech since the Wingate case, and he liked both his work ethic and his attitude.

"Sergeant McQueen," Cahill said, when he came on the phone. "What can I do for you?"

"I've got a new cases, Cahill, and I need your help."

"I'll do whatever I can. What do you need?"

"I need a phone number from a phone and address book."

"I assume the book belongs to the victim?"

"You assume correctly."

"And that you can't get the number the old-fashioned way? By looking it up?"

"That page is missing."

"Ah," Cahill said. "Well, send it over. If there's an impression of the number on the next page we can raise it."

"That's what I was hoping for."

"Don't do that trick everybody's learned from TV with the pencil," Cahill said. "You might screw it up."

"I leave that sort of thing to the professionals."

"Good man."

"Thanks, Marty. I'll get it right over to you."

"And I'll get it right back."

McQueen hung up and started rifling through his desk, looking for an envelope to put the phone book in.

"Got it!" Sommers said, startling him by appearing in front of his desk.

"Got what?" he asked.

"The picture you took of Thomas Wingate that day at Coney Island," she said. "It was still in the memory of your phone and now it's in my computer."

"Can you print it out?"

"I can, but it wouldn't come out clearly," she said. "You won't be able to see the scratch clearly."

"But you can see it on the screen?"

"It's clear as day on the screen."

"Great. Can you get me a print photo?"

"I can have it done at Kinkos," she said.

"Good, do it."

"Today?"

"No," he said, "not today . . . now!"

"Okay, boss. What are you looking for?"

"An envelope. I'm sending the phone book to Cahill at the lab. He's gonna get the phone number for us from the next page."

"The impression? Good thinking, Dennis. I guess that's why you get the big money."

"That's not even funny," he said.

"I'll get you an envelope from my desk and then get right on this photo."

"Good. Thanks, Bailey."

When she brought him an envelope he thanked her again and she was out the door with her partner.

Now that he had a photo—when she returned with it—he needed to work out some roster changes that would enable him to work the serial case. He really wanted to work on the serial case, and he wanted Bailey Sommers with him on it. He didn't know Tolliver well, though, so he didn't know how the man would feel about McQueen taking his partner away, or about being reassigned to another case. He decided to give that case to the Double Ds—Dolan and Diver—but to also assign Tolliver. He'd tell Sommers's partner it was for the sake of continuity. Meanwhile, he'd take Sherman and Silver to work the serial case with him. (Idly he wondered why nobody ever referred to them as the Double Ss? Probably the missing double entendre.)

He went to work putting this all down on paper for his boss.

47

Owen stared dispassionately at the woman's body that was hanging from a hook in his freezer. He was excited that things had started up again. Waiting the entire year had been difficult, but he knew it was necessary. The only way to go about this and not get caught was to do it as no one else had ever done. That was why it took three separate entities—the Observer, the Ice Man and the Killer. One would have been hard enough for the police to find, but three would be impossible.

As for the bodies, the fourth one had been found. Now it was time to decide how and where this fifth one would be found. And the sixth one—maybe that one should be a woman. It would serve two purposes. First, it would even things up, three and three, men and women. And second, killing two women in a row would again throw the police off, because there was no discernable pattern. As he had seen and heard at all the seminars, and read in all the books, the profilers worked from serial killer patterns. And the police—well, they waited for mistakes to be made, but that would not happen here.

He tore his eyes from the dead woman hanging by her bra—he liked that touch—and left the freezer to go back and see to his customers. The next move belonged to the Observer . . .

48

McQueen presented himself at the door of the lieutenant's office at 5:05 that afternoon. Bautista was studying something on his desk. When he looked up he saw McQueen and waved him to a chair.

"You must want this pretty bad, Dennis," he said.

"Yes, sir, I do."

"Why?"

"This nut has killed four people that we know of," McQueen said. "It's my best guess that he's got another one on the hook now, and is probably staking out a sixth. To put it plainly, he's pissing me off."

Bautista smiled and sat back in his chair.

"Let me ask you something," he said, "and this is just for my own edification."

"Go ahead."

"It doesn't piss you off that I'm about, what, ten years younger than you? And you have to report to me?"

"No, sir, not at all."

"As you said earlier today, I am ambitious," Bautista said. "I do not try to hide that from anyone.

Because of that I guess I can't understand a man who lacks ambition."

"I don't lack ambition," McQueen said. "Right now my ambition is to put this sick fucker away. My ambition is just not as lofty as yours, or someone else's, might be. I don't aspire to a higher rank, Lieutenant, because that would keep me from my ambition in life."

"To put bad guys away."

"Exactly."

"Well," the lieutenant said, "as ambitions go I suppose that's not a bad one."

"We got a photo of the scratch on the first victim's back," McQueen said. He placed the file on Bautista's desk. Inside was a photo Sommers had gotten from Kinkos.

Bautista opened the file and took a look.

"And these are my suggestions for how we can handle these cases in-house."

"Why not a task force, Sergeant?" Bautista asked.

"Because word would get around, that way," McQueen said. "It would end up in the papers. We can run this just like a task force without announcing it."

"With you in charge?"

"With you in charge, sir."

Bautista picked up McQueen's report and scanned it.

"Sommers?"

"She's got good instincts, sir."

"Diver and Dolan," Bautista said. "I am not impressed with them. They seem to me to be too . . . trivial."

"They get the job done."

"And what about Tolliver? He seems an up and comer to me. Why not assign the case to him and let them assist him?"

"Because having to assist him—someone a lot younger—would piss *them* off, sir. It would work out better this way."

"What about the others? Vadala? Mollica? Chapin?"

"They can continue to rotate and catch cases on an individual basis," McQueen said. "In the event they need help, we can deal with each case individually."

"And how long do you anticipate this reorganization would last?" Bautista asked.

"Until we catch the bastard."

"The serial killer."

"And the child killer."

"You really think you can keep this under your hat, Sergeant?" Bautista asked.

"Nobody knows about it now, sir. Why should that change? It would only happen if someone was to leak it to the press."

Bautista seemed to bristle at that.

"And you think I would do that? As part of my ambitious plan to advance in rank?"

"No, sir," McQueen said. "I didn't mean that. Besides, there'd be plenty of credit when the bastard is finally caught. Letting it out now, letting him see himself in the papers, would jeopardize that."

"You don't think that reading about himself in the newspapers could possibly force him into a careless act of bravado?"

"Can I be perfectly frank, sir?"

"As I told you this afternoon, I would appreciate that."

McQueen leaned forward.

"This nut isn't going by the rules the profilers have set down in all the books," McQueen said. "That much is obvious from the MO in each case."

"All being killed in a different manner, you mean."

"Yes, sir."

Bautista nodded and waved for McQueen to continue.

"In addition," McQueen said, "his activity is not escalating. He waited at least nine months to take victim four. That's unusual patience for a wacko."

"Are you convinced he is a . . . wacko?"

"Oh, he's a nut, all right," McQueen said. "He's not sick, he's not acting out, he doesn't need treatment, he needs to be caught, and put down."

"Put down?"

"Figure of speech, sir."

"I don't see anything in your record to indicate you are trigger-happy, Dennis," Bautista said. "I wouldn't want you to start this late in your career."

"I just meant he needs to be put away . . . sir."

"How long do you have in, Sergeant?"

"Better than twenty-five, sir . . . about twenty-seven years."

"You are not ready to retire, are you?"

"No, sir," McQueen said.

"Why not?"

"What else would I do?"

"So I don't have to worry about you wanting to go out in a blaze of glory, and taking my career with you?"

"Not at all, sir."

Bautista studied his second-in-command for a few moments, then said, "I'm inclined to go with you on this, Sergeant. Do what you have to do to get this done. I'll back you."

"You got the okay from above?"

Bautista made a steeple of his fingers and regarded McQueen over them.

"We're going out on our own here, Dennis—you and I," he said. "I haven't checked this with anyone."

"Sir . . . you're taking a big chance."

"I'm counting on you, Dennis," Bautista said. "Is that taking a big chance?"

McQueen hesitated, then said, "Yes, sir, you are."

Bautista smiled.

"Honest to the end, eh, Dennis?"

"I'm afraid that'll be on my tombstone, Lieutenant."

"Well," Bautista said, "get to work, Sergeant, and keep me informed."

"Yes, sir. Thank you."

When he left the office he closed the door behind him. He tried to catch a glimpse of what his boss might be doing at that moment, but failed to. He decided that if the lieutenant was willing to take a chance on him, he'd have to do the same with the younger man.

The squad room was empty. He walked to his desk and sat down, and as he did, Bailey Sommers and Andrew Tolliver came in.

"What have you got?" he asked them.

"Nothin'," Tolliver said. "False alarm."

"What's happening here?" Sommers asked him.

"I got the go-ahead to pursue our case as a serial."

Her eyes sparkled and she said, "A task force?"

"No," he said. "In-house, right here."

"All right!" Tolliver said. "When do we start?"

"Tomorrow, the morning. I'm gonna call the Double Ds, Silver and Sherman and have them come in tomorrow at ten. The two of you be here, as well. You're all coming off the chart."

"What about the rest of the squad?"

"They'll keep catching cases. If we get jacked up, I'll have to deal with it then."

"This is so cool," Tolliver said.

"You guys are off the clock, so go home and come back in the morning."

"Yes, sir," Tolliver said.

"You go ahead, Andrew," she said. "I'll do the paperwork on our false alarm."

"Okay," Tolliver said. "See ya tomorrow."

"One thing," McQueen said, before Andrew Tolliver could get out the door.

"Sir?" Tolliver said.

"I'm telling you both what I'm gonna tell the rest tomorrow," he said. "Anyone leaks this to the press and I'll have his or her head. Got it?"

"Yessir," Tolliver said.

"Got it," Sommers said.

After her partner left, Sommers turned to McQueen and said, "What aren't you telling us, Dennis?"

"I'm putting the Double Ds on the Richards case, and I'm assigning your partner to assist them."

"He's not going to like that."

"I know," McQueen said, "but he has to learn how to be a role player."

"And me?"

"You'll work the serial case with me, Silver and Sherman."

From the look on her face he knew she was mentally rubbing her hands together with glee.

"Go do your report, finish up any other paperwork you have. Any cases you have that are still active give them to Paddy Vadala."

"Yes, sir!"

"And Bailey?"

"Yes?"

"I'm counting on you to keep your partner in check," McQueen said. "Make him understand that his part in this is important."

"I'll do my best, Dennis."

As she went to her desk to do her paperwork he turned and pulled out a blank roster sheet. As he stuck it in his typewriter he couldn't help feeling excited himself. Somewhere out there a nut had somebody on a hook. He hoped to God he and his people could make it the last one.

49

The next morning at ten sharp the squad room was full. McQueen had set up a bulletin board and on it had pinned all of the facts of both cases he was going to be talking about. Sommers and Tolliver had been the first to arrive, followed by the Double Ds, Silver and then Sherman. McQueen had wondered if the lieutenant was going to put in an appearance, but apparently the man had decided to let him handle this alone.

"I know I don't have to tell all of you this, but I'm going to, anyway," he began. "Everything that's said here stays here. If it leaks out and I find out who did it, your head is mine. Are we clear?"

They all nodded and agreed that they were clear. McQueen had worked with most of them for a long time, and in the time he'd worked with Sommers he'd come to trust her. Tolliver was the only real newcomer and he was going to count on her to keep him in line.

"As of right now you're all off the chart," he announced.

"We got cases to clear, Sarge," Silver complained. He knew that Silver and his partner, Sherman, enjoyed working cases as long as they could work them together. When partners clicked it was often better than a marriage.

"If you can clear them while working on this, fine," he explained, "otherwise we're gonna ship 'em off to someone in the squad who's still catching cases."

Silver wasn't thrilled with that, but he subsided.

"What are we gonna be workin' on, Sarge?" Dolan asked.

"I've got two cases up on the board," McQueen said. "One we caught yesterday, a mother and daughter killed in their home. We think it's the boyfriend, but we're not sure. Diver and Dolan, you're gonna be workin' on that. Tolliver, you're assisting them."

"Wha—" the younger detective started, but Sommers grabbed his arm to shut him up.

"I read about that in the paper," Dolan said. "We got a location on the boyfriend?"

"Not yet, we're working on it," McQueen said.

"Does he have a sheet?" Diver asked.

McQueen looked at Sommers.

"Small stuff," she said. "Nothing like this, but the way it looks it was spur of the moment, maybe an argument over the way he disciplined the woman's daughter."

"And how was that?" Dolan asked.

"Apparently," Sommers said, "he put her arms in hot water and scalded her to teach her a lesson."

"Jesus," Diver said.

"Everything's on this board," McQueen said, "but

pick up the case file from Bailey when we're done here."

"Right, boss," Diver said.

"And what are we gonna be workin'?" Sherman asked.

"Jack, you, Jimmy, Bailey and me are gonna be working a serial case."

"What?" Sherman asked. "I haven't heard anything about a serial killer."

"For good reason," McQueen said. "Listen up, because this gets complicated. It goes back about ten months . . ."

After he'd outlined all the deaths—the three the previous winter, and the new one—McQueen settled his butt onto the edge of his desk and waited for comments.

"What happened with the list of slaughterhouses and such?" Diver asked.

"Bailey and I have been checkin' them on our own time. It's been slow going, and the ones we've checked haven't revealed anything. In fact, I think it's been a waste of time. We can't check all the hooks in all the slaughterhouses and meat-packing plants in the state, or even the city, for skin samples from our victims."

"What about the cow's blood?" Tolliver asked.

"It's gonna be on every hook we look at," McQueen said.

"So the scratch," Dolan said, "whether it's made by a hook or not, is the link between the cases?"

"And the method of disposal," McQueen said. "Storing the bodies on ice, and then getting rid of them."

"Don't serial killers usually kill in the same manner?" Tolliver asked. "I mean, every book I've read—"

"Forget the books," McQueen said to all of them. "This killer is writing a new one."

"Only we're gonna write the last chapter, right?" Diver asked.

There were some groans and McQueen said, "I'm glad you said it, Jimmy, and not me."

"That's what I'm here for, boss," Jimmy Diver said. "To state the obvious."

"This is cleared with the Loo?" Dolan asked.

"I got his okay yesterday, Artie. You want to check with him?" McQueen asked.

"Hell, no, I trust you, Sarge."

"Who's gonna tell Paddy and the others that they're endin' up with our cases?" Silver asked.

"I'll pass the word along," McQueen said. "Everybody clear on what they're workin' on, and what we're doin'?"

"Clear on what we're workin' on," Dolan said.

"Not what we're doin'," Diver said.

"Collect your case files from me," McQueen said. "I've made copies for everyone."

He moved around behind his desk and handed out files. When he gave Tolliver his file, the younger man obviously wanted to say something. McQueen waited, but the young detective walked away without a word.

When Diver and Dolan came over McQueen said, "Check with Cahill at the crime lab. He's working on getting a phone number from the victim's phone book."

"We need the crime lab to do that?" Diver asked.

"We do when the page we want is missing."

"Gotcha," Diver said.

"You get something solid let me in on it."

"You got it, boss," Dolan said.

When Silver and Sherman came over Jack Sherman asked, "What do we do first, boss?"

"I want you fellas to work the new case," McQueen said. "I'm gonna have Bailey going over the three old cases, and then you can all compare notes."

Telling them to work the case was good enough. They were experienced detectives and didn't need to be told how to work it.

Sommers came up to him last.

"Bailey, work the computer. We didn't have it last year, and maybe you can come up with something."

"I'll input all the case notes as a start," she said, "and do some cross referencing with—"

McQueen held up his hand and said, "Don't give me the details, just the results."

"Okay, Dennis," she said. "Can I ask what you're going to do?"

"The first case, the Wingate kid," he said. "That one bothers me. There was something else going on there."

"With the daughter, and the husband?"

"Yeah," he said. "I'm gonna check into that a little, maybe talk to the mother again."

"What about looking for meat hooks?" she asked.

"Forget it," he said. "It's needle-in-a-haystack stuff. When we find the right guy we'll find the right hook."

"This is exciting, Dennis," she said. "I hope you're not going to keep me on the computer the whole time."

"Don't worry, Bailey," he said. "You'll get your street time on this one. The computer's gonna help, but I think the answer is on the street."

50

During his ride to Lydia Dean's house, McQueen thought about the murder of Thomas Wingate, and the fire the boy had died in. He wasn't sure why, but he thought that first case was the key to catching the serial killer. The whole thing just didn't sit right with him. Most of all it was Lydia Dean. She'd lost her brother, her husband had been gone missing and she was forced into a situation where she had to interact with her estranged mother. And through it all she had remained so calm, so in control. On top of it all she was beautiful. A woman like that might have attracted him—should have attracted him—and yet she didn't.

Because there was something . . . off about her, and he wanted to find out what it was.

When she opened the door to him the first thing he noticed was that she looked different. She still looked like herself, only more so—younger. Yeah, that was it.

251

The body was the same, well-toned and shapely, but the face . . . she'd had some work done. That was it. Her eyes, maybe around her mouth. Why did women do that, he wondered. He would have found her more attractive before the work, had it not been for that something "wrong" that he'd detected.

"Sergeant McQueen," she said. "What a surprise."

"Mrs. Dean."

"It's been a while," she said, leaning on the door, "but I thought we'd dispensed with the need for 'Mrs.'" She was wearing a tank top in shimmering green, and a pair of black pants. There was not an ounce of excess flesh on her arms. "You must be here on business."

"I am . . . Lydia," he said. "Can I come in and speak with you?"

"Of course." She backed up, then closed the door behind them. She turned and pressed her back to it, hands behind her back, breasts thrust out. She was doing it again, the flirting. He still maintained there was no reason for her to do that except as a cover-up. He was not the kind of man women flirted outright with, despite what Bailey Sommers might have him think.

Although some women were incurable flirts and would do so with anything in pants, he just didn't get that vibe from this woman.

"Coffee, tea, or something stronger?" she asked.

"Coffee would be fine."

"Come into the kitchen, then," she said, leading the way.

"Have you heard from your husband?" he asked as they went down a hallway.

"Not since the fire," she said. "I must tell you I much prefer my life this way."

"And how is your mother?"

He thought he noticed her shoulders tense, but then they reached the kitchen and she was able to busy herself at one of the counters while he sat at the kitchen table.

"She's not well, I'm afraid," she said, scooping coffee into an expensive-looking coffee maker. "This past year has been hard on her. As long as my brother's killer isn't found . . ." She let the line hang there.

"I understand," he said. "We haven't made much progress, but we're starting again."

Again, her shoulders hunched slightly, or did he imagine it?

"Are you?"

"Yes," he said. "We now believe that your brother's murder is part of a pattern, so I'm starting from scratch again."

"Interesting."

"What about the fire?" he asked. "Any progress on that?"

"None," she said.

"Did you collect the insurance?"

"Yes, finally," she said, turning to face him. She leaned against the counter, but there was no posing now. "Although the police and fire department haven't found whoever set the fire, the insurance company was satisfied that I did not."

"The insurance was in your name? Not your husband's?"

"That's correct."

She turned to get cups down from a cupboard. As she stretched he was sure it was for his benefit. She seemed to turn it on and off.

She put the cups down on the counter, turned to face him again.

"So what is it you think I can do for you, Dennis?"

"I just have some questions," he said. "Some of them may be repetitive, but if you'll bear with me I'll go through them quickly."

"Very well."

"Do you know why your brother was in your building that day?" he asked.

"I assume he had some work to do."

"What kind of work was he doing?"

"I don't know."

"It was your company."

"Victor ran it," she said, "badly, I might add. He would have had Thomas doing something or other."

"But you did the designing?"

"Yes."

"Are you still?"

"I'm trying to start up a smaller company right now, but it's hard." She didn't elaborate on what made it so hard, and he didn't ask.

"What were your brother's skills?"

"I'm not aware that he had any."

"Then why would your husband give him a job?"

"For two reasons," she said. "First, because Thomas was my brother. And second—as I said—he ran the company badly. How do you take your coffee?"

"Black," he said. "Thanks."

51

While McQueen was having coffee with Lydia Dean, trying to figure her out, Bailey Sommers was inputting information into the computer. The work was drudgery, but she also thought it was important to the squad to start using the computer more extensively. She created files for each victim, then a master file with all the information. As she was finishing that up she was so intent on what she was doing that she didn't notice the man enter the squad room and come up behind her. He leaned over her, brought his hands to her breasts to cup them and whispered into her ear, *"Querida."*

She jumped, then leaned back against him just for a moment, long enough for his thumbs to find her nipples through the fabric of her blouse and bra, and for his scent to waft gently into her nostrils—and then she realized where they were.

"Ernesto," she said, pushing his hands away.

Lieutenant Bautista straightened up, then came around her desk to face her.

"Anybody could walk in," she said.

"Then come in my office with me," he said. "No one will disturb us there."

She'd left his warm bed only hours ago, sated from a long bout of early morning lovemaking, and yet here he was, making her heart race and her palms sweat. The first time Bautista had approached her for a date months ago she'd refused, because of their working relationship, but the handsome Latino had pursued her relentlessly, and finally she had given in. They had dinner that night, and she ended up in his bed. He was her boss, was several years younger than her, this was wrong on so many levels, and yet she'd never been so happy—or satisfied—with a man. She'd been embarrassed that first night in bed, when she cried after they'd had sex, to tell him she'd had her first orgasm with him. He, on the other hand, was loving and gentle. He made love to her again and she had several orgasms. He was the most considerate lover she'd ever had, although she was no expert, having slept with only three men in her life. She was slow to develop, remaining a virgin until she was twenty-five when she finally decided "Fuck it," went out, picked up a guy in a bar and had her cherry popped. She never saw him again. The other two men were relationships that didn't last, and the sex was never good.

This man, however, had swept her off her feet, but she struggled to maintain some distance at work so no one would suspect anything. She especially didn't want McQueen to know, because she respected him as a man and as a professional, and she wanted the same respect from him. She thought she had it after all these months, and she didn't want to lose it.

"I can't come into your office," she said. "I have work to do."

"Ah, the good sergeant has begun his investigation."

"Yes, he has."

"And he is wasting your talents on the computer?"

"Ernesto, some of my talents lie in the computer."

He leaned over her desk and said smoothly, "And I know where some of your other talents lie."

If he'd tried to take her right there on her desk, she probably would have let him, but he stood up and said, "Very well. I also have much work to do."

"Ernesto, thank you for letting Dennis do this."

"I would say *por nada*, but I didn't do it for you, my love. If Sergeant McQueen can prove his point and catch a madman, it will reflect very well on me."

"And on him."

"Yes," he said, "of course. Back to work then, *mi corrazon*."

She watched him as he walked back to his office. She knew—and no one else in the squad did—that he had gotten the computer for her. She'd thought him an extraordinarily generous man, but the squad ran more smoothly with the computer, and so that benefited him. Now she found herself wondering, had it been for him? As allowing McQueen to pursue his serial killer angle was for him? And would Dennis McQueen share in the glory—would any of them—if and when they caught this killer she'd started thinking of as The Cold Man?

She shivered, not from cold or from fear, but because she could still feel the touch of Ernesto Bautista's thumbs on her nipples. She shook her head to clear it, bent to her keyboard and went back to work.

52

At that same moment Detectives Diver and Dolan were sitting in chairs at the crime lab, waiting to see Marty Cahill.

"You the guys Sergeant McQueen sent over?"

They looked up, saw a young guy, fit, good-looking, and they both took an instant dislike to him.

"That's us," Diver said. He was approaching fifty, his partner, Artie Dolan, was mid-forties, and neither of them was in anything approaching the shape this man was in.

"This is for you, then." Cahill handed Diver a slip of paper.

"That the address?" Dolan asked.

"That's it. I got it from the impression of the page that was beneath the one that's missing. Of course, that page had a bunch of numbers on it, so it took some doing to separate the impressions."

"Are you sure this is accurate?" Diver asked.

"Oh, it's accurate," Cahill said. "The address is, anyway. The phone number was a little harder. Lots of ohs and eights, which are hard to tell apart when you're dealing with shapes. But the address was pretty distinct, and I checked the phone book to be sure it was an actual address."

Dolan took it from Diver. It was accurate, all right. He knew exactly where it was.

"Let's go, then," he said to his partner.

They both turned and left without another word to Cahill, who said to their retreating backs, "Hey, you're welcome, any time."

The address was in the Bay Ridge section of Brooklyn, a street of houses very similar to each other near Eighty-second Street. They parked in front and approached the door.

"I'll cover the back, in case he rabbits," Diver said.

"And if he does?" Dolan asked. "You gonna chase him?"

"Good point," Diver said. "You cover the back."

"I ain't in as good shape as that guy Cahill, but I can still run," Dolan said.

"I didn't like that guy," Diver said.

"Me, neither."

They'd said that several times to each other during the drive from the crime lab to Bay Ridge.

"Okay, I got the back," Diver said. "Gimme five."

"Gotcha."

Diver waited the five minutes and then rang the bell. He was about to ring it again when the door opened. A pretty young woman with choppily cut blonde hair stood there, leaning on the door, standing hip shot. She was about fifteen, but had developed early. She was wearing cutoff jeans and a tight top that showed off what Diver thought of as "bowling ball" tits. She stood about five eight and was what could only be described as a big girl.

"A little cold out for that kind of outfit, ain't it?" he asked.

"The cold makes my nipples hard," she said. He could see she was telling the truth. He could also see she had the kind of nipples his partner called "puppy dog's noses."

Okay, he thought, get a hold of yourself. This is a kid.

"I'm looking for Allan Hansen."

"He ain't here," she said. "You a cop?"

"I am," he said. "Wanna see my badge?"

"Yeah."

He took it out and showed it to her.

"Nice," she said, touching it. "Blue and gold. I like those colors."

"Does he live here?"

"Yeah," she said, "but he ain't here now."

"What's he to you?"

"My asshole brother. What's he to you?"

"An asshole suspect."

"Cool," she said. "Suspected of what?"

"When did you see him last?"

"I dunno," she said, with a shrug. "Days ago. He comes and goes as he pleases."

"Does anyone else live here?"

"My mom."

"Has she seen him?"

"Probably not," she said, then added, "she's been blind for years."

He didn't know if she meant literally blind, or blind to the action of her brother.

"What's your name?"

"Terry," she said. "What's yours?"

"Detective Diver," he said. "Would you mind if we came in to talk to you and your mother, Terry?"

"We?"

"My partner is out back."

"Out back?" She screwed up her face, then brightened. "Oh, you thought if Allan was here he might try to run?"

"It had occurred to us, yes."

"Is you partner better-lookin' than you?" she asked.

"Tons," he said, "and younger."

"Ohh," she said, "well come on in and let's go get him."

There it was, he thought, the invitation. He'd been afraid the kid might ask for a warrant.

She turned and he followed her big, round ass into the house, shaking his head in both disbelief and admiration.

53

Terry was thrilled with Artie Dolan's appearance and, even though he was over forty, he was still younger than Diver, so she turned her considerable charms onto him.

"Where's your mother?" Dolan asked.

"She's out, at the center. She old, and blind, and they help her out, there. Give her something to do."

"How old?" Diver asked.

"Like sixty," she said. "I was a change-of-life baby."

"So you're alone in the house?"

"Well, no," she said. "Duh. You guys are here. So, are you married or what?"

She leaned forward in her chair and the move pressed her breasts together. Diver noticed his partner's eyes almost bulging out of their sockets. He waved to get his attention, then made a circling motion with his finger, indicating he was going to have a look around.

Terry was still asking questions of Dolan as Diver moved into the kitchen. He looked around a bit but didn't find anything of interest, like a phone book or a note pinned to the refrigerator door with a magnet. He was about to leave the room when he caught a whiff of something odd. He sniffed around and finally came to a door near the back of the house. He assumed it led to a basement, opened it and discovered he was right. He looked around for a light switch, found it and flipped it on. One single bulb appeared at the bottom of the steps, and he went down.

It was a tiny basement and it was musty and damp. There was that smell in the air, even stronger, the one he couldn't identify. There was very little down there. A flimsy wooden table, a metal folding chair, an old sink and, off to one side, some boxes. Inside one of the boxes he found plastic bags, like baggies for sandwiches, but larger. They were all empty.

The smell persisted and he searched for the source. There were more boxes on the floor piled under the staircase. The base of some of them was stained with dampness. He nudged one with his foot, wondering if there might be a dead mouse or rat inside. Briefly, a childhood memory intruded on the moment, a memory of opening a bread drawer in his mother's kitchen only to have a mouse jump out at him. Actually, it hadn't jumped at him, it had simply jumped out and run away, but at five years old he didn't know that, and it didn't keep him from yelling in terror.

He pulled the box closer to the light, crouched down by it, opened the top—it was not sealed, the flaps had simply been folded to close it—and looked inside. The smell he hadn't been able to identify came out at him full force. He reached in to take out a small, damp box, and read the name of the contents on the side.

Mothballs.

* * *

McQueen wasn't getting much out of Lydia Dean except for some more flirting—which he decided she wasn't very good at—coffee, and more of that feeling that there was just something wrong about her.

He was about to leave when his cell phone rang.

"Excuse me," he said. "McQueen."

"Hey, boss," Diver said, "Artie and me are over at Allan Hansen's house."

"Is he there?"

"No, but his sister is. She's upstairs with Artie. Man, she's about fifteen but what a set of—"

"Upstairs with Artie? Where are you?"

"In the basement."

"I hope she let you in, Jimmy," McQueen said.

"Don't worry, we got invited," Diver said. "In fact, she's givin' Artie a big invitation right—"

"Why did you call me, Jimmy?"

"Mothballs."

"What?"

"I found mothballs."

"How many?" McQueen asked.

"I'm looking at three cartons of mothballs," Diver said into his cell phone.

"At the Hansen house?"

"Right."

"Well, maybe they've got lots of moths."

"Could be," Diver said, "but amateur firebugs also use the stuff for fires. It's got, whataya call it, naphthalene in it. It's used in making homemade fire bombs."

"How do you know that?" McQueen asked.

"I worked arson a few years, before they got all specialized. Didn't that first case you're workin' on have somethin' to do with fire?"

"It did," McQueen said, "but this is a stretch, Jimmy. That would connect my serial case to your homicide."

"Stranger things have happened."

"Why don't you keep looking around there and see what you can find that has to do with your case?"

"Okay, boss. Just tryin' to help."

"I know it. Where are you going from there?"

"According to the case file, our girl had a job at some telemarketing place." He gave McQueen the address. "We thought we'd talk to some of her coworkers. Maybe they know something about the boyfriend."

"That address is near here," McQueen said. "Let me take that. Why don't you check Hansen's job?"

"Okay," Diver said. "I think he was a mechanic some place near here."

"Good," McQueen said. "I'm about done here, anyway."

"Well, I better go up and save Artie. She's probably got his pants off by now."

McQueen closed his eyes and broke the connection.

"Are we done here, Dennis?"

"I think so."

"I'm afraid I haven't been very helpful."

"Maybe you have," he said, standing up. "I won't know for sure until later."

She walked him to the front door.

"It was nice seeing you again."

"Yes," he said, "nice to see you, too."

"If you find out anything you'll let me know, won't you?"

"Yes, I will."

"Or," she added, "you could come and see me, anyway."

"Good-bye, Lydia," he said, and went out the door without addressing her last words.

Kathy Stephens had worked at a telemarketing firm near Utica Avenue. He found it without much trouble.

It was a huge building that looked like it had once been a warehouse. He pulled into a parking area behind it, got out of the car and found a door. He wasn't sure if it was the front door, but he went in, anyway. Now all he had to do was find his way to the personnel department and he'd be all set. He only needed to find a couple of people who worked with Kathy Stephens, who were either friends, or just wanted to gossip about her.

He knew he wasn't sticking to his own plan by crossing over to the Stephens homicide, but that was a failing he admitted to as a boss—he wasn't very good at delegating. Also, he was already in the area, so what was the point of making the Double Ds drive all the way over here?

It took him a while, walking down hallways, sticking his head in the doorways, fending off security guards with a flash of his badge—security guards who didn't know where personnel was. Finally he stopped a pretty girl wearing white jeans and a tight purple top.

"You looking for a job?" she asked, brightly.

McQueen showed her his badge, thinking how very young she was. "No, I'm just looking for the personnel department."

She gave him a smile and directions.

"Thanks."

When, he wondered, did businesses start hiring babies?

54

He found personnel and approached a middle-aged woman seated behind a desk. She was attractive, in her forties, and much closer to McQueen's age than the girl in the hallway had been. This one was wearing a sensible business suit, and was not flirtatious, at all.

"May I help you?" she asked.

"Yes, my name is Detective Sergeant McQueen, N.Y.P.D," he said, showing her his badge and his ID. As he started to put it away she clamped her hand on his wrist, holding it there until she could examine both fully.

"Are you interested in moonlighting, Detective?" she asked, releasing his wrist.

"Not really," he said. "I need to talk to someone about an employee."

"And who would the employee be?"

"A woman named Kathy Stephens. Do you know her?"

"I know Kathy," the woman said, her attitude becoming warmer. "I hired her."

"When would that have been?"

"Oh . . ." she said, frowning, searching her memory, ". . . had to be about two years ago."

"Have there been any problems with her?"

"What kind?"

"Boyfriend problems?"

"That would be personal," she said, her tone scolding, "not personnel . . ."

"Very good," he said, smiling.

She gave him a sly look. "I don't think I should be talking to you about this."

"Well then, who should?"

"Probably my supervisor."

"Can I see him—or her—please?"

"Wait here."

She stood up and left the room. There were several other desks in the room but none of the people occupying them looked up from what they were doing, or showed the slightest interest in him.

After a few minutes the woman returned. "Will you come with me, please?"

"Lead the way."

She did, taking him to a smaller office, on the door of which was the name: FRED HICKMAN, PERSONNEL SUPERVISOR.

"Detective McQueen?" the man behind the desk asked.

"That's right."

The man stood up to his full height of about five-eight and said to the woman, "That's all, Grace. Thank you."

"Yes, sir."

Grace gave McQueen another sly look and left the room. He wondered if she thought there was some private joke existing between them that he wasn't getting?

"Fred Hickman," the man said, sticking out his

hand. McQueen shook it briefly. The man's hand was clammy, and unpleasant.

"Now what can I do for you, Detective? Grace said something about Kathy Stephens. She's not in trouble, is she?"

"She's dead, Mr. Hickman," McQueen said.

"Oh, my."

"Somebody killed her and her daughter."

"Oh . . . oh *my!*" Hickman said, looking very distressed. "That poor child."

"I really need to talk to some people who knew her," McQueen explained.

"I'm the supervisor of the personnel department," Hickman said, "but I don't know if I can help you."

"Then point me in the direction of someone who can."

"Well, that's just it," Hickman said. "I'm not sure."

"I'll make it easy for you, Mr. Hickman," McQueen said. "Send me to the department where Kathy Stephens worked. I'd like to talk to her coworkers, and possibly her boss."

"Well, her immediate superior would be whoever was on duty at the same time she was."

"How many people would that possibly be?"

"There are three supervisors on the project where she was working," Hickman said.

"So she must have worked with all three at some time or other, right?"

"Yes, that's true."

"And did she work the same shift each week?"

"Well, yes—"

"With the same people?"

"One would assume—"

"Good," McQueen said. "I need to talk to them, also."

"Well—"

"So just have somebody walk me over there," Mc-Queen went on, "and this problem is out of your hands."

McQueen could see that this solution immediately appealed to Fred Hickman.

"All right," the man said, "I'll have Grace walk you over."

"And what's Grace's last name?"

"Hoffman, Grace Hoffman—*Mrs.* Grace Hoffman."

"All right, then," McQueen said, "why don't you just put me back into Mrs. Hoffman's capable hands and we'll go from there?"

55

"What department did she work in?" McQueen asked Grace Hoffman as she led him down a long corridor.

"She handles—handled—incoming calls, specifically from people who want to purchase beepers."

"She only dealt with people on the phone?"

"That's right."

"Did she give her name?"

"If asked, yes."

Suddenly, Grace Hoffman slowed down and seemed to falter for a moment.

"Are you all right?"

She kept her back to him. "I'm sorry, it's just that . . . well, I told you, I hired Kathy. It's just a shock to hear . . ."

McQueen put his hand on her shoulder. "You can go back, if you like. Just give me directions."

"No, no," she said, "it's all right." She turned and smiled at him. "You're very kind, but I'm fine. I'll take you there."

They started off again.

She took him into a room filled with partitioned cubicles, and behind each partition was a person sitting in front of a computer, talking on a phone.

"Kathy worked there," Grace said, pointing to one desk, behind which another woman was sitting and working.

"Has she been replaced?" McQueen asked.

"No," Grace said, "that was her station when she was here. When she's not—wasn't—here, someone else would work there. The only thing that belonged to her was her headset. Everything else was shared."

"I see. Did she work with all these people?"

The room was very large, easily holding about thirty employees.

"She might have known some of them, but she mainly worked with the people on either side of her. Those four stations all dealt with the same project she was on."

"I see. And where would her supervisor be?"

"Over here," she said. "I'll introduce you."

The supervisor's partitioned area was only slightly larger than those the other workers were sitting in.

"Frank? Can I talk to you a minute?" Grace called out.

The man named Frank turned and McQueen thought he was young—probably twenty-six or seven—to be a supervisor.

"What can I do for you, Grace?" he asked.

"Frank Kovac, this is Detective Sergeant McQueen, from the police. He'd like to talk to you about . . . about Kathy Stephens. I'm sorry." The introduction made, Grace rushed off.

"What's wrong with her?" Kovac asked. "Did something happen?"

"As a matter of fact it did, Mr. Kovac," McQueen said. "Kathy Stephens and her daughter have been killed."

"What?" Kovac's eyes seemed to go out of focus behind his wire-rimmed glasses. "Was it . . . a car accident?"

"No," McQueen said, "they were murdered."

"Murdered?" McQueen hadn't noticed the man's Adam's apple before, but now it seemed to bob up and down. "God." He groped for his desk and sat heavily in his chair.

"Did you know her well, Mr. Kovac?"

"What? Well? Uh, no . . . I mean, we worked together, that's all."

"Never saw her outside of work?"

"No," the man said, and then hurriedly, "say, you don't think—"

"I'm just asking questions, Mr. Kovac. I don't think anything, yet."

"Oh . . ." Kovac said, but he looked dubious.

"What about her coworkers?"

"What about them?"

"Did she get along with them?"

"Sure, I guess so."

"Anyone in particular?"

"Are you asking if she was seeing any—"

"Mr. Kovac, I just want to know if anyone here was close friends with her, male or female."

"Well . . . she spent most of her break time talking to Jen . . . uh, Jennifer Douglas."

"And is Jennifer Douglas here today?"

"No, she'll be in . . ." He paused to look at his watch. "Well, soon. She and . . . uh, Kathy . . . would have been coming in at one."

McQueen looked at his watch. It was quarter to one.

"What about the people who are here now?" he asked. "Did they know her?"

"Sure . . . I guess . . ."

"I'd like to talk to all of them," McQueen said, "but I don't want to disrupt your workday. Would you go and get them and bring them here one by one?"

"They're on the phones . . ."

"I won't keep them long. I promise."

"Well . . . I guess it would be all right . . ." Kovac said, haltingly.

"It would be very helpful, Mr. Kovac," McQueen said. "You want to help, don't you?"

"Oh, yes, of course—"

"Good," McQueen said, "I'll just wait here while you go and get one of them."

56

McQueen questioned the three people who were presently assigned to the same project that Kathy Stephens worked when she was there—two girls and a young man. They all told him the same thing. They saw her sometimes at the end of their shift, when she was coming in, or at the beginning of their shift, when she was going home. No, they didn't socialize with her outside of work.

"She was old," one of the girls said. She looked to be all of eighteen and McQueen knew from Kathy Stephens's driver's license that Kathy was thirty-seven. Old.

They were all shocked that she was dead, but they knew nothing about her home life.

By the time McQueen had finished questioning them their shift was over. Kovac told him that Jennifer Douglas had arrived.

"Did you tell her anything?"

"No, sir."

"I want to talk to her before she starts working."

ROBERT J. RANDISI

"I'll get her."

"Wait," McQueen said. "Is there someplace more private?"

"Uh, you could use the break room."

"How do I get there?"

Kovac gave him directions that were easy enough to follow.

"Give me two minutes and then send her in."

"All right."

McQueen found the break room empty. It was the end of one shift and the beginning of another. There were long tables, chairs, and some vending machines. Also a microwave, and a small refrigerator.

He turned when the door opened and a rather chubby, plain-looking woman in her mid-twenties walked in, looking nervous.

"Miss Douglas?" he asked.

"Mrs. Douglas."

"I'm sorry," he said. "My name is Detective Sergeant McQueen. I'm with the N.Y.P.D."

"Is . . . has something happened?"

"How do you mean?"

"I mean, to my husband, or my kids?"

"Oh, no, Mrs. Douglas," McQueen said, "your family is fine. Don't worry."

The woman heaved a sigh of relief and looked less nervous.

"What's this about, then?" she asked. "I have to get to work."

"I won't keep you long. Why don't you take a seat?"

"I really don't have time to—"

"I think it would be better if you sat."

The woman hesitated, then said, "All right," and sat down.

"Can I call you Jennifer?"

"Sure," she said, with a shrug of her round shoulders. Her hair was shoulder length, brown, rather lank, her clothes were KMart rather than J.C. Penney or Macy's.

"I'm here about Kathy Stephens."

"Kathy."

"You do know her, don't you?"

"Sure, Kathy and I are friends. We're in the same boat, you might say."

"The same boat?"

"We both have kids. We're a little older than the others on our project."

"I see."

"Has something happened to her?"

"Yes, Jennifer. I'm sorry to have to tell you that she's dead."

Jennifer's mouth dropped open and for a moment she was speechless. Her eyes filled with tears; she covered her mouth with both hands. She gagged for just a moment, leading McQueen to think she might vomit, but she didn't.

"W-where's Miranda?" she asked.

McQueen hesitated, then said, "I'm afraid Miranda is also dead, Jennifer."

"Oh, Gohhhhd!" she said, drawing it out and covering her mouth again. She said something behind her hands that McQueen didn't catch.

"I'm sorry, I didn't under—"

"I said, 'Did he do it'?" she repeated, dropping her hands into her lap.

"Did who do it?"

"That boyfriend of hers," Jennifer said, "Allan."

"Allan Hansen?"

She nodded.

ROBERT J. RANDISI

"Why would you ask that?"

"Because he used to hit her, and Miranda," Jennifer said. "How was she killed?"

"I don't think you want—"

"Please?"

"She had a broken neck," McQueen said, "and Miranda was . . . kicked in the head."

Her mouth quivered, her eyes filled even more, but she did not dissolve into tears. Instead, she became angry.

"That dirty sonofabitch!" she snapped. "He finally did it."

"Jennifer—"

"Do you have him?" she asked. "Did you arrest him?"

"No, we don't have him," McQueen said. "That's why I need your help, Jennifer. Can you answer a few more questions?"

"I'll tell you everything I know if it will help put him away."

McQueen sat down opposite her.

"Do you know where he lives?"

Anxious to help she looked crestfallen at the first question.

"No, I don't," she said, sadly.

"He didn't live in the house with her?"

"No, but he stayed there a lot. He used to get some mail there, too. Oh, and he used her basement."

"For what?"

"Storage."

"What did he store there?"

"I don't know," she answered. "Kathy never said."

"Is it possible she didn't know?"

"Yeah, it's possible," Jennifer said. "That bastard never told her anything. He took her money, and didn't tell her what he was spending it on."

"Did he work?"

"Sometimes."

"What did he do?"

"He was a mechanic."

"Jennifer, did Kathy give you any idea where he might have lived when he wasn't with her?" He wondered if Hansen had an apartment somewhere that his sister and mother didn't know about?

"Well . . . I think she said that he stayed with his mother and sister."

"Did he live with her?"

"No, just stayed there sometimes, like he did with Jennifer. Like he probably did with other women."

"He had other women?"

"Kathy always said no, but I think he did."

"Did you ever meet him?"

"Once," she said, "when he came here to pick her up. He even looked mean, Detective. I don't know what she ever saw in him."

"I'm going to give you my card. I'd like you to call me if you think of something I should know. Will you do that?"

"I'll do whatever I can to help you put that bastard away," she said, with feeling.

He handed her his card.

"Are you all right to go back to work?" McQueen asked. "Would you like me to try and get you the day off?"

"No, I want to work," she said, standing up. "It'll keep me from . . . thinking about it too much."

McQueen stood and said, "Jennifer, thank you for your help."

"You get him, Detective," she said, "you get that monster."

"We will," he said, realizing he had made the same promise a couple of times before.

57

Finding an address for Allan Hansen turned out to be stupidly simple. Diver and Dolan found the garage where the man worked, and the bookkeeper there gave them the address she had to send Hansen's checks to if he didn't come in and pick them up.

"Some of these guys," she said, "you don't see 'em for days. Sometimes they just find other jobs and never come back, so we mail 'em their last check."

She had fake red hair, and painted-on eyebrows, and was sixty if she was a day, but her clothes were as tight as they could be without strangling her.

"Say," she said to Dolan, "you married?"

In the car Dolan said, "What is this, my lucky day? First the kid, now this old lady with the creepy, painted-on eyebrows."

"I wouldn't take too much credit for the girl," Diver told his partner. "She was just teasin' a coupla old men."

"Hey," Dolan said, "she was into me."

"Yeah," Diver said, "that'll happen."

"What the hell happened to kids?"

"Whataya mean?" Diver asked.

"They didn't have fifteen-year-olds like that when I was a kid," Dolan said. "Shit, twelve- and thirteen-year-olds got tits these days."

"Yeah, I know what you mean," Diver said. "It's scary—especially when you have daughters."

"Your daughter's only—holy crap, she's fifteen, right?"

"Yeah," Diver said, "but she don't look like that kid Terry—and thank God for that."

This time the address was for a two-family brick house in Bensonhurst, around Sixty-third Street.

"This guy's got a lot of addresses," Diver said, as they approached the door. "I wonder if he lives anywhere permanently?"

"If this is another girl like the sister . . ." Dolan said.

"If she was even his sister," Diver said.

"Damn, but she was built . . ." Dolan said.

"Back or front?" Diver asked.

"Let's see if he's here," Dolan said. "I don't want to go all the way around the back for nothing."

"Yeah," Dolan said, "you're in shape, all right. Fifteen-year-olds with Jayne Mansfield bodies are really into you."

"Speakin' of Jayne Mansfield," Dolan said, as they went up the stairs. "You ever watch that *Law & Order SUV*?"

"It's *SVU*, you dunce."

"Yeah, well, the broad on there, what's her name, Mariska? That's Jayne Mansfield's daughter."

"With Mickey Hargatay."

"What?"

"That was her father. Mickey Hargatay. Played Hercules in the movies."

"He didn't."

"Yeah, he did."

"Steve Reeves was Hercules."

"There were lots of Herculeses," Diver said.

"Yeah, but Steve, he was the real Hercules."

"There was no real Hercules, you dumb fuck."

"Then what are we arguin' about?"

When they reached the top of the steps Diver was already huffing and puffing.

"Shoulda called for backup, this time."

"Yeah," Dolan said, "and last time they coulda helped us with Terry Big Tits, right? Ring the bell, Hercules."

When McQueen got back to the house, Sommers waved him over to her desk.

"I've got all the cases entered in the computer, Dennis."

"That's good," he said. "Did Detective Dell solve it yet? Or whatsit? Detective Pentium?"

"Don't make fun, Dennis," she said. "This computer has been invaluable to the squad since we got it."

"Seems to me the computer wouldn't be any good without you, Bailey," he said. "And what about that?"

"What about what?"

"The computer?" McQueen said. "How come this lieutenant can get us one, but Jessup couldn't?"

"I dunno," she said. "Maybe Jessup never tried."

"Yeah."

As he walked to his desk she asked, "Where've you been? Did you talk to Lydia Dean again?"

"I did."

"She still comin' on to you?"

"Bailey . . ."

"She did, didn't she?"

"I told you," McQueen said, "I thought she had something up her sleeve last winter, and I still think she does."

"Like what."

"Well," he said, leaning back in his chair, "what if her husband's not missing? What if she killed him?"

"We don't have enough murders to deal with?"

"No, think about it," he insisted. "Nobody's seen him or heard from him in all this time."

"Maybe because he doesn't want to be seen or heard from."

"And the fire . . . that's also an odd piece, here," McQueen said. "Who chooses to kill that way?"

"Lots of people have used fire to kill someone."

"But then they go in, take the body out and store it for two weeks before getting rid of it? I wouldn't go back into a burning building—or a burned-out building—to get a dead body out."

"So it's just the entire Wingate case that bugs you," she said.

"Yes," he said. "It bugs the hell out of me. It's an odd way for a serial killer to get started. There are too many other people involved."

"Okay," she said, "I've got one for you. Try this. The Wingate murder is entirely separate from the fire, and from Victor Dean's disappearance."

"O-kay, keep going."

"The killer goes in the building after Thomas Wingate, and suddenly finds himself in the middle of a fire . . ."

". . . set by Victor Dean, or somebody working for him."

". . . right," she said, "And Lydia Dean is right in there with him. They're after the insurance . . ."

". . . and she later kills him to get rid of him. So, she is a widow, and she collects the insurance."

"And her brother happened to be in the building at the time."

"I can accept her brother being in the building and succumbing to the smoke," McQueen said, "but then you bring an entirely different person into it, the serial killer."

She bit the end of her pen as she tried to ponder that one.

"What if he's there to kill Thomas Wingate, but the smoke gets to him first?"

"So he takes him anyway, puts him on ice as he planned, and then disposes of the body two weeks later?"

"Sure, why not?" she asked. "He meant to kill Thomas, but the kid is dead anyway. Why not go ahead with the rest of your plan?"

"And then continue from there with the others? The Sheepshead Bay guy, Melanie Edwards and now John Bennett."

"And whoever this nut has on ice now."

"Boss," she said, "nobody's worked the Bennett angle yet."

"Jesus," McQueen said, covering his face with his hands. There it was, his glaring flaw, delegating.

"Why not give it to Andy?" she asked. "The Double Ds really don't need him."

"Where is Tolliver?" McQueen asked. "I spoke with Diver and he didn't say."

"I hate to say it, Dennis," she said, "but I think they ditched him."

McQueen sighed.

"Find him, Bailey," he said. "I'll give him Bennett

to follow up on. That puts him on the serial case, which is what he wanted in the first place, right?"

"I'll get right on it."

McQueen watched her walk back to her desk and hoped he hadn't bitten off more than he could chew.

58

"What've you got?" McQueen asked Sommers, looking at her computer screen over her shoulder.

"Basically," she said, "we've got absolutely no connection between any of the victims. A couple of them are in the same age group, but the woman was a thirty-year-old housewife. They don't match up as far as jobs go, or lifestyles. Thomas Wingate was perpetually unemployed, but John Bennett had a good job. And we still don't know anything about victim number two."

"Okay," McQueen said, rubbing his face vigorously with both hands. "Did you get a hold of Tolliver?"

"Yes," she said, "I got him on his cell. Diver and Dolan sent him on a wild goose chase, just like we figured. I told him you were giving him the Bennett murder."

"Good. Keep working the machine, Bailey, see what you can find out about all these victims."

"That's what I've been doing," she said. "There's nothing to connect them."

"Sure there is."

"What?"

"They're being killed by the same person, aren't they?"

As he went back to his own desk Bailey Sommers thought, "We think."

A couple hours later, McQueen was ready to go home and come back in the morning to start fresh. He stopped short when he saw Jimmy Diver enter the office.

"Boss."

"Jimmy, what you and Artie did to Tolliver—"

"We got him, boss."

"Got who?"

"Hansen," Diver said. "We got him."

"Where is he?"

"In a holding cell downstairs."

"Where was he?"

"At another girlfriend's house," Diver said. "We tracked him to a house in Bensonhurt. There we found a girlfriend who was pissed at him. She gave us the address of another girl and we literally found him napping on her couch."

"Napping?" McQueen asked. "He kills a woman and her daughter and he's napping?"

"Hey," Diver said, "innocent until proven guilty, right, boss?"

It was a valid point. They had no solid evidence that Hansen had killed Kathy Stephens and her daughter, Miranda.

"Okay, Jimmy," McQueen said. He was about to tell Diver that he wanted to question Hansen, but then thought better of it. He was supposed to be working the serial case. "You and Artie see what you can get out of him."

"Glad to, boss, but I thought you might want to hear what he has to say."

"And why's that?"

"Well . . . he confessed."

"What?"

"In the car," Diver said. "He said he did it."

"Jesus, I hope you Mirandized him."

"We arrested him for suspicion and read him his rights."

"He didn't ask for a lawyer?"

"No," Diver said, "he confessed, and said he wanted to speak to my boss."

"What for?"

"He wants to make a deal."

"A deal?" McQueen asked. "What's he think he has to deal with?"

"He says," Diver answered, "he can give us Thomas Wingate's killer."

"What?" Sommers asked. "He can give us our serial killer?"

"He doesn't know anything about a serial killer," Diver said. "He just says he can give us the kid's killer."

"How?" McQueen said. "How can he do that?"

"Remember the mothballs I said I found at his house?" Jimmy Diver asked.

"Yeah. So?"

"Hansen's an amateur torch," Diver said. "He says he's the one burned down that Lydia Dean building."

59

Allen Hansen was moved to an interrogation room. McQueen decided to go ahead and conduct the interrogation himself, with Diver and Dolan present, and one other detective—Bailey Sommers.

"He's got a real low opinion of women," Diver told McQueen, which is what persuaded McQueen to put Sommers in the room. He sent Diver down to move Hansen from the cell to a room, and spoke to her while they were alone in the office.

"I want you to sit right in front of him," McQueen told her. "Don't say a word. Just keep your eyes on him."

"You think me being there is going to rattle him?"

"I hope so," he said. "I'm gonna hit him hard if I have to, belittle him, and doing that to him in front of you just might do it."

"Do what?"

"Bring out the truth."

"Dennis, he confessed."

"I know," he said, "but I want to make sure he really did it. And that he really does have something to deal with."

"You'd actually make a deal with him after what he did to that woman and her little girl?"

"What would you do, Bailey?" McQueen asked. "We've got a serial killer out there ready to take another life. What would you do?"

"I'd take the bird in the hand," she said. "If he confessed, then we know he did it. We don't know what that nut out there is going to do—or if there really is one nut. Who's to say that whoever this guy gives us is a serial killer?"

"That's what I want to find out."

"You wouldn't cut him loose, would you?" she asked, incredulously.

"It's not my call," McQueen said.

"Then whose is it?"

"It would be up to the D.A."

"Who doesn't know anything about a serial killer," she pointed out.

"Maybe not, but we do have an unsolved homicide on the books," McQueen said, "and an arson."

"I just can't see letting this . . . this child killer go, no matter what he says."

"Let's see what he's got for us, Bailey," McQueen said, "before we fight about it. All right?"

"All right," she said. "I'll do it—I don't approve, but to be truthful I can't pass up the opportunity to be in on this."

"Then let's do it."

60

"This interview with Allan Hansen is being conducted by Detective Sergeant Dennis McQueen. Also in attendance are Detectives First-Grade James Diver and Arthur Dolan and Detective Second-Grade Bailey Sommers."

"What's this for?" Hansen asked, looking at the tape recorder. His blonde hair was a mess, since the Double Ds had dragged him straight from a nap. He was wearing torn jeans and an Aerosmith T-shirt. "I said I killed the bitch."

"We need to conduct an interview, Allan, and get it all on tape. Is that all right with you?"

"Ah, sure," the young man said, "why not?"

"And you've been given your rights and have understood them?" McQueen asked.

"Sure."

"And you waive your right to an attorney."

"Yeah, yeah," Hansen said, "what do I need a lawyer for. I killed Kathy and Miranda, but I got something to trade."

"We'll get to that in a minute, Allan," McQueen said. "First, where do you live?"

"Here and there?"

"You move around?"

"A lot," Hansen said. "Depends on which girl I'm wantin' to fuck, ya know?" He leered at Sommers. "I got a lot of 'em."

"What's your legal residence?"

"My mother's house, I guess."

"You lived there with her and with your younger sister?"

"Yeah," Hansen said, "my sister. You guys seen her?"

"The detectives spoke with her, yes," McQueen said.

"Don't think I ain't tapped that gash, even though she's underage."

"And your sister," McQueen reminded him.

"I know that."

"You're admitting to incest and statutory rape?"

"What the hell?" Hansen said, leaning back and lacing his fingers behind his head. He looked directly at Sommers. "I confessed to murder. What can they do to me for rape and incest? Besides, if you seen my sister you know what I'm talkin' about. I mean, who wouldn't tap that?"

"Let's go through what happened when you were at Kathy Stephens's house on . . ."

Hansen was very forthcoming when it came to talking about Kathy and Miranda Stephens. Kathy was a whiny bitch who nagged him, and Miranda never shut up. The only reason he stayed around was because Kathy was good in bed.

He leered constantly at Bailey Sommers, who had not said a word.

"She gave great blow jobs," he told her, "and she was a natural blonde, ya know?"

Sommers remained silent.

"Whattsa matter with this cunt detective?" he asked. "Don't she talk?"

"She'll speak when she has something to say, Allan," McQueen told him.

"When's that gonna be?" Hansen asked. "Maybe she's in love with me, ya know? Struck dumb? Maybe she wants to fuck me?"

"I doubt it, Allan," McQueen said. "Let's talk about the fire."

"I thought you wanted to talk about murder?"

"We'll get to it, Allan," McQueen said. "I have to do this by the book, you know? Rules?"

"Rules," Hansen said, spitting the word out. "I hate rules."

"Not as much as you hate women, I bet," Sommers said.

"Hey, she talks!"

Sommers realized she had spoken out of turn and fell silent again.

"You were hired to set fire to the building that housed Lydia Studios?"

"Yeah, that's right."

"Who paid you?"

"She did."

"Who is 'she,' Allan?"

"Lydia Dean, her and her husband, they paid me." He looked at Sommers. "I fucked her, too." He pursed his lips and blew her a kiss.

"Oh, I doubt that," McQueen said.

"What?" Hansen asked.

McQueen took a second to lean in and hit the Stop button on the tape recorder.

"I doubt that a woman like Lydia Dean would let an arrogant little snot like you touch her."

"Wha—"

"You want us all to believe what a big man you are, Allan. You screwed your sister, you have lots of girlfriends . . . I might have believed all that, but when you try to claim Lydia Dean . . . you know what I think of men who claim they've screwed lots of women, Allan?"

Hansen didn't answer.

"Jimmy?" McQueen said.

"They're usually gay, boss."

"That right, Artie?"

"Fruits, boss," Dolan said, "every one of them."

Suddenly, Allan Hansen's faced suffused with red—more from the small smile on Bailey Sommers's face than the words of the other detectives in the room.

"Get her out," he said.

"Excuse me?" McQueen asked.

"I want her out!" He glared at Sommers. "Get out!" Spittle dotted his chin and he wiped it away with the back of his hand.

"She's not going anywhere, Allan," McQueen said, "so just settle down."

"You can't talk to me that way in front of her," the prisoner complained. "She's a . . . a broad. We're men!"

"You're a man, Allan?"

"That's right."

"All right, then. Tell me about something a real man would do?" McQueen hit the PLAY button. "Tell me about the fire?"

"I set the damn fire!" Hansen said. "I burned that whole mother to the ground."

"But something else happened while you were

there, didn't it, Allan?" McQueen asked. "Isn't that what you wanted to talk to me about?"

Hansen glared at Sommers for a few more seconds, then switched his gaze to McQueen.

"I wanna make a deal."

"I can't make a deal, Allan, until I know what you've got."

"I want out from under the murder charge."

McQueen shook his head.

"Ain't gonna happen, kid," McQueen said. "You confessed. There's no way the D.A. is gonna cut you loose."

"Then I'll take it back," Hansen said. "I'll take my confession back."

"You can try, Allan," McQueen said, "but we all heard you, and we've got it on tape. In fact, we've got you on tape saying you'll take it back."

Hansen looked like he was going to cry, his chin quivering before he firmed it.

"This ain't fair!"

"Life ain't fair, kid," McQueen said.

"What kind of deal can I get, then?"

"If you help us solve the murder of Thomas Wingate, I'll tell the D.A. you cooperated."

"That's it?"

"That's the best I can do for you, Allan," McQueen said. "What do you say?"

"Well . . . first of all . . . who the hell is Thomas Wingate?"

"What?"

"I never heard of no Wingate."

McQueen turned and looked at Diver and Dolan.

"You said you had information about the murder in the Lydia Studios building."

"Yeah, but I wasn't talkin' about no Wingate."

"Then what were you talking about?" McQueen asked.

"The woman, Lydia."

"What about her?"

He looked at all four of them like they were the crazy ones.

"I saw her do it."

Frustrated, McQueen said, "You saw her do what, Allan?"

"Well, for fuck's sake," the kid said, "I saw her do her husband!"

61

"You have been on this one day and you've come up with another murder?" Lieutenant Bautista asked.

They were all in his office, so it was pretty quiet. McQueen hadn't known how to get in touch with the lieutenant, but Sommers had volunteered to try and locate the man. Not only had she found him, but she had convinced him to come in to the office. McQueen decided not to wonder how she had done that until later.

"Well, sir," McQueen said, "Victor Dean has been listed as a missing person since January. This is the first real indication we'd had that he might be dead."

"But you suspected?"

"I . . . thought his wife was hiding something," McQueen admitted, "but her business had burned down, her brother was dead, and her husband was missing. I thought she might be . . . acting out of sorts."

"And now?"

297

"Now I think she may have been . . . well, just acting."

Bautista sat back in his chair and regarded the four of them.

"You two," he said, to Diver and Dolan. "You did good work coming up with this Hansen."

"Thank you, sir," Diver said.

"We were following Sergeant McQueen's orders, sir."

"Yes, yes," Bautista said. "You can leave. Have Allan Hansen's confession typed up."

"Yes, sir," Diver said. He and Dolan left the office after a nod from McQueen.

"Detective Sommers," he said, "I'd like to speak to Sergeant McQueen alone."

"Yes, sir."

McQueen thought something might have passed between Sommers and Bautista, but maybe he was imagining it.

After Sommers had gone and closed the door behind her Bautista looked at McQueen.

"Although you've managed to come up with yet another homicide, this was quick work."

"Yes, sir."

"How would you suggest approaching this?" the man asked.

"We could go to the D.A. with Hansen's confession, and his statement about Lydia Dean."

"Let me ask you something, Dennis. Do you think Lydia Dean may have killed her brother?"

"No, sir."

"Why not? Because it flies in the face of your serial killer theory? By your own admission you've had trouble reading this woman."

"That's not the—"

"Is she attractive?"

298

"She's . . . very well-preserved."

"There's not something . . . going on that I should know about, is there?"

"Absolutely not, sir."

"All right, then," Bautista said. "We'll go to the D.A. and see if he wants to file charges against the woman. I'm seeing various conspiracy and fraud charges, but most of all the murder of her husband—although murder is hard to prove without a body."

"Yes, sir, it is."

"And now that you have the killers of the woman and child you'll concentrate your efforts on the potential serial killer case?"

Now it was a "potential" case, McQueen thought.

"Yes, sir."

"What kind of a deal did you make with Allan Hansen?"

"No deal, sir," McQueen said. "I told him I'd speak to the D.A. about him offering up the statement on Lydia Dean."

"Excellent," Bautista said. "I'll call the D.A. Meanwhile you just . . . carry on."

McQueen hesitated, then said, "Yes, sir."

In the squad room he found Sommers and Diver.

"Where's Artie?"

"Downstairs, getting someone to take Hansen's statement," Diver said.

"Okay," McQueen said, "Jimmy, you and Artie are gonna come aboard on the serial case."

"Boss," Diver said, "if it turns out the Dean woman killed her husband, what about her brother?"

"I guess when we go to make the arrest," McQueen said, "we can ask her."

"You think the D.A. will file without a body?"

"I don't know," McQueen said. "The lieutenant is gonna check in with him."

"I'll go downstairs and see how Artie is coming along."

As he left McQueen turned to Sommers and looked at her.

"What?"

"Is there something you want to tell me?"

"About what, Dennis?"

He just stared at her.

"Dennis . . ."

"Let's go get some coffee."

62

They walked two blocks up to Church Avenue and had several choices for coffee. They chose a luncheonette, where they'd be able to have some privacy in a booth.

"I didn't mean for it to happen," she said. "In fact, I fought it for a long time."

"Did he force you?"

She reached out and covered one of his hands with both of hers.

"Oh, no, Dennis, it's nothing like that," she said. "You're very sweet to ask, but this isn't a case of sexual harassment. Just a mutual attraction."

"This is not good, Bailey," McQueen said.

"We're keeping it out of the workplace."

"If I noticed something, you don't think someone else will?" he asked.

"With all due respect, Dennis, you're the smartest person in the squad and you only just noticed."

"That's a left-handed compliment if I ever heard one."

"You know what I mean."

"So what, you've got his private cell phone number?"

"I've got all his numbers."

McQueen studied the surface of his black coffee. There was no guidance there on how to handle this situation, but was it his to handle? Wasn't this between two consenting adults?

"Dennis . . . you're not going to do anything . . . are you?" she asked.

"Like what? Blow the whistle?"

"Or say anything to Ernesto—to the lieutenant?"

"Ernesto?"

"That's his first name."

"I don't think I knew that."

"Are you?"

"Bailey, this is none of my business if it doesn't interfere with the squad. Do you agree?"

"Yes."

"Then as long as that doesn't happen, I've got no business doing anything."

She sighed and said, "That's a relief. It's also a relief to finally tell somebody."

"You don't have a friend you can talk to?"

"I have no girlfriends," she said, "and the only male friends I have are at work."

"What about a mother, or sister?"

"No siblings, and my mother's got Alzheimer's, so there's no talking to her."

"I'm sorry."

"She's in a nursing home," she said. "I send money. I used to feel guilty about not going to see her, but she never remembered me, and it used to upset her."

He didn't know what else to say.

"Are you going to go and get Lydia Dean yourself?" she asked.

"Me and the Double Ds, I think. That is, if the D.A. decides to charge her."

"Dennis . . . don't you want some credit for this? I mean, shouldn't you be talking to the D.A.?"

"Bautista is the C.O.," McQueen said. "We'll play however he wants. I don't care about credit, Bailey, I just want to get these killers off the streets. I know that's corny, but it's what I'm all about."

Sommers worried her bottom lip with her teeth. She knew Bautista intended to take credit for whatever collars McQueen came up with in the serial cases, and as long as the sergeant was okay with it, why should she worry? What she didn't know was, if things went wrong, was McQueen going to take the fall himself?

"We better get back," McQueen said. "He might be looking for us."

"Okay."

As they stood up McQueen asked her, "Bailey, you sure you know what you're doing?"

"Actually, Dennis," she said, "no, I'm not."

When they returned to the office and walked in together, Lieutenant Bautista gave them a long look. He was standing next to McQueen's desk with file folders in his hands.

"Something I can help you with, Loo?" McQueen asked.

"I'm sending copies of the case files over to the Brooklyn D.A.'s office, Sergeant," Bautista said. "He would like to see you in his office at ten A.M."

"Okay, Loo," McQueen said. "I'll be there."

"How is Allan Hansen's statement coming?" Bautista asked. "I'd like to include it."

"Bailey was just going to go downstairs and check on that," McQueen said, "weren't you, Bailey?"

"Oh, uh, yeah, I was," she said. "I'll be right back."

"Bailey," McQueen said, before she could leave,

"why don't you take the files from the lieutenant and make copies for him while you're down there?"

"Sure."

She grabbed the files from Bautista, gave both men a look in turn, each meaning something different, and then left the office.

"Was there something you wanted to talk to me about, Sergeant?" Bautista asked.

McQueen decided not to let on he knew about Bautista and Sommers unless the man flat-out asked.

"No, sir," he said. "Nothing."

Bautista studied him for a moment before continuing. He didn't know if the man had come to any conclusions about him.

"The D.A. didn't sound very encouraging on the phone, but I think he'll change his mind when he sees the files."

"I hope so."

"If not," Bautista added, "maybe talking to you will give him the push he needs to file."

"I'll do my best."

"Yes, I'm sure you will. I'll wait in my office for Detective Sommers to bring back those files, and the statement. Send her in when she returns, will you?"

"Sure thing, boss."

The man hesitated long enough for McQueen to expect him to say something else, but then he turned and went into his office.

McQueen sat at his desk. He thought it odd that after talking with Sommers, and now seeing Bautista, he felt . . . dirty.

When had he turned into an old prude?

63

McQueen had both Diver and Dolan accompany Allan Hansen to Central Booking on Gold Street in downtown Brooklyn. Sommers delivered the file copies and Hansen's statement to Lieutenant Bautista, who called an outside messenger service to get it to the D.A.'s office quickly. After that was done he came out and bade them all good night. By that time the next shift was on, and Paddy Vadala was seated at his desk, across from his partner Tom Mollica.

"Looks like you're makin' progress, boss," he said to McQueen. "Maybe we'll get some people back on the charts sooner than we thought?"

"One day and you're complaining already?" McQueen asked.

"Don't listen to him, Sarge," Mollica said. "His wife's giving him a hard time, again."

Sommers came over to McQueen's desk and asked, "Anything else before I head out, Dennis?"

"No, Bailey, you can go."

"Good luck at the D.A.'s office in the morning."

"Thanks."

She hesitated, like she wanted to say something else, but then turned and left.

"I heard some talk down in the precinct," Vadala said to his partner.

"What's that?" the gray-haired Mollica asked around his ever-present pipe.

"Seems our lady detective might be makin' nice with the new boss. Maybe she's buckin' for a promotion."

"Knock off that kind of talk, Paddy," McQueen said.

"Hey, it's not me, boss," Vadala said, defensively. "It's goin' around downstairs."

"Well, don't pass it around up here if you don't have proof."

"Sorry," Vadala gave his partner a look, but Mollica just shook his head and lowered his eyes to his desk.

This was what McQueen had been afraid of, only he'd hoped he wouldn't hear it for a long time—or not at all. If the word was going around maybe somebody saw something, unless it was just all conjecture and rumor. Maybe somebody downstairs had made a pass at Sommers and she'd rejected him. There were enough cops who were jerks who would start that kind of rumor because their pride was hurt. Or somebody may have been trying to get at Bautista that way, like another lieutenant who had it in for him.

He had just about decided to go home when he changed his mind and made a phone call.

"Meet me for dinner," he said into the phone. "I've got some stuff to talk to you about."

"Where?" Mace Willis asked.

"I was surprised to get your call," Mace said as they were seated.

In the end he had given her the choice of places to meet, and she picked a restaurant in Greenpoint.

"Why out there?"

"I don't want to go too far from home. My son's got the flu. I want to be close by in case the sitter calls on my cell."

When he reached the restaurant she was already there, sitting in the front waiting for a table. She was dressed more casually than he'd seen her, and wearing a pair of wireless glasses that were almost invisible on her face. Still, they gave her a softer look.

While waiting they engaged in the weakest kind of small talk until he said, "I didn't know you had kids."

"One," she said. "Andy's six, and he's a big baby when he's sick, like most men."

"Aren't they all?"

"Do you have any kids?"

"Yes," he said, but didn't elaborate.

As soon as they sat down she said how surprised she was that he'd called.

"Why is that?"

"I don't know," she said, shrugging. "Except for the other day I hadn't heard from you in months."

"So why'd you agree to come?"

"I heard you collared a suspect," she said. "I figured that was what you wanted to talk to me about."

When the waiter came they each ordered a hamburger platter. Neither one wanted to spend too much time deciding.

"Did your source happen to give you the suspect's name?" he asked.

"No," she said. "I figured I'd get that from you."

"Okay," he said, after a moment, "the name Allan Hansen ring a bell?"

"Sure," she said, "amateur firebug, but a talented one. I've been tryin' to hang a couple of fires on him. He's who you have for the Lydia Studios fire?"

"We've got him for more than that," he said, and explained.

"Wow," she said. "I wouldn't have figured Hansen for murder."

"What about the fire?"

"Well, yeah," she said, "it could've been him. It's a little different from some of the other fires I've suspected him of, though."

"In what way?"

"The others were residential," she said, "and probably just malicious. This one would have been for pay. I mean, I'm not surprised if he's started to hire himself out. I am kinda disappointed with myself that I didn't look at him for this. How'd you get onto him, anyway?"

He told her the steps they'd taken in their investigation, and how Diver and Dolan had simply followed up some leads and found him sleeping on a girlfriend's couch.

"And then there's the mothballs."

"What?"

"My guys found the basement of his mother's house was filled with mothballs."

"Filled with them?"

"Well, three cartons. According to my detective, who spent some time working Arson years ago," he explained, "someone could make a device using that?"

"That's plenty. Do you think the Stephens case could be connected to the string of murders?"

308

"I'm thinkin' this is a helluva coincidence," he said, "and it makes me antsy."

"You think he's lying?"

"I don't know," he said. "He could just be trying to make a deal for himself to get out from under the murder charge."

"You'd trade for that?"

"Not me," he said, "but maybe the D.A. would. I'm gonna see him tomorrow morning."

"About making a deal?"

"That," he said, "but mostly about something else."

"What's Hansen lookin' to trade for?"

He told her what Hansen had told them about Lydia Dean. She looked stunned.

"I didn't see that coming. Do you believe him?"

"Again, I don't know, and again, it doesn't matter."

"The D.A."

"Right."

"Well," she said, frowning, "it would sure close out the fire for me and for your Arson Task Force—"

"—if they're even still lookin' at it," he said.

"—and it would close out the case on Victor Dean. You think the D.A. will file without a body?"

"Depends on how strong he thinks Hansen is as a source, and how much mileage he thinks he can get out of the Lydia Studios fire. She collected the insurance, so even if he can't get her for murder, he can get her for fraud."

"And what does all this mean for your case?"

"This is what's drivin' me batty," he said. "I thought you might have a fresh perspective."

"Why me?"

"I wanted to talk it over with someone outside my squad," he said. "You came to mind."

"I'm flattered," she said. "Go ahead."

"I'm convinced I've got a serial killer working, and that Thomas Wingate—Lydia's brother—was the first intended victim."

"Intended? Isn't he dead?"

"That's where this gets dicey," McQueen said. He went on to explain the theory he and Sommers had spitballed.

"So basically what you're saying is the killer took credit for Thomas Wingate, even though he didn't actually kill him. He just . . . removed him, put him on ice and then dumped him two weeks later."

"Right."

"And that was the first of—how many?"

"Three last winter, one so far this winter."

She shook her head.

"I've got good sources, McQueen, but I ain't heard a peep about this one."

"What about your parallel investigation?"

"Well, like I told you, I never once looked at Hansen for the Lydia Studios fire. I did, however, suspect the husband and wife of fraud. Obviously, I couldn't prove it, and she collected. I gotta tell you I like her for all this."

"Even the murder of her husband?"

"That's one cold bitch," Mace said. "Yeah, I think she probably did her old man."

"And left the body in the fire?"

"Not in that building," she said. "We didn't come up with a body, or the remnants of one."

"So, according to my own theory, we've got her hiring Hansen to set the fire. Then she goes in, kills her husband and pulls his body out of the building while her brother is overcome by the fire, dies of smoke inhalation, and is, in turn, removed from the building by my killer."

"That's what you're saying."

"And they never ran into each other."

"That's not what you're saying," she said. "Hansen says he saw Mrs. Dean."

"Right."

"What if Mrs. Dean saw something, too?"

64

McQueen arrived at the Brooklyn D.A.'s office at nine-fifty, but was kept waiting until exactly ten. The D.A., Edward Delaney, was a notoriously punctual man.

"Please, have a seat, Sergeant," Delaney said.

McQueen sat across from the man with a case file in his lap. He'd stopped by the office first and had gotten some good news, which he brought with him.

Ed Delaney was a good-looking district attorney on the rise. In fact, he reminded McQueen of Lieutenant Bautista. They both had the youth and the looks to go far. All they needed was the judgment. From what the veteran police detective knew of the young D.A., he didn't have it. Of course, what he did have he had in abundance, and that usually made up for whatever was lacking.

McQueen hated politics, and politicians. He hated how they interfered with him doing his job.

There were other men in the room, and Delaney made the introductions.

"Detective Sergeant Dennis McQueen, these are ADA's Kearney and Worth."

Kearney was another in the mold of Delaney, and was probably next in line for the D.A. job when Delaney ascended. Worth was white-haired, florid-faced, and looked to be several months from retirement. McQueen knew him from other cases over the years. The man had been in the D.A.'s office for a long time without any danger of ever moving into the top job. In that room, though, he was the voice of experience and he was—in McQueen's estimation—the man with the judgment.

"Sergeant McQueen and I have met before," Worth said.

"Oh," Delaney said, "well, maybe that will help here."

"Uh, we're waiting for one other person, Ed," Kearny reminded his boss.

Delaney looked around the room as if surprised and said, "So we are."

At that moment the office door opened and the D.A.'s secretary ushered Lieutenant Bautista into the room. It had been McQueen's understanding that he would be meeting with the D.A. Bautista's presence was a surprise.

"Sergeant," Bautista said, taking a seat away from McQueen.

"Sir."

It wasn't lost on McQueen that the seating arrangements in the room had left him quite on his own.

"Sergeant," the D.A. said, "it's been brought to my attention that you have been handling the case of— well, several cases, I guess, involving the same people.

313

The, uh, Dean family?" Delaney made a show of looking at his notes.

"It started as the Wingate case, sir," McQueen said. He explained about Thomas Wingate's murder, and how it had led to the arson case involving Lydia Designs and then to the disappearance and possible murder of Victor Dean.

"Right," Delaney said, "the Deans. Prominent people in the borough, I'm sure you know."

"No," McQueen said, "I wasn't aware of that."

"Contributors to the mayor's last campaign, I understand."

The Brooklyn D.A. was definitely not someone who had voted for the last mayor. If he could use any case to make the mayor look bad, he would. McQueen already had a bad feeling about where this was going.

"I knew they had a design business," he said, "but I didn't think they were influential."

"I suppose it's not your job to know those things, Sergeant," Delaney said, "but it is mine."

McQueen remained silent.

"So, tragedy has befallen this family on more than one occasion, it seems. Murder, arson . . . hmm," Delaney said, still looking at notes undoubtedly supplied to him by Lieutenant Bautista. "Yes, I see . . . after the arson the husband disappears, the fire is deemed suspicious, but nothing can be proved against the wife." He looked up abruptly at McQueen, met his eyes. "Looks like the insurance company paid off, even though the case was never closed."

"Looks like it."

"So, now you have evidence that Mrs. Dean killed her husband?" Delaney asked.

"No, sir," McQueen said, "we have a prisoner who says he saw Mrs. Dean kill her husband."

"An eyewitness," Delaney said. "That's very good."

"Not so good, I'm afraid," McQueen said. "The eyewitness is himself a confessed murderer."

"Confessed?"

"Yes, sir."

"And he made this confession under proper Miranda conditions, I hope?"

"Yes, sir," McQueen said, "he was advised of his rights and waived the right to counsel."

"Is that a fact?" Delaney asked. "And then he confessed?"

"Yes, sir."

"Why, I wonder?"

"I wondered the same thing myself," McQueen said, "but the fact remains we have a confession."

"But, as I understand it," Delaney said, "we also have the offer of a deal?"

"Allan Hansen, the man we have for killing a woman and her four-year-old daughter, claims he was in the Lydia Studios building on the day of the fire."

"And what does he say he was doing there?"

"Setting the fire."

"Wait a minute," the white-haired Dan Worth said. "This guy confessed to arson and murder?"

"Yes, sir."

"Go ahead, please," the D.A. said, tossing Worth a dirty look.

"Well, he claims he saw Lydia Dean kill her husband by hitting him on the head with . . . something. A bat, a club, some blunt object."

"How does he know the man was dead?"

315

McQueen opened his file and refreshed his memory from the printed version of Allan Hansen's confession.

"He says she hit her husband at least ten times. 'There was blood everywhere,' he says."

"And was blood found at the scene?" Delaney asked.

"The scene was a burnt-out husk," McQueen said. "No blood could be detected."

"What about a body?"

"There were no remnants of a body found."

"Anything in the ashes?" ADA Kearny asked.

"Both the fire department and our Arson Task Force—that is, our crime lab—sifted the ashes. They found nothing."

"But that doesn't necessarily mean the body wasn't there," Kearney said. "Right? It could have been completely burned."

"It's possible that the respective labs could simply have not been able to find any trace, yes," McQueen said.

"Or," Delaney said, "it could be that she removed the body from the scene and disposed of it."

"Yes, sir."

"Now," Delaney said, "you are investigating other murders that you think are connected to this case, is that correct?"

"Yes, sir," McQueen said, "connected to the murder of Thomas Wingate."

"Are you prepared to present me with any evidence in those cases?" Delaney asked.

"No, sir, not today."

"Then the question before us is this," he said, wrapping things up. "Do we want to make a deal with one killer to catch another?"

When no one responded McQueen said, "I suppose that's where you are, sir, yes."

"All right, then," the D.A. said. "Sergeant, if you'll step out of the room, we'll discuss the matter and call you back in when we've made a decision."

65

The Observer thought he needed another name. Here he was, transporting the fifth victim. He'd done his job in the beginning, finding this victim, staking him out. The Killer had done his job killing him, and the Ice Man had done his job keeping the body on ice. Now it was time for the body to be found, and here he was again, only this time not observing, but transporting.

The Transporter. Yeah, that's what he should be now, not the Observer.

Okay, he thought, driving the van with the body in the back, now I'm the Transporter.

He liked that better. He didn't feel out of place, or out of control. Everything was as it should be again.

Briefly, he had thought about dumping this one somewhere in Manhattan or Queens, but no, this was a Brooklyn thing. As a serial killer he was going to put not only himself on the map but Brooklyn as well. And one was almost as important as the other.

When he came within sight of the Brooklyn Bridge

he started to get excited—and as he got excited he started to think about victim number six. He'd already picked her out, and he knew the Killer was growing impatient to take her. The Ice Man, too, liked when he had them on a hook in the back. He often went back there, brought a stool with him, and sat and talked to them. They were almost like his friends, and as soon as one friend left, he grew impatient for more company.

But right now he had to concentrate on victim number five. He was going to dump this one so that it was found sooner. He was impatient for this one to hit the newspapers. He wondered when the tabloids would catch on, when they'd first start talking about him as a serial killer. What he didn't want to have to do was call them himself. That had been done before. He wanted them to catch on by themselves, with no help from him.

He wondered who the police detectives were who were investigating this. They must have caught on by now that he was a serial. Three victims last winter, now two this winter. He knew he was smarter than they were, but for Chrissake, if they never caught on where would the fun be in that? He wanted it to come out in the open so he could discover who his adversary was.

Or was he overestimating them? Were the cops in New York that stupid? That dense? The men and women who policed the greatest city in the world?

It couldn't be. At least, he hoped not. Without a worthy opponent, this would all go to waste.

And he hated waste.

66

McQueen thought he'd made a mistake.

He'd made a lot of them in his life, but he thought that, like most mistakes, they went unnoticed, unidentified. This time he felt like he'd made a mistake, but he couldn't put his finger on it.

Maybe he should have let all of this lie. Who else cared as much as he did? Bailey Sommers? She was just looking to make her mark, looking to work her first serial killer case.

What about Mace Willis? She was just working one case, the Dean arson. What did she care about the other victims?

Not the other guys in the squad. Not the Double Ds, or Sherman and Silver. They were just working for their paycheck—and there was nothing wrong with that. They—like McQueen—considered this a job, not a career. It was only a career to men like Bautista and Delaney, men who were on the way up and didn't want to stop until they got to the top.

McQueen also considered it a job, as he had told

Bautista, but it was a job he enjoyed doing, one he often took home with him at the end of the day.

The only part of the job men like Bautista took home with them was the political part. Parties, fundraisers, dinners at the homes of men who could do them some good.

Right now Delaney and Bautista and the others were trying to decide what their most expedient political move would be. If they chose to issue a warrant for Lydia Dean's arrest, it would be McQueen's job to pick her up. If they decided there wasn't enough evidence, it would be up to him to keep looking for more. Once Allan Hansen told him that Lydia had killed her husband, that became his case, as well. So he was charged with finding out who killed the four people with the scratches on their backs—and any future victims—as well as determining whether or not Lydia Dean actually had killed her husband. And as far as Kathy Stephens and her daughter Miranda was concerned, Allan Hansen's confession would put him away for those murders.

What McQueen needed to decide was, did he believe Hansen? If he decided he did not, then he was giving himself still more to do. If Hansen didn't kill them, why confess? But no, he had the proof in his hands that Hansen had done it, so that was not in question. What was in question was what Hansen said he saw at Lydia Designs.

He was still mulling over his next moves when the intercom on the secretary's desk buzzed.

"You can go in, Sergeant."

"Thank you."

He opened the door and entered. All four men were exactly where they had been when he left.

"Have a seat, Sergeant," Delaney said.

He sat back down where he had been before.

"All right," Delaney said, "I'm issuing a warrant for the arrest of Lydia Dean. Suspicion of arson, fraud, and murder. It'll be up to you and your squad to bring her in."

"Yes, sir. What about Allan Hansen?"

"What about him?"

"Will you be cutting a deal with him?"

"That depends on what we find out about Mrs. Dean when we bring her in," Delaney said. "If I'm convinced we have a case against her with his testimony then it's very likely I will."

"But . . . he killed a mother and her little girl."

"He won't walk, Sergeant," Delaney said. "I guarantee that. He'll just serve a lighter sentence."

"For murder?"

"Manslaughter two, probably," Kearny said.

"And with good behavior he'll be out in eight," McQueen complained.

"Come on, Sergeant," Delaney said, "do we even know that he did it?"

"He confessed."

"Still—"

"And I have the proof here that he did it," McQueen said, holding up the file on Kathy and Miranda Stephens.

"What proof?" Worth asked, with interest.

"The lab has matched the shoe print of Allan Hansen's shoes with a clear footprint on Miranda Stephens's side," McQueen said.

All the men fell silent for a moment, and then Delaney said, "That wouldn't be the killing blow, though."

"Well . . . no. The killing blow was the kick to her head."

"And was there an identifiable footprint there?" the D.A. asked.

McQueen hesitated, then said, "No."

"Well—"

"But he still confessed."

"A confession he could recant at any time," Delaney said, "if we don't cut a deal."

"But . . . if she killed her husband he was a grown man," McQueen said, "This maniac killed a child and her mother."

"A good defense attorney could argue involuntary manslaughter," Kearny said. "He could walk."

"What?" McQueen asked, not believing what he was hearing.

"That's enough, Sergeant," Bautista said, speaking for the first time. "Either have your men pick up Mrs. Dean, or do it yourself. But get it done . . . today."

"But—"

"There is no need of any further input from you into this matter," the lieutenant said. "You're dismissed."

McQueen sat still for a moment, trying to decide whether to argue or not. In truth, though, he wanted to talk with Lydia Dean. What these clowns decided to do could always be overturned later, depending on what he found out.

"Yes, sir," he said, standing up, thinking, *we'll see what gets recanted later on.*

67

"How did it go?" Sommers asked as soon as McQueen entered the squad room.

"Let's go," he said. "We're picking up Lydia Dean."

"We?'

"You, me," he said, then waved across the room at the Double Ds, "them. Let's move, boys."

Both detectives got to their feet, grabbing their jackets from the backs of their chairs.

"Separate cars," McQueen said as they all went out the door.

"Uniforms?" Sommers asked.

"We don't need any."

They took the stairs instead of waiting for the elevator.

"So, what happened?" Sommers asked again, as they went down.

"I'll tell you in the car."

* * *

COLD BLOODED

"So they're going to cut him a deal?" Sommers asked, in disbelief.

"Looks like it."

"To walk?"

"They say no," he replied.

"And you don't believe them?"

"Actually," he said, "they can't just let him walk. That would look too bad. They'll work something out, though."

"Providing he's telling the truth about Lydia Dean, though," she pointed out.

"Exactly."

"And do you think he is?"

"That's what we're gonna find out."

Because of the fire, and because the fire marshal's office was still working on the arson, McQueen had agreed the night before to call Mace Willis if he was, indeed, to go to Lydia Dean's house and arrest her.

When they got out of their cars in front of the Dean house McQueen introduced Fire Marshal Willis to his detectives. They all stood there wrapped in their coats and scarves, their cold breath mingling.

"How long have you been here?" McQueen asked.

"Just a few minutes. I think she's inside."

McQueen turned to Diver and Dolan and said, "You boys take the back in case she tries to run. I don't think she'll be armed, but you never know."

As the Double Ds made their way to the back of the house McQueen, Sommers and Willis walked to the front door.

"You armed?" he asked Willis.

"Yeah."

"Don't draw your weapon unless I do."

"Okay."

325

He could see that Bailey Sommers was puzzled about the presence of Mace Willis, but he didn't have time to explain.

When they reached the door he waited a few minutes until he was sure the Ds were in position, and then he rang the bell.

When Lydia Dean opened the door she glanced at them coldly, then looked directly at McQueen.

"Dennis," she said, "can't you take a hint?"

"Lydia—"

"I keep inviting you to visit me," she went on, "and you keep showing up with other women. This time, two?"

"This is Detective Sommers," McQueen said. "You know Marshal Willis."

"And why are we all here?" she asked.

"Detective Sommers?" McQueen said. He told Sommers in the car that he was giving her the collar.

"Lydia Dean," Sommers said, taking out her handcuffs, "I'm placing you under arrest."

"On what charges?" Lydia asked.

"Conspiracy to commit arson, fraud, and murder," Sommers said, "Turn around, please."

Lydia obeyed, without argument, which surprised McQueen.

"You have the right to remain silent . . ." Sommers began, reading Lydia her rights while she applied the bracelets.

When she turned the woman back around Lydia looked at Mace Willis.

"I'll bet this gives you a lot of satisfaction," she said.

"I've suspected for a long time that you and your husband started that fire, Mrs. Dean."

"But you couldn't prove it."

"No, I couldn't."

Lydia looked at McQueen.

"And you think you can?" she asked. "You think you can prove I killed my own brother?"

"You're not under arrest for the murder of your brother, Lydia," McQueen told her.

For the first time since he'd met her, Lydia Dean looked totally confused.

"Then . . . for what?"

"You're under arrest for the suspected murder of your husband, Victor Dean."

"Victor—that's crazy. You can't prove that!"

"Maybe I can't," McQueen said. "But I have an eyewitness who says he can."

68

When Mrs. O'Brien entered the butcher shop on Sackett Street, Owen watched her approach the counter and was struck at once with an urge, and an idea.

"Owen," she said, "some of that wonderful veal again, please?" the old woman asked.

Owned looked around the shop. As Mrs. O'Brien had entered, another customer had left, and now he was alone with the old woman. This woman, who knew his father and constantly compared the two of them, would have nothing whatsoever in common with the other five victims. It made her the perfect sixth victim, but it was too soon.

"And exactly how fresh would you like it, Mrs. O'Brien?" he asked her.

"As fresh as your father would have given it to me, Owen," she replied. "He was a wonderful man, you know. Everybody in the neighborhood loved him."

Yeah, Owen thought, especially the women. More than once he'd caught his father in the back room with one of the neighborhood wives. He'd grin at the little boy and say, "Full service, Owen. Don't ever forget to give the customers full service."

Even now Owen wondered how his father knew that he'd never tell his mother what he saw.

Then his father bought that big freezer for the back room. On sale, he said. Having the huge freezer would enable them to keep much more fresh meat on hand.

It also gave his father some place else to take the ladies.

"It was a shame how he and Mrs. Levinson got locked in the freezer that time," Mrs. O'Brien said. "It was you who found them, wasn't it, Owen?"

"Yes, ma'am. It was."

"Terrible accident, wasn't it?"

"Accident," Owen said. "Yes, ma'am, that's what it was."

"No one ever did figure out what Sadie Levinson was doing in there with him, did they?"

Didn't they? Owen thought.

He looked at the shriveled-up face of Mrs. O'Brien and wondered how many times she'd been in the back room with his father.

"What about that veal, Owen?" she asked.

"Mrs. O'Brien," he said, "I think you should come back to the freezer with me."

69

"I want to make a deal," Lydia Dean said.

McQueen looked over at Sommers, who stared back at him, shaking her head.

Behind the two-way glass were Lieutenant Bautista, D.A. Delaney, and ADA's Kearny and Worth. Bautista had been livid when McQueen brought Lydia Dean in with Bailey Sommers . . . and Fire Marshal Mason Willis.

"What the hell is she doing here?" he demanded.

"She's been workin' this case for almost a year," McQueen said. "I thought she deserved to be in on the end."

Bautista got real close to McQueen and said, "I did not wish to share this with anyone."

"I know," McQueen said. "And that probably includes me, but then, here we all are."

The arrival of the D.A. had driven the two men apart, and McQueen had gone into the interrogation room with Lydia Dean, where Sommers had been talking to her. Off in another corner of the room Mace

COLD BLOODED

Willis just watched. She fully expected to be put out at any moment, and she considered every moment she was allowed to stay as gravy.

"What kind of a deal, Mrs. Dean?" Sommers asked. "We have an eyewitness who saw you bludgeon your husband to death. Do you think you can deal your way out of that?"

"I know who your eyewitness is," she said. "An arsonist."

"He's an arsonist, all right," Sommers said. "And a murderer."

"He didn't kill my brother."

"We know that, Mrs. Dean," Sommers said. "He's not being charged with the murder of your brother. His charges stem from an entirely different case."

"Then why is he—"

"He's giving you up to save his skin," Sommers said.

"I can give him up," Lydia said. "Victor paid him to burn the building down."

"Victor did it."

"Yes," she said. "I knew nothing about it."

"That's not what he says."

"You've just said he's an arsonist and a murderer," Lydia Dean said. "How hard is it to believe he's a liar, as well?"

"Mrs. Dean," Sommers said. "You and your husband hired Allan Hansen to burn down your business, and then you killed your husband so you wouldn't have to share the insurance money with him. We've got you. All you have to do to make things easy on yourself is confess."

And it was at that point that Lydia Dean said, "I want to make a deal."

70

In the end Owen killed Mrs. O'Brien because the urge was too great. It had become the Urge. He knew it was too early, but he also knew that she lived alone and had no family. It would take even longer for her to be missed than the others.

He wasn't quite sure how he was going to do it, and then it came to him. She should die someplace truly cold, the same place his father and his whore, Sadie Levinson, had died—and the same way.

"Owen," she said, as he opened the freezer, "why would I want to go in the—"

"Just go in, Mrs. O'Brien," he told her, "just go in," and shoved her. She staggered forward and, because of her age and frail legs, fell to her knees. She cried out, but the sound was cut off when he slammed the freezer door on her. He looked through the rectangular window in the steel door, thinking he'd enjoy watching her freeze to death. He had just decided to go to the front of the store and turn the OPEN sign to

CLOSED when suddenly the old woman, still on her knees, clutched at her chest . . . and died!

"Nooooo!" he wailed. Not a heart attack! Where the hell was the fun in that?

He opened the freezer door, rushed inside, turned the old biddy over and started CPR, but it was no good. The old cunt was gone. He stood up and kicked her in the side. He was angry—angrier than when he found out his first victim had already died from smoke inhalation by the time he reached him. Luckily he was not the type to panic. He went ahead with his plans for Thomas Wingate, even though he hadn't actually gotten to kill him personally.

And he was going to have to do the same thing now, with Mrs. O'Brien. Just put her on a hook and let her hang there for a while, until it was time to get rid of her. Of course, he was going to have to keep her longer, because he'd only just gotten rid of number five. He didn't want the police to think his activity was escalating. That was too much of a serial killer cliché.

But even as he stripped off her dress so he could lift her and hang her on a hook by her bra—scratching her back in the process—he was feeling very unsatisfied by this kill. His hands were shaking when he left the freezer and closed the door behind him. He realized he might need to go out and get another one. As long as they were on hooks and being kept fresh, why did it matter when he killed them?

He heard the bell ring on his front door, indicating a customer had come in. With one last look at poor Mrs. O'Brien, still swaying a bit to and fro on her hook, he wiped his hands on his apron and went to wait on his customer.

71

McQueen, Sommers and Willis stared at Lydia Dean. Her lawyer had arrived, and was seated next to her.

"I don't appreciate having my client questioned before my arrival," he'd complained.

"Don't worry, Walter," Lydia told him. "I didn't say anything incriminating."

"The hell she didn't," Sommers said. "She said she wants to make a deal."

Walter Gibson, attorney-at-law, glared at his client.

"What?"

"Walter—"

"I need to confer with my client," Gibson said. "Do you officers mind?"

"No," McQueen said, "not at all. Ladies?"

Sommers and Willis preceded McQueen out of the interrogation room and into the hall.

"Sergeant," Gibson said.

"Counselor?"

"You may have blown this one."

"You sayin' there's something to blow, counselor?"

Gibson turned away. McQueen left the room and pulled the door closed behind him. No sooner had it snapped shut than another door opened and D.A. Edward Delaney came storming out, Bautista right behind him. McQueen was willing to bet that the two men had gone to the same college.

"What does she have to deal with?" Delaney asked.

"We didn't get a chance to ask her, did we?" McQueen replied.

"Her lawyer's going to make her dummy up," Sommers said. "He'll never let her talk, now."

"She asked for a deal," Delaney said. "That's as good as a confession."

"In what state?" McQueen asked.

"Sergeant—" Bautista said, warningly.

"Look," McQueen said, "this lady's got a mind of her own. If she wants to deal, she'll deal. Believe me, she's telling her lawyer how it's gonna go down, not the other way around."

At that moment there was a knock on the door of the interrogation room. Delaney and Bautista went back into the adjoining room to observe. McQueen opened the door.

"My client wants to talk to you," Gibson said.

"Fine," McQueen said. He stepped aside to allow Sommers and Willis to precede him, but Gibson blocked their path. "Just you, Sergeant. No other detectives. No fire marshal. No two-way glass."

"What's on her mind, counselor?"

"Like she said," Gibson replied, "she wants to make a deal." The man didn't look happy, at all.

"All right," McQueen said. "Go on in. I'll be right there."

As Gibson went back into the room and the door slammed shut Sommers said, "Dennis—"

"She's gonna deal, Bailey."

"Yeah, but for what?"

"That's what I'm gonna find out."

When McQueen entered the room the lawyer, Gibson, stood up.

"Just for the record," he said, "I'm against this."

He gave McQueen a look, and left the room.

"Sit down, Dennis," Lydia invited.

He sat across from her.

"Alone at last," she said, "that is, if I take your word there's no one on the other side of that glass."

"You've got my word, Lydia."

It had taken some doing. Delaney had wanted to remain, telling McQueen just to lie to her.

"Not a chance," McQueen had said. "This has to be on the up-and-up . . . sir."

"Okay if I turn on the tape recorder now?" he asked her.

"Not yet," she said. "I want to talk."

"About what?"

"I'm not sure what my best option is here, Dennis," she said. "I thought you might help me figure it out."

"Isn't that what you pay your attorney good money for?"

"This is all . . . very convoluted, Dennis."

"Are we gonna talk deal?"

"Are you authorized?"

"What do you think, Lydia?" he asked. "I'm a sergeant of detectives. I'm not high on the food chain, here. We've got a D.A. out in the hall, chompin' at the bit because he's got an eyewitness that has you killing your husband. He wants to make headlines with you. And my lieutenant is out there, ready to take the credit if all of this goes right."

"Well," she said, "your D.A. can have his headlines, and your lieutenant can have his credit, but it won't be at my expense."

"The D.A.'s ready to file, Lydia," McQueen said. "My advice is to cop a plea."

"I'll admit to the arson," she said. "Walter and I hired Allan Hansen to burn the business so we could collect the insurance."

"This has to be on tape, Lydia."

"Wait," she said, putting her hand out to stop him. "I don't want to go to prison."

"Then you better have a heckuva lot to deal with."

"I do," she said, withdrawing her hand.

He waited, and when nothing was forthcoming asked, "Well, what is it, Lydia? What've you got for me?"

"Your serial killer," she said. "I can give you your serial killer."

72

He sat with his back to the freezer door, the steel cold against his back. How had it gotten out of hand so fast? When he reached inside for that cool, calm, collected person who was always there for him, there was nothing.

Where was the Ice Man?

Where was the Killer?

Was he alone now?

He stood up and looked through the small window at the bodies hanging on the hooks—and then the bell above the front door rang as someone entered.

He'd forgotten to turn the sign to CLOSED.

Again!

"Hello?" a man's voice called out. "Is anyone here? Some service, please?"

The impatience in the voice did something to calm him. His father always sounded impatient with him, all through his childhood, his teen years, up until *that* day.

This time, he thought, as he headed for the front of the butcher shop, this time he had to remember to turn the sign on the door.

73

McQueen stared at the tape reels going around as Lydia Dean told her story. Ed Delaney and Lieutenant Bautista were also in the room. The rest—Sommers, Willis, the ADA's Kearney and Worth—were in the adjoining room, watching through the two-way mirror. Also in the room, next to Lydia Dean and not looking happy, was her attorney.

"It's true Victor and I hired Allan Hansen to burn our business. We needed the insurance money. But at the last minute I got cold feet. I drove to our building to stop it, but by the time I got there it was in flames."

"Had the fire department responded?" Delaney asked.

"Not yet," she said. "But I knew that both Victor and Thomas were in there."

"You knew your brother was in there and you still had Hansen set the place on fire?" the D.A. asked.

"Victor was supposed to get Thomas out."

"And he didn't?"

"No."

"Why not?"

"I don't know," she said. "I don't know what happened to Victor. I—I always assumed he died in the fire."

"All right," Delaney said. "Go ahead, Mrs. Dean."

"I was worried about both my brother and my husband, so I ran into the building."

"You ran into a burning building?" Delaney asked.

"That's right," she replied. "Is that so hard to believe?"

"Just continue, Mrs. Dean."

"The smoke was thick and I couldn't find my husband. I kept looking and looking and finally, when I got to the third floor, I saw them."

"Saw who?"

"My brother and . . . and his killer."

"You actually saw your brother's killer."

"Yes."

"What did you do?"

"Nothing," she said.

"Why not?"

"I was frightened," she said. "I thought if he saw me he'd kill me, too."

"What about Hansen, Mrs. Dean?" McQueen interjected. "Did you see him in the building, at all?"

"Briefly," she said. "Just long enough to know he was definitely there."

Just long enough to put a nail in his coffin, McQueen thought. The story was utter bullshit. He and Lydia Dean both knew it, but the D.A. allowed her to continue.

"I'll have to tell it my way," she'd told him.

"Your way meaning copping to hiring an arsonist, but not admitting you killed your husband."

"How many times do I have to tell you I didn't kill my husband?" she'd demanded.

"Too many times, I think," he said, but he'd then let the D.A. into the room.

"Mrs. Dean," Delaney said now. "Who killed your brother?"

"My client wants immunity on the arson charge, and the conspiracy charge."

"Conspiracy to commit murder?" McQueen asked.

"Arson," Gibson said, impatiently, "conspiracy to commit arson."

"So she's not admitting she killed her husband?" Delaney asked Walter Gibson."

"Not at all," the man said.

"But I know who your serial killer is," Lydia said. "Don't you want to catch him?"

Delaney looked at McQueen, and then at Lydia Dean.

"Did Sergeant McQueen tell you that we have a serial killer at work in New York, Mrs. Dean?"

"No, of course not," she said. "But he did show me a photo of a man he said was likely killed by the same man who killed my brother. I read between the lines, Mr. Delaney. You have a serial killer at work, and you want to stop him. I can help you."

"And in return you want immunity."

"Yes . . . but there's more."

"What?"

"I don't want to have to fear Allan Hansen for the rest of my life," she said. "I want him behind bars."

Delaney sat back in his chair and looked as if he were actually considering the request.

"All right," he said, finally.

"What?" McQueen said. "You have an eyewitness that she killed her husband."

"And she can give you your serial killer, Sergeant," Delaney said. "Which do you think is more important?"

"But she killed her husband," McQueen argued. "You were going to let a child killer go free to nail her. Now you're willing to let her go to get someone else. Where does it end?"

"Hopefully," Delaney said, "with you and your people putting handcuffs on a serial killer, Sergeant."

He turned to look at Lydia Dean.

"Mrs. Dean, who killed your brother, Thomas?"

"His name is Owen Feinstein."

"And how do you know this man?"

"He's my butcher."

74

The sign on the front door said CLOSED.

"Jimmy, Artie," McQueen said.

"Yeah, we know," Diver said. "The back."

McQueen turned and looked at Sommers and Willis. The fire marshal's chief had spoken with the chief of detectives and, after threatening to go over his head to the commissioner, it was decided that the FDNY and Marshal Mason Willis would be part of the arresting team—even though her connection to the case was "tenuous, at best."

They also had two uniformed teams from the local precinct.

"Secure the block," McQueen told them.

Sommers was looking at the card taped to the door with the store's hours on it. It was supposed to be open until eight P.M. but here it was almost four and it was closed.

"Should be open," she said.

"I can read," Willis said.

The two women exchanged a hard look. They did

not like each other. McQueen didn't know if that was just NYPD/FDNY rivalry, or something else.

Silver and Sherman were with them, also, since they were part of the team. The odd man out of the whole scenario was Tolliver, which McQueen admitted to himself wasn't quite fair. But he was the last man into the squad, and McQueen really couldn't afford to give him any more thought.

"Okay, guys," McQueen said to Sherman and Silver, "let's get this door open."

Before either of them could move, though, Mace Willis slammed her shoulder into the part of the door nearest the doorjamb and it popped open, the bell above the door jingling.

"Looked like a flimsy lock," she said with a shrug, as the others stared at her.

McQueen produced his gun and led the way in. The others drew their weapons and followed.

The inside looked like an old-fashioned butcher shop. The bare wood floors and sawdust brought McQueen right back to his childhood. Glass cases filled with various cuts of meat, and a gleaming slicer on top of the cases completed the picture. All along the glass cases and on the wall behind were taped sale prices for different meats.

"Wow," Sherman said, "this takes me back."

"Yeah."

"It was owned by Abraham Feinstein for years," Sommers said, reading from a computer printout she had gotten that morning, "but has been run by his son, Owen, for the past twenty years."

"Twenty years in the old man's business," Silver said, shaking his head.

"What kind of name is Owen for a Jew?" Sherman wondered.

No one commented.

Abruptly, the bell above the door jangled as some-one tried to enter.

"Jack," McQueen said.

Sherman went to intercept the potential customer, who complained that he needed his round chuck. Ushering the man out with the suggestion that he go and buy some good fish—"Tuna almost tastes like steak"—he locked the door.

"If he's here," Sommers said, "he already knows we're here."

"If he tries to get out the back the Double Ds'll get him," Silver said.

There didn't seem to be anywhere in the front of the store for a man to hide. They went around behind the meat display cases, found some storage places beneath them. Silver and Sherman opened them while they all stood by with their weapons ready.

"Okay, then," McQueen said, when they didn't discover a murderer hiding under there, "let's go in the back. My guess is we'll find a freezer back there."

He could have sent Sherman and Silver ahead of him, but that wasn't his way. He led the way into the back, followed by the two men, with the two woman bringing up the rear.

"Look at that," Silver said, pointing to the large walk-in freezer. "Somebody bought that baby second-hand—maybe even third."

"Jesus," McQueen said. "That thing'd never been on your list, Bailey."

"Yeah, that list turned out to be a bust."

"I know, I know," he said. "It was my idea."

"Hey, Sarge," Sherman said, "you're the boss, all the ideas are yours."

"Yeah, right."

At that moment Sommers's cell phone rang. Mc-Queen was annoyed that she hadn't turned it off. Between the bell over the door and her cell, their suspect definitely knew they were there—if he, indeed, was there at all.

"Got it," she said. "I'll tell him." She broke the connection and tucked the cell back into her purse.

"What is it?" he asked.

"Vadala and Mollica got called out on a body," she said. "Looks like our guy's fifth victim popped up down by the Brooklyn docks."

"Damn!" McQueen said.

Silver was over by the freezer, looking through the small rectangular window in the door.

"Sarge, you better look at this."

"Fan out," he told the others, "see what you can find," and went to join Silver. "What's up?"

"Take a look."

McQueen looked through the window and saw three bodies hanging from hooks. One was an elderly woman hanging by her bra. The other two were men, hooked behind their pants. McQueen was sure if he looked they'd all have scratches on their backs.

"Jesus," Silver said, "he's got them backed up."

"But why?" McQueen asked. He looked through the window again. "They don't look like they've been in there very long." He frowned. "Could he have lost it today, started killing customers? If he just got rid of the fifth recently, why start killing again?"

"He's escalating," Sommers said from across the room. "It's textbook."

"There's been nothing textbook about this guy, so far," McQueen said.

McQueen put his hand on the door handle and pulled. The door opened cleanly. They stood that way quietly for a few moments, and then there was a thump from above them.

"Bailey?"

"Yep?"

"You got a home address on this guy?"

"No," she said, "just this place."

They all looked up at the ceiling as there was a scrape.

"Maybe he lives upstairs," Sherman said, saying what they were all thinking.

"Bailey, you and Willis check the bodies in the freezer. Maybe they're alive."

"What are you gonna do?" Willis asked.

"The boys and I are going upstairs, soon as we find a door or a stairway."

"Found it!" Sherman chimed in.

McQueen and Silver went to join him while the women entered the freezer together.

Sherman was standing by an open door. When McQueen looked inside he saw a stairway leading up.

"Close quarters," Silver said.

"Yeah."

There was only room for them to go up the stairs one at a time, and at that McQueen was large enough that his shoulders might brush the walls. There was a crack of light at the top, but there didn't seem to be a door.

"Sarge?" Silver said. "Want us to go first?"

"Nope," McQueen said. "Follow me."

He started up.

"What do you think?" Willis asked.

Sommers inspected the bodies closely, touched one of the men.

"They're dead," she said. "I don't know how, but they are."

Willis went around behind the bodies. She saw the deep scratch on the woman's back between her shoulder blades.

"This guy's a sicko," she said.

"Tell me about it."

"Shouldn't we take them down?" she asked.

"No," Sommers said. "Not until the M.E. gets here. I better make the call."

She tried her cell, but there was no signal inside the freezer.

"I'll have to step outside."

Momentarily alone with the three stiffs Willis shivered; she started to follow Bailey out. She stopped short, though, when she noticed something. There were three bodies on hooks, two other empty hooks, and then there was a chain hanging down, but no hook.

"Hey, Detective . . ."

McQueen held his gun ready as he went slowly up the stairs. He was aware of Sherman and Silver following close behind him. As they ascended his eyes got used to the gloom. He saw that there was, indeed, no door at the top, just a landing. He didn't like the close confines of the stairway, there was no room to maneuver. Also it was hot and he was sweating inside his heavy coat.

The stairs creaked beneath their feet, and he abruptly wondered if the thing would hold them, or collapse beneath their collective weight.

As he neared the top stairs he thought anything could be waiting for them at the top. It was only that attitude that saved him, because at that moment someone stepped out and swung something at him.

"Jesus—" he shouted. He tried to duck, and while he succeeded he lost his balance and fell forward, onto the landing.

Meanwhile Silver, unprepared, wasn't as lucky. A metal hook struck him in the face and he fell backward, his full weight landing on his partner. Together, they tumbled down the stairs.

Owen Feinstein, feeling swollen with power, turned to address the fallen McQueen. He raised the heavy meat hook that he'd removed from the freezer, felt his thin arms surge with strength.

McQueen was stuck, his bulk working against him in the confined space. He tried to bring his gun around but slammed his hand into the wall. He looked back over his shoulder and his eyes widened as he saw the sharp point of the meat hook coming down at him.

Then the stairway filled with the sound of shots. Owen staggered, frowned, dropped the hook and fell on top of McQueen . . .

At the bottom of the stairs both Sommers and Willis were looking up over their extended guns.

"Sarge?" Sommers called. "Are you all right?"

At their feet Silver and Sherman both moaned, and Willis leaned over to check them.

"Dennis?"

It was dark near the top of the stairs, but Sommers thought she saw someone moving.

"Damn it—" she said, but she was cut off by McQueen's voice from above.

"I'm okay, Bailey," he said, "but you better call for an ambulance. This guy's hit twice and I don't want to lose him."

EPILOGUE

McQueen's left arm was in a sling. The dropped
meat hook had taken a chunk out, but there was no
broken bone.

Silver and Sherman had both been treated. Silver
had been hit in the head with the hook. A gash had
been torn and it had bled like a stuck pig, but the
wound wasn't bad. The doctors were keeping him
overnight for observation. Sherman had gone home,
suffering from a sprained shoulder. Within the confines of that staircase they had slowed each other's
progress down the stairs, effectively saving each
other from more serious harm.

The D.A., Delaney, and Lieutenant Bautista were
down the hall, conferring with each other and with
Delaney's ADAs, Kearney and Worth. They already
had a psychologist in with Owen Feinstein, who was
still alive after major surgery to remove the two bul-
lets, one from Sommers's gun and one from Willis's.

Sommers was down the hall with Bautista. Willis
was seated with McQueen.

"She's sleeping with him, ain't she?" Willis asked. "The Latino dreamboat?"

"Yeah."

"You care?"

"Yeah," he said, "but not the way you think. By the way, thanks. You and Bailey saved my life."

She shrugged.

"We heard the commotion and came runnin'."

"It was dark at the top of those stairs," he said. "How'd you know who you were shootin' at?"

"We didn't."

McQueen looked at her.

She grinned.

"We took a shot."

"Yeah," he said, "one each. It worked."

They both looked up as Bailey Sommers came walking over to where they were sitting.

"How is he?" McQueen asked.

"He might make it," she said. "At least, the head doctor hopes he does. He says he's a fascinating subject."

"In what way?"

"He refers to himself by four different names," she said. She took out her notebook. "The Observer, the Ice Man, the Transporter, and the Killer."

"Split personality?" Willis asked.

"That's just it," she answered. "The doctor says no. He's only going by one given name, Owen Feinstein. The other . . . titles are how he referred to himself when he was doing a certain job. The Killer when he was killing, the Ice Man when he was putting them up on hooks, and so on."

"Sick man, either way," McQueen said, "split personality or not."

"Yeah."

"I don't mean insane sick," he went on, "but that's what they'll say. He'll be in a hospital for a long time, instead of jail."

"That sucks," Willis said. "They know why he was killing?"

"No, not exactly," she said. "The doctor says he'll have to study him. He said something about waiting the nine months between victim three and four pushing him over the edge. Apparently, you can't put off an urge for that long. He flipped out today and started killing more people, one after the other."

"Well," McQueen said to Willis, "you got your firebug."

"You got your husband killers, and your serial killer," Willis said. "Is everybody happy?"

"Dennis," Sommers said, "can I talk to you?"

Willis said, "I gotta go check in. I'll call you."

"Okay, Mace."

"Detective," she said to Sommers.

"Marshal."

"Nice shooting."

"You, too," Sommers said.

Willis went off down the hall and Sommers sat next to McQueen.

"How's your arm?"

"It hurts."

She looked off in the direction of Willis.

"You like her?"

"Yeah," he said, "but not the way you think."

She fell silent.

"You wanted to tell me something?"

"Yeah," she said. "I'm done with Ernesto."

"Good for you," he said. "Not because of me."

"Maybe a little," she said. "He turned out to be an asshole. He and the D.A. are gonna spin this so that they come out looking like supercop and super D.A. Not only a serial killer, but a child killer, a husband killer, an arsonist . . ."

"Forget it, Bailey."

"It was you, Dennis," she said. "All you."

"It wasn't, Bailey."

"What do you mean?"

"They can study Feinstein all they want," he said. "He had us beat. His victims were chosen at random, had nothing to do with each other."

"But the scratches from the meat hooks—"

"The fact remains we never would have found him if not for a series of fortunate—and unbelievable— coincidences that occurred in that burning building."

"There sure was a lot going on in there."

"Yeah."

He shifted, moved his arm around a bit, then cradled it with the other one.

"Want me to drive you home?"

"As long as you're not going home with the Latin heartthrob."

"Never again."

"Well, that's good."

They stood up.

"What happens now, Dennis?"

"We go on with our jobs, Bailey," he said. "Move on to the next case. As far as we're concerned this one's over. Case closed."

THE PEGASUS SECRET

GREGG LOOMIS

What started as a suspicious explosion in a picturesque Parisian neighborhood could end in revelations that would shatter the beliefs of millions. American lawyer Lang Reilly is determined to find the real cause of the blast that killed his sister. But his investigation will lead him into the darkest corners of history and religion. And it may cost him his life.

Lang's search for the truth begins with a painting his sister bought just before she died. Could there be something about the painting itself that made someone want to kill her? Every mysterious step of the way, Lang unearths still more questions, more hidden secrets and more danger, until finally he arrives at the heart of a centuries-old secret order that will stop at nothing to protect what is theirs.

VENGEANCE

BRIAN PINKERTON

How far would you go for justice? Rob and Beth are very
much in love. He has just proposed to her, but she won't live
to see the wedding. Instead, Beth is intentionally sideswiped
by an angry driver and knocked off her bike—to her death.
Rob witnesses the whole thing, but he can only stand by as the
driver gets off with a slap on the wrist.

Rob is devastated. He becomes obsessed with making
Beth's killer pay. Then, one day, a strange man approaches
Rob. He offers Rob the justice he's been seeking. He tells Rob
about "The Circle," a small group of people with one thing in
common: They all want revenge for something. But Rob will
learn only too late that there is a catch....

VICKI STIEFEL
THE DEAD STONE

It starts with a mysterious phone call, summoning homicide counselor Tally Whyte back to the hometown she thought she'd left far behind her. Almost as soon as she arrives, Tally hears that a young woman she knew as a child has been found ritualistically murdered and mutilated.

The deeper Tally probes into the bizarre murder, the more chilling it becomes. Each glimpse into the killer's dark mind only unnerves Tally more. Despite frustrating secrets and silences, Tally suspects she's getting close to the truth, but perhaps she's getting too close for her own good. As each new body is found, Tally has to wonder…will she be next?

MAX McCOY

HINTERLAND

Andy Kelsey is a reporter who may have just stumbled on the story of a lifetime. He's infiltrated a white separatist group in the Ozarks, an underground organization ready to fight and die—and kill—for their extreme beliefs. The deeper Kelsey gets in the group, the more he's trusted, and the bigger his story becomes. Until he realizes the shocking extent of their scheme…

The separatists have finalized plans for a spectacular cataclysm that they hope will bring about Armageddon. What terrifies Kelsey is that they have the weapon and the means to achieve their mad goal. Will he be able to fight them from the inside without being discovered? Or has he gotten in too deep to ever get out?

THE CRIMINALIST
WILLIAM RELLING JR.

Detective Rachel Siegel is a twelve-year veteran of the San Patricio Sheriff's Department. But she's never seen anything like the handiwork of the Pied Piper, the vicious serial killer who's been terrifying that part of California for months. Because she's the best at what she does, it's now her job to catch this maniac—but she has very personal reasons, too, for wanting him stopped

Kenneth Bennett works for the Department of Neuropsychiatry at St. Louis's Washington University. There's something special about the Pied Piper case that draws Bennett almost against his will to the west coast. He has no choice but to help Siegel in her frantic search—even if it gets both of them killed in the process.

- -

JOEL ROSS
EYE FOR AN EYE

Suzanne "Scorch" Amerce was an honor student before her sister was murdered by a female street gang. Scorch hit the streets on a rampage that almost annihilated the gang, but it got her arrested and sent away. That was eight years ago. Now Scorch has escaped. The leader of the gang is still alive and Scorch wants to change that.

The one man who might be able to find Scorch and stop her bloodthirsty hunt is Eric, her prison therapist. Will he be able to stand by and let Scorch exact her deadly vengeance? Or will he risk his life to side with the detective who needs so badly to bring Scorch back in? Either way, lives hang in the balance. And Eric knows he has to decide soon. . . .
